I0655293

dry river bed

river

mountains

fort

Santa Fe

Mora

Conchas

Rio Grande

Apishapa

Purgatoire

Lake Meredith

Cimarron

Beaver

Canadian

Arkansas

Smoky Hill

Walnut

North Canadian

Cimarron

Salt Fork

Ninnescah

Cane

Kaw Lake

Oologah Lake

Fort Arbuckle

Fort Gibson

Verdigris

Neosho

Cottonwood

Illinois

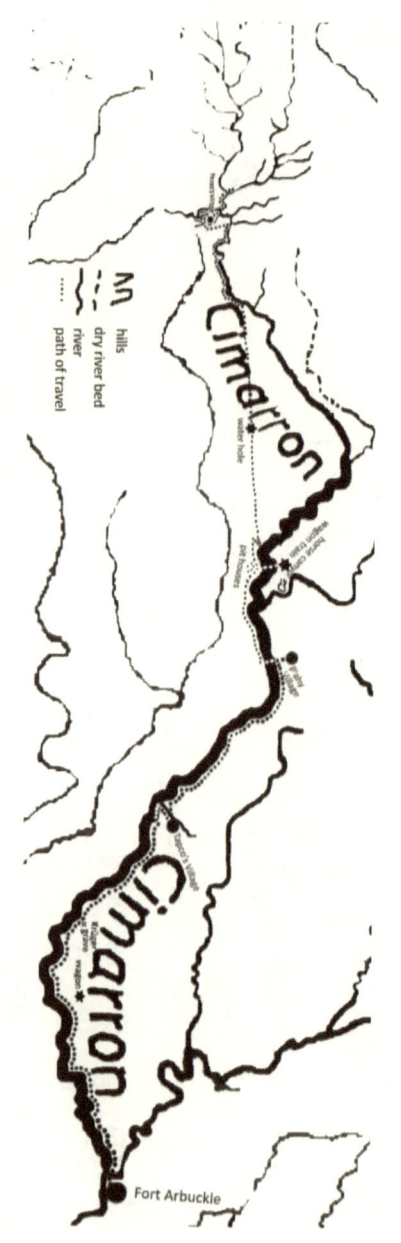

ALONG

THE

WAY

A Chance and Choices Adventure
Book Nine

Lisa Gay

Illustrations by
W.R. Michael Mattingly

Copyright © 2021 Elisabeth Gay
All rights reserved.

This book is a work of fiction. The names, characters, places, and incidents either are the product of the author's imagination or used factitiously. Any resemblance to an actual person, living or dead, business establishment, or event is entirely coincidental.

ISBN-13: 978-1-945858-19-2

Those Involved in these incidents:

Place of Origin – Dover
Starlight – a mule, bought by Eli and then traded to Roscoe
Brandy – a mule bought by Eli and then traded to Roscoe
Gumdrop - mule bought by Noah
Glory - mule bought by Noah

Place of Origin – Fort Arbuckle
Joy - baby girl

Place of Origin – Fort Smith
Promise – army horse purchased by Noah
Biscuit – army horse purchased by Noah

Place of Origin – Harmony
Ann Williams – oldest sister and Noah's wife
Stephanie Yates – middle sister and Eli's wife
Sally Williams – the youngest sister
Eli Yates – Stephanie's husband
Tom Yates - Eli's father/first owner of Yates Mercantile
Eyanosa – Noah's horse
June- horse purchased for the trip

Place of Origin – Little Rock
Daniel Hall – Judge of State of Arkansas
Beauty – a mule, given to Sally
Honor – a mule, purchased by Noah
Justice – mule purchased by Noah

Place of Origin – Indian Territory
Quapaw Land:
Noah Swift Hawk – Ann's husband (Tahatankohana)
Christopher – Noah's and Ann's baby son (Chris)
Ehawee – Noah's sister
Cherokee Nation:
Adahy - Ehawee's husband

Kiowa:
Gomda - Mystery man-in-training
Tapco- Mystery man-in-training, traveling with
Noah
P'ahy – Girl Tapco loves
Guipago – P'ahy's father
Ankímä - P'ahy's mother
Akea – P'ahy's sister
Settan – Akea's husband
Haungooah – Guipago's village leader
Dohosan – village leader of 5th group to trade site
Adoeette – warrior of Dohosan's village

Comanche:
Pecos – met while hunting bear
Nacoma - chief of Peco's village
Quanah – Nacoma's daughter

Place of Origin – Maumelle
Zi- Noah's mare

Place of Origin – New York
Helen Yates – Tom's mother
Woodrow Yates – Tom's father
Lemonade – Helen's horse

Place of Origin – Pine Bluff
Roscoe Bacon – the first owner of Bacon's Trading
Post/adopted grandfather of the family
Roscoe's donkeys:
Little Jenny – miniature donkey
Little Jack – miniature donkey
Roscoe's mules:
King
Rose
Hector
Eli and Stephanie's mules:
Redeemed
Ace

Place of Origin – Unknown
Warren Stringer - carried Tom across the Arkansas
River in his wagon
Emily Stringer– Warren's wife
Oscar –Emily and Warren's son
Nicholas Wolfgang Krüger – met on the prairie
(Nikki)
Greta Adele Krüger – Nikki's sister (Adele)
Otto Krüger – Nikki and Adele's father
Freda Krüger - Nikki and Adele's mother

Wagon Train
Jedidiah – Wagon Train leader
Ruben – lost an arm in the storm
Hortense - Ruben's wife
Ken – lost wife in storm
Cleo – Ken's son
Abigail – wagon blew away in the storm
Josiah – Abigail's husband
Heath – one of 3 brothers who survived the storm
Henrietta – girl with abdominal pain

One

The translucent leaves of spring changed to deep green. The fresh air that flowed through the open doors and windows erased the smell of the wood fires that had kept them warm that winter. The planned start day for the journey came and then went. The family grew antsy. The young man delaying their departure looked into the green eyes that enchanted him. "I can't go. They might be on their way back."

His wife didn't believe Noah's family would return. His grandmother was too afraid of another wolf attack. However, the raven-haired woman didn't want her husband to spend his life wondering if any of his family had decided to go with them, but he had left too soon. She handed him a brass telescope that glittered in the morning sun. "Go look, my husband." The woman admired her husband's sleek Indian physique as he climbed the watchtower of the abandoned fort where they had spent the winter.

From the ramparts, Noah Swift Hawk scanned

the horizon. "They're coming. Thank you, God!" He flew down the stairs. "They're coming!"

Eli, Noah's brother-in-law, scrambled up to look. He put his spyglass to his eye. "I don't think so; too many wagons."

"You're right." Noah slammed the telescoping pieces of his looking tube together and jammed the thing into his pocket. "Find out who they are. Let me know if I should open the gate." Dejected, he strode away.

When the wagon train arrived, Roscoe Bacon, the sixty-year-old man they had adopted into their family, pretended to be feeble as he spoke to the wagon train leader. "I'm an old man. It might not be safe for me to let you in."

"We won't hurt anybody, and it is truly perilous out here. The colonel at Fort Smith said there'd been a lot of unrest in the Indian tribes around here."

"You are in Indian Territory, and it is their land." Roscoe contemplated. *One man has already come searching for Noah and Ann, but I doubt a whole wagon train would have been sent. We probably only need to make sure these people don't plan on killing us to rob us.*

"Just let the women and children in."

"You'll all rush me if I open the gate."

"The rest of us will ride far enough away that we can't get back before you close up."

"All right. The rest of you leave." When Roscoe saw that the men were true to their word, he told Noah, "Open the gate."

The women and children hurried into the

protection of the fort the army had deserted shortly after building. The men came back believing they would camp outside Fort Arbuckle. Noah still held the gate open. "We trust you now. Come in. How long are you planning to stay before you continue on?"

"Just long enough to clear the path to the river."

That night, Ann lay in her husband's arms. "Noah, would it be safer if we went with this wagon train?"

"I want to give my family more time, and I'd rather not anyway. We're on the run, and I don't want to cross the entire prairie pretending to be somebody else. We created enough problems from the last two times we did that."

"We might not be alive, and for sure, our backs wouldn't have any flesh on them if we hadn't, so don't think we did the wrong thing."

"I don't. With my blue eyes, nobody would know that I'm part Indian, but our names would allow Judge Hall to track us, and you know how upset your sister was when I pretended to be Dr. Luke Smith."

"Stephanie is over that now. She knows how qualified you are to give medical treatment. Besides, you wouldn't have to use that name."

"Ann, I don't want to be around other people."

"All right, my husband. It was just a thought."

When the wagon train moved out, they left Noah praying that somebody in his family loved him enough to travel with him to the western sea.

Two weeks later, their large herd of animals had

eaten all their hay. The prairie, however, was full of lush green grass. Noah's birth family could have gone all the way to their village at the western edge of the Boston Mountains and still had time enough to return to Fort Arbuckle. Roscoe spoke up, "We won't be able to travel fast because of the goats and sheep. If we wait any longer, we might not get over the Sangre de Cristo Mountains before winter. We have to get going."

With a very heavy heart, Noah agreed. "You're right. We'll leave in the morning."

Noah prayed the entire night. "If my family is coming, don't let me leave without them." In the morning, he changed to, "Keep my family safe in our village." When Ann woke, Noah told her, "I'm ready to go."

With her passion, Ann let him know she loved him desperately. Later, she told her sad husband, "I've prayed that your family would stay with us ever since we found out they were going home, but I think you're making the right decision to move on without them."

Ann nursed their fourteen-week-old son, Christopher. Noah played with Joy, the red-haired baby girl they had taken as their own when they had first arrived at Fort Arbuckle and found the child's parents dead. By God's grace, they had gotten there in time to save the tiny baby born a few days after theirs. When Chris was full, Noah took him and went to tell the others to get ready to move out.

Mid-morning of March 27th 1841, Noah Swift

Hawk and Ann Williams, along with Ann's family, left Fort Arbuckle. They lowered the bar on the outside of the gates to secure the fort for other travelers emigrating to the West who might want to take refuge.

Weeks before, they and the wagon train folks had cleared a path through the wild hops, brush, and trees. This morning, they followed it to the Arkansas River crossing just north of the Cimarron's convergence from the west. Roscoe tried to see across the water. "Last time, there was a bear in the glen just on the other side. We should keep a sharp lookout."

Stephanie handed a sledgehammer to her father-in-law, Tom Yates. For nearly two decades, Tom had carried heavy merchandise in Yates Mercantile. He was very strong and easily pounded an iron stake into the ground. "Can we get the wagons up on the bank before we're in the glen?" he asked.

Roscoe stood beside Tom with hundreds of feet of rope and a large wooden pulley. "Yes, but two of us should go in the first wagon with all four Lefaucheux revolvers. We'll have eighty shots if we need them."

Noah strapped on two of the twenty-round French revolvers he had purchased in Little Rock the previous spring. "I'll go in the first wagon with Roscoe." He climbed into the driver's box.

Roscoe handed Tom's son, Eli, the end of the rope attached to the pulley. Before he climbed into the wagon, Roscoe rubbed his favorite mule's head.

5

"I appreciate all you do for us, King." From the wagon seat, he commanded, "Forward ho!" They started into the Arkansas River. "I hope this wagon is heavy enough to stay on the bottom."

"I do too, my friend," Noah replied.

Hector, another of Roscoe's mules, walked beside King, followed by four more of their largest mules. Molly, Redeemed, Jumper, and Blue still walked on the solid river bottom as the rear wheels rolled in. Ann stood on the eastern shore with Chris on her hip. Her youngest sister, Sally, stood next to her, holding Joy. The water touched the wagon's bed before it was halfway across. Ann called out, "Tom, make sure that stake is deep!"

The wheels still pressed against the rocky bottom when Roscoe gave the command, "Forward, swim!" He pulled King's reins and instructed him to lead the team upstream. Since the donkeys and mules were swimming, the current pushed the animals downstream. As Roscoe had hoped, the wagon prevented them from washing away. He pulled the reins hard to the right, "King. Hector. Upstream."

Tom watched the water rise up the sides of the wagon. "I think we made the wagon heavy enough. Still, if the water gets too deep, the wagon does need to float. I hope it won't come to that." As the words left his mouth, the water reached the ash logs lashed to the sides of the wagon. The wheels lifted off the riverbed. The wagon rapidly traveled downstream.

The color drained from Ann's face. "Please, God, get them safely across."

Sally added, "And keep the bears away."

As the wagon floated away, it pulled the animals downstream and the slack out of the rope. Tom hammered the only hope they had deeper into the ground. His son, Eli, ran circles and wound the part of the rope beyond the pulley to the stake.

Stephanie hugged Eli's tiny baby to her chest but kept a close eye on the rope. "Now!" she screamed. Eli dropped the rope just as it snapped tight. The stake remained in the soil, neither the line nor the pulley broke, and the wagon stopped.

"It worked!" Eli slapped Tom triumphantly on the back.

Tom's mother, Helen, let out the breath she had been holding. "Thank you, God." She realized how much she had come to care for Roscoe. *It's only been eight months. How can I be feeling this way?*

As planned, if the wagon ended up floating at the end of the rope, Roscoe climbed out to the closest mule to release the harness from the doubletree. He did something he had found himself frequently doing the last few months. "Lord, let the ropes be long enough to get to the other side." His next request went to his animals. "Forward, swim!" As the team crossed the channel, the ropes tied between the wagon and the animals followed them. The line grew short. *Why can't anything work out?*

Helen saw the line pull tight and started biting her fingernails.

Ann moved closer. "It will get easier to watch the man you love doing very dangerous things. In the beginning, I was scared out of my mind that Noah was going to kill himself. I still worry a little, but I believe in Noah's ability to know what he can do. And remember, Roscoe made this trip before."

"He was much younger then."

"Roscoe is very smart and very tough. He and Noah will figure this out."

Helen turned to Ann. "How did you know?"

"You always want to be close to him, and you look at him that way, but mostly, it's the smile when you're around him."

"Tom is going to be so mad when he realizes. His father died only eight months ago, and I'm already in love with another man."

"I think your son wants you to be happy."

Roscoe directed King and Hector slightly downstream toward the inner side of the river bend. Before long, the lead mules rose a little. Immediately after, Molly and Blue did the same. Two by two, the animals made contact with the ground. Roscoe turned upstream and toward the far shore. He pulled out his spyglass and examined the land beyond the water. *The space between the trees is wide enough, and I don't see any bears.* The mules struggled up the bank fifty feet downstream from the glen, then continued due west and hauled the wagon the rest of the way across.

Once at the bank, Noah hollered, "We're over!"

They reattached the team to the wagon and walked in the river toward the glen. The water deepened until it again skimmed under the wagon bed. Roscoe stopped the team. "Maybe we should secure our end of the rope here. I'm afraid we'll lose contact and float downstream again if we go any farther."

"I guess there's no reason we have to go straight across, and the bank is shallow enough to get out." Noah tossed a sledgehammer and an iron stake out of the wagon. With powerful strokes, Roscoe pounded the stake into the hard soil. Noah sloshed to the riverbank with their other pulley. "I'm going to untie the rope from the wagon. We can get the mules to pull the rope tight before we thread it through."

On the west side, Roscoe attached the harness Eli had made, like the one they had used in 1839 when they had crossed Cadron Creek at full flood. He had bolted large "c" clamps from end to end of a heavy board. At one end, he had attached two very long, wide, and thick leather straps that went around a wagon. At the other end, fastened on with leather straps, a harness slid over an animal's legs and then buckled around its body. In this case, however, they didn't slide the contraption along a stationary line. They hooked the harness to loops in the rope. People on both sides could pull the opposite line and draw the wagon. Roscoe and Noah joined the chains secured to eyebolts run through the ash logs to the loops and sent them back to use on the next wagon.

Helen marched their goats into their empty wagon. Behind them, Sally led in the miniature donkeys. "I'm glad they're accustomed to riding in the wagon. It's much easier since we don't have to sedate them anymore."

Ann secured her two children in the ten-gallon washtub tied to the driver's seat. "So am I. Stephanie, bring Hattie."

"I want to ride with the children." Stephanie put Hattie, her six-week-old daughter, beside Joy.

Sally got into the driver's box. "The three of us can go on this trip. Helen can come with Eli or Tom." She drove the wagon to the rope.

Tom and Eli attached the logs and strapped the wagon into the harness. Ann and Stephanie raised the side of the wagon cover to get ahold of the top rope and help pull the wagon when the water got deep. Eli kissed Stephanie and Hattie. "I'll help pull you from here. I'll see you on the other side."

Six horses towed them until they had to swim. Then, Ann and Stephanie helped haul them from inside the wagon. Tom, Eli, and Helen pulled from the east while Noah and Roscoe drew the opposite rope from the west. They came up out of the river, unhitched, and then unloaded the animals and children.

Noah and Roscoe sent the empty animal wagon back to the east. Tom, Eli, and Helen loaded the last of the goats and the sheep. Six donkeys pulled them across. The following sets of mules, horses, and donkeys went across harnessed to the traveling board without drawing anything. Eli secured the ash logs and then hitched up the remaining mules to the last wagon. "I can dig out the stake and come across in the buffalo-hide boat."

Tom spoke up. "Son, it's going to be a dangerous

ride with only one end of the rope attached. Stephanie and Hattie need you, so take your grandmother across in the wagon. I'll come over last."

"The ride in the buffalo hide boat is going to be exciting. I would have liked to be the one to take it, but you're right. I'll go in the wagon." Eli helped Helen get in. After an easy crossing, Eli drove the wagon onto the far bank next to the other two. "It'll probably take a month of Sundays for Pop to dig out that stake. He was really going to town on it."

Helen rummaged around in the wagon. "It's almost noon. I'll lay out dinner. By the time Tom gets here, we'll be ready to eat."

"I'll help you." Roscoe worked closely beside the first woman he hadn't walked away from since he was fifteen.

Helen told him, "I was worried about you."

All alone across the river, Tom heard a noise. *That sounds like something coming. Bears are probably on this side of the river too.* He ran into the woods, climbed into an oak, and then pulled the shovel and boat up with him. He watched a momma bear with two cubs come into view. *I hope it doesn't want to put its cubs in danger and keeps going.*

The large bear stopped, smelled the air, and then ran the cubs into the trees that lined the river. Alone, it examined the stake and rope with the offensive aroma.

Eli looked across the river to see how the stake removal was going. "Oh, no!" He pulled his spyglass from his pocket. "There's a bear over there! I thought they were supposed to be on this side. I don't see Pop anywhere!"

Everybody hurried to the riverbank. Sally spotted Tom. "He's in that oak almost directly behind the stake."

"By the horn spoons! He's in a pickle!" Roscoe put his spyglass back into his pocket. "I can't shoot it from over here. I could pull myself closer, but it looks like Tom might have the stake too loose for it to hold."

Noah said, "I think he's safe in the tree. He'll wait up there until it leaves."

They watched the bears as they ate dinner. Sally sketched the momma bear sitting on her rump at the edge of the river with a large fish in her mouth and two more fish she had thrown to her cubs. Sally's second drawing was of the big bear asleep on the ground with its legs splayed out with her babies asleep on her back. Last, she drew the cubs playing together.

As darkness fell, the bears had made no indication that they planned to leave the area. Therefore, so Tom wouldn't fall out of the tree and become bear food, he found a place to wedge the buffalo skin boat, climbed in and slept.

By the light of the slender crescent moon, Eli tried to see what was happening on the other side of the river. Helen sat beside her grandson. "I can't lose him again. I just got my beautiful boy back."

"Grams, Pop always told me that you are the most dedicated Christian he has ever known. I haven't heard you say one single prayer since I've known you. Maybe now is the time to start doing that again."

"God let my son disappear in the middle of the night and be gone for twenty years."

"I've read the Bible every day for the last three years. It seems to me that God gives us free will. That includes letting a man pick a woman his mother doesn't like and letting a woman drive a wedge between herself and her son."

"It's not that I didn't like your mother. Hattie always did so much to help others, and I could see how much she loved Tom. I thought over time they would tear out each other's hearts because a Christian and a non-Christian intrinsically walk different paths."

"This is a case of God allowing people to exercise their free will and create a mess, and then God making it all work into something good."

"How is that?"

"God allowed your son to leave with his wife. Twenty years later, your husband was dying, and you thought you had nobody. But God brought your son back in time for Woodrow to know that his son still loved him, had missed him all those years, that he had a grandson, and that you wouldn't be alone. Tom was there when both of you needed him. Then, God brought you to this big family of yours. You even got to meet Noah's part of the family. Count how many people God gave back to you."

The two of them counted on their fingers as they named everybody. Helen said, "Twenty-nine. Plus, I don't even know how many if you count the families of James' new sons-in-law."

"And there are five more babies on the way."

"You're right. I had prayed for a big family. God was making it happen. I just didn't know it."

"Something else you don't know is that God answered Pop's prayer too. My mother did accept God on her deathbed. We found out about that last year."

Helen took Eli's hand. "God, please send the bears away and keep my son safe. God, I'm going to pray for something wildly outrageous. Tom deserves to be loved. Give him another wife. Whoever she is, I promise I'll love her. In Jesus' name, amen."

"Amen." Eli hugged his grandmother. "Thank you, Grams, but I don't know how he'll find a wife in the middle of the prairie."

"That's why it's wildly outrageous."

Two

The sun rose, the wind shifted direction, and the mother bear smelled a human. She roared and then followed the scent drifting from the trees. The angry roar woke Tom. He peeked over the rim of the boat he had dragged into the tree eighteen hours earlier. *I might not have to choose between dying of thirst and being eaten by a bear.*

The bear reared up under the smelly creature above. It slammed its feet against the tree. The tree lurched. Tom grabbed a branch and held on. The buffalo hide bowl flew out of the tree and landed upside down over the bear's head. It walloped the thing and sent it crashing through the woods. Its giant paws battered the tree.

On the other side of the Arkansas River, Eli saw what was happening. He snatched up two of the Lefaucheux revolvers and ran to his mule. He urged Ace into the water. As Ace swam the river, Eli held the guns above his head with one hand and clutched the mule's tail with the other. The current carried them downstream. Soon, Eli could no longer see his father. When he and the mule came out of the water, they were back where they had been the day before, at Fort Arbuckle.

A wagon came out of the gate. Eli hollered, "Help! Bears ahead! Get out your weapons!"

The man driving the wagon reached under the seat. "Where did you come from?" He pointed his rifle at Eli.

"I crossed the river. A bear has my father trapped in a tree. It's trying to knock him out. It may have already gotten him." He charged up the cleared path.

The man backed the wagon into the fort. The woman looked at her husband. "We should help."

"You know I'm not well. I can't fight a bear."

The woman grabbed the rifle. "It's not that difficult to shoot one." She ran the same way Eli had gone. Ahead, shots rang out. She arrived as a large black shape, leaving behind a trail of red, ran into the forest with her two small cubs close behind.

The man who had asked for help still held revolvers in his hands, but he looked at another man's arm.

She ran over. "Are you all right?"

The handsome, well-muscled, forty-year-old man with dark brown hair and eyes replied, "Blessedly, it's only cuts from holding onto that branch up there." Tom pointed to a bloody branch. "I think the ornery animal broke our boat." The three of them examined it. The branches over which the hide had been stretched were indeed smashed. "I guess I won't be ridings in this."

The woman offered, "You can ride in our wagon."

"That would be nice. We have a pulley system rigged that you can use to take your wagon across. I almost had the stake out when that bear showed up. We'll have to tie it to a tree. Right now, I need water. I've been in that tree for a long time."

Eli waved at the people across the river before he helped Tom drag the mangled boat.

The woman led Ace. "I'm Emily. Sorry I didn't get here sooner."

"I'm Tom. It wasn't something you would have known to do. Besides, Eli, my courageous son, saved the day."

"Even if Eli hadn't already told us his father was in danger, I would have known you're his father. Eli looks just like you."

Inside the fort, the man saw his wife returning with the young man who had flown past earlier, along with an older man. He went down the stairs from the rampart and opened the gate. A seven-year-old, blond-haired boy ran to the woman. "Ma, I'm glad you saved them."

"I didn't save them, Oscar. Eli had already run the bear away before I got there. Meet my son and my husband, Warren. I'll get you that water, Tom."

Tom watched the blonde-haired woman draw a bucket of water from the well inside the fort. *She's beautiful.*

Emily handed the water to Tom and then climbed into her wagon. A few minutes later, she had bandages and wrapped Tom's arm. Once Tom's wounds had been dressed, they put the smashed buffalo hide boat into the wagon and made their way back to the river.

Eli finished removing the iron stake while Tom, Warren, and Emily held their guns at the ready and kept a sharp lookout. Oscar stood beside Eli. "You swam across this river to save your father?"

"My mule swam across. It pulled me."

"You're brave. My Pa wouldn't even try to help you."

"He has to protect the most important people."

"Who is that?"

"You and your mother, of course."

"Oh. I'm glad to know that's why." Oscar walked over to his father. "Pa, thank you for thinking me and Ma are the most important people. I love you."

"You're welcome, son. The two of you are the most important." Warren hugged his son.

Eli pulled out the stake. He tied the rope to Ace and then signaled for those across the river to give him slack. "Come on, Ace, pull the rope to the tree." Ace easily accomplished the task. By the time Eli and Tom had untied the rope from the mule and secured it to the tree, Noah and Roscoe had the harness on the line. Warren pulled it over, then attached his wagon. Tom, Emily, Warren, and Oscar got in the wagon with its floats permanently attached. Their one horse pulled them into the river.

Noah, Roscoe, and the people in the wagon

pulled them along the rope. With his revolvers out, Eli sat on Ace a short way into the river. Eli had shot the bear five times before he had run it off and seriously doubted that the bear had survived. Even so, and although he still had thirty-five rounds, he was worried that the bear would come back.

The wagon lurched. The right front wheel went up onto a large stone. Everything slid to the left. Before they could stop, the cart went over the top and slammed hard onto the rock.

Oscar flipped out of the wagon. "Help!"

Tom grabbed Oscar's wrist. The current sucked the boy from his grip and beneath the water. Warren jumped into the river and followed his son under the wagon.

Emily ordered Tom, "Hold me." She leaned far over the edge. The only place Tom could hold her that would allow her to go far enough down was around her hips. He couldn't help but notice her very shapely bottom as he held her tightly. Emily stuck her head under the water.

Oscar's leg had gone into the space between the axle and the wagon bed. Warren tried to pull him out. As he had said, he wasn't a healthy man. He couldn't extract his son against the current, so he worked Oscar around until his head was downstream.

Emily waved her hand. Tom pulled her in. She dashed to the downstream side of the wagon. "We've got to grab them as they come out. It should be right here. Hold me under again."

They repeated the process of getting Emily's head under the surface. Through the crystal water, she saw Warren trying to pull Oscar loose from the broken axle. She got ahold of the only thing she could reach – Oscar's hair – then pulled. Oscar's pants ripped off his body as he came free. Emily waved her other hand to signal Tom, then got both hands on her son. Tom pulled up Emily.

Warren was out of air under the wagon, but he didn't want anybody trying to catch him when they needed to recover Oscar. His lungs screamed for air. Oscar's one foot with a shoe and one with only a sock rose out of Warren's view. *You can do it. Just a few more seconds.* He saw Emily's face again and pushed off.

A half-second later, Emily grabbed him. Her head rose above the water. "Help!"

Tom seized Warren's shirt and then saw his ears. "Grab the side."

Warren clung to the wagon and gasped for air. Tom found a better place to hold on. He hauled Warren in by the back of his belt.

Oscar reported what he had seen. "The wagon is broken. We don't have another one of those bars that hold the wheels."

Tom flicked the reins to get the horse that had been standing in place to resume its trek to the far side. "First, we have to get the wagon across. Then, we'll worry about the axle."

Everybody pulled with all their might to drag the wagon off the rock and into water deep enough to float. On the west side, Noah commented, "It's a good thing that didn't happen to our wagon carrying the dynamite."

"You ain't just whistlin' Dixie," Roscoe replied.

"If we need to fix their wagon, it would be easiest while it's floating!" Noah hollered, "Tell us as soon as you feel a wheel touch the bottom. Get your spare parts ready!"

Warren replied, "I couldn't afford spare parts."

Roscoe quietly told Noah, "If they couldn't afford what they needed, they shouldn't have tried to make the trip."

"I agree. Let's at least see what they need."

"We've touched." They were close enough that Emily didn't have to yell.

Everybody stopped hauling. Tom quickly made all the introductions then said, "First, we need to get Eli over here. That bear may come back, and it's going to be one heck of a mad bear. Eli will tie the rope to Ace. Secure our end to a wagon and get the animals into the harnesses. We'll pull them over." Not much time passed, but Tom was worried. "Are you ready yet?"

"Just about," Noah replied.

A minute later, Roscoe said, "Let him know we're starting."

Tom waved. Eli urged Ace farther into the river as Roscoe started the wagon forward. As soon as Ace began to swim, the strong current moved them toward Fort Arbuckle. Roscoe increased the speed to pull Ace as close as possible before the rope was against the trees. As they assumed, it didn't take long for that to happen. However, they had Eli and Ace more than halfway across.

Everybody else was already at the downstream side of the tree around which the rope was pulled. They only drew the line, rider, and horse for a short time before the current and the tether had forced them to the western shore. Eli rolled up the rope as he rode upriver just offshore. He walked into camp. "How bad is it?"

Warren had had a long close-up view of the problem. "The axle and right front wheel are smashed. You moved the pulley to that tree and lined me up with that big rock. This is your fault." *I hope they'll accept the responsibility and fix my wagon.*

Eli looked at his family. "I did move the line, but there was no other place to secure it."

Sally felt the tension. "It will be better if everybody is rested and not hungry. Let's eat dinner before you decide what to do." While Sally, Helen, and Emily fixed the mid-day meal, it started to rain. The men put up one of the huge floorless tents they used as a shelter for their animals.

Three

Three hours later, they had the wagon jacked up on the soggy ground. An hour after that, they had removed all the broken pieces and had hammered the bent metal parts still attached to the wagon back into shape. Eli and Tom carried one of their spare axles to Warren's wagon. Ann made coffee for the men working in the cold rain.

"I can't get it on. The jack is sinking into the ground." Roscoe continued trying to slide a wheel onto the axle.

Noah looked down. "Same with this one, and the jack is as high as it will go."

Warren, who had been unable to help because of his weak heart, offered a suggestion. "You could all raise it while I slide on the wheel. Then, we can do the same on the other side." The other men spaced themselves from one end of the wagon to the other. Warren stood beside the axle. "One, two, three, lift!" The four men raised the wagon. Warren slid on the wheel. "I got it!" The men gently lowered the wagon into a cock-eyed, three-wheeled angle. "Together, we do good work," Warren wiped the rain from his eyes.

Roscoe pulled his foot from the muck the wagon had pressed him into. *You've hardly done enough work to consider this working together.* He walked to the other side. "Let's put on the other and be done. I want to get dry and warm."

The second wheel went on the same way. Warren checked to make sure everything was securely attached. He changed into dry clothes in his wagon before he went to the tent and took a cup of hot coffee. "We're going to move on. We're trying to catch up to the wagon train."

Roscoe told him what he knew from experience. "They're two weeks ahead. You can't do that with only one horse to pull your wagon."

"They had been stopping for several hours in the middle of every day. If we push straight through, we can catch up."

"Animals need to rest and graze during that time."

"Our horse can rest after we join them."

"You'll kill your horse, and then you won't get anywhere," Roscoe warned them.

Emily had enjoyed all the women she had helped for the last several hours. She put her hand on Warren's arm. "Maybe we should stay with these people."

Warren didn't like it. "Don't tell me what to do. Nobody tells me what to do! You and Oscar, get in the wagon." Emily stayed where she stood. He ordered her, "NOW!"

For just a second, her brows furrowed, and the

corners of her mouth pulled down. "Come on, Oscar." Emily took her son's hand and walked through the rain to their wagon. She waved as they rode away. "God keep you!"

Tom waved back. "Thank you for helping with my arm." He turned to his son. "What do women see in men like that?"

Eli replied, "Some people are so hard-headed," then added, "It's already late. I suggest we stay here until morning."

"I bet we'll see them again. I'll help get our evening meal started." Still in his wet clothes, Roscoe went to the river to draw water to make beef stew.

Ann chopped shriveled potatoes. "Two days, and we've only gotten a few hundred yards."

"I guess a few days won't make a difference." Sally dumped meat into the water.

Everybody heard a gunshot, hit the ground, and shielded the babies. Noah looked in the direction of the shot through his spyglass. "Only by the grace of God!" He jumped up and ran toward the river, waving his arms. He screamed back to the camp. "It's Ehawee and Adahy! The river's going to rise from all this rain! We have to get them across now!" *Except for the day I married Ann*, he paused in his thoughts, *and the day at Pine Bluff when I got her back*, he stopped again, *and the day my white eagle baby boy was born.* He paused one more time. *Well, this is one of the happiest days of my life.*

When Noah arrived at the river's edge, his sister and brother-in-law were already halfway across the river but far downstream. Noah ran along the river, keeping pace with his sister's unwanted but unavoidable progress back toward Fort Arbuckle. Ehawee and Adahy rode two of the horses Noah had given his family to get home. Two other horses, carrying packsaddles full of supplies, swam with them. Tears of happiness joined the rain on Noah's face. They met just beyond the fort. Noah pulled his sister up the bank. He hugged her fiercely. "You came back! Is everybody safe at home?" He helped Adahy up, then hugged him too. "I hope you're here because you want to come with us."

Adahy pulled his horse out of the river. "So that I could marry Ehawee, I promised your father that I would walk to the western sea. I'm going to keep that promise even if nobody else does. Also, Ehawee and I want to go."

"But your brother."

"I've always been nothing but Dustu's twin. Now, I can be my own man."

Noah looked at his sister. She told him, "I think it was cruel for everybody to leave you. I didn't know Adahy was willing to go. He told me if we could see you from Fort Arbuckle that God wanted us to go with you. I prayed and prayed that you would still be here. Do you think God kept you here?"

"God sent a bear and broke a wagon to keep us here. We would have been gone yesterday morning."

Adahy exclaimed, "So He is real!"

"Yes, He is!" Noah pulled in his sister's horse as Ehawee and Adahy pulled up the other two.

They started back to camp. Noah asked, "Why did you bring all four horses?"

"This one is mine. You bought these from Petang. They belong to you. The family said, 'Thank you for letting them use them to get home.' And besides that, they did keep the wagon and one of your horses."

"Everybody is safe at home?"

Ehawee replied, "Yes, but it was traumatic getting there. Luyu is sure that wolves are going to eat her for trying to take Waya away. He wanted us to stay in the village until after he got his new name. He felt he needed to not be 'wolf' anymore."

"What's his new name?"

"Alisdelisgi."

"Protector. I like it," Noah replied.

His sister continued, "He promised Luyu he would protect her no matter what."

Back at camp, everybody hugged the new arrivals. Ann kissed Ehawee's cheek and whispered into her ear. "I love you so very much. I can't tell you how much this means to Noah and me."

Ehawee held her sister-in-law tight. "I'm sorry we left."

Four

Roscoe looked at the ground in the early morning light. "This is how we did it back in 1820." He stomped his foot. Mud spewed in every direction. He picked up his foot and looked at the hole. "Only a few inches. I think we can go."

Noah looked at the result of Roscoe's test. "The wagons should be able to roll through mud only that deep." They walked into the tent. "We need to round up all the animals. I think we should try what Ann suggested last year. Let's take apart some rope and make nets to go between the wagons. If we space them out as far as we can, there should be enough grass for one night."

Ann volunteered, "I could ride in the wagon with Chris and Joy and start making one."

"I'll help. It will be easier to keep the babies safe inside the wagon." Stephanie rocked her crying baby, who they had named Hattie after Eli's dead mother.

"All you women could work on the net if you'd be willing." Roscoe assisted in taking down the tent.

Helen sweetly smiled at the man she had grown

to love. "I would be glad to do as you suggest, Roscoe."

Since the whole group going west was together, God sent no further complications and allowed them to move out. Roscoe told them, "I don't even have to read my journal to remember this. On the prairie, there is no wood to use as fuel. We have to keep a lookout for dried buffalo droppings. They're called buffalo chips. Collect and put them into the storage nets under the wagons. We'll burn them to cook."

After a day of sloshing through the mud and finding every buffalo chip too wet to gather, they baked bread in their sheet metal ovens over a fire of the last of the wood they had brought from Fort Arbuckle. That night, they ate hot bread fresh from the oven.

For breakfast, they ate the bread cold during the extended time they spent finding the animals.

They stopped for four hours mid-day of every day to allow the animals to graze. Tom frequently volunteered to scout ahead. Riding Spirit, his horse that he had brought from their home in Harmony, he searched the horizon. Tom often thought about Emily. He hoped she and her family would catch the wagon train ahead without wearing out their horse and not become stranded and vulnerable.

For two weeks, the three wagons, ten people, twenty mules, ten donkeys, fifteen horses, eight goats, four sheep, and one cow that no longer produced milk forded streams and rolled across the mostly flat prairie. They uneventfully avoided the plentiful rattlesnakes visible in the short grass from many yards away. Every evening, they read and discussed the Bible while Noah and Eli spent time enjoying their babies. Ehawee taught the women how to separate a hemp rope into strands, then tie them into sheet bends to make the three-inch bars and rows of the net's mesh. After using up three one-hundred-foot ropes, they had made a ninety-foot-long, four-foot-high net.

The ten of them stretched the net from one wagon to the next. Noah admired the work. "This is beautiful. The mesh is so even, but we used up three ropes. We can't use any more to make another."

Tom added, "We might find a way to make more. It would save so much time if we could make the corral. In case we can, I'm going to make stakes to support this one. It sags too much."

Roscoe swept his hand across the horizon. "I don't see anything but grass. What would you use to make stakes?"

"You're right. Still, it's such good work; I hate to not use it." Tom unhooked the net from the wagon.

Eli helped him roll it up. "Even though it would only be half this length, we could tie together the nets that are under the wagons and make a second net."

Roscoe nixed that plan, "First, I don't want to handle the nets after they've held the buffalo chips. Second, it wouldn't do any good until we can close in the third side."

That night, Ehawee jumped up from the fire. "I've got it! Let's cut a handful of hair from each mule and horse's tail, wash it, and braid it. We should be able to get more than enough without even taking very much from any individual animal."

Ann walked to Eyanosa with Chris in the cradleboard on her back. "Would a handful be enough?"

Sally looked at her favorite mule's tail. "I don't want to take more than we need. Let's only take an inch section and see how long of a braid we get." She pulled together the hairs from all around Beauty's tail and cut a clump of three-foot-long tail hair.

"Do you remember that horsehair bowl in Kangee's lodge? If we separate them by color, we can make a very strong, lightweight, and gorgeous net." Helen looked at her horse. "All of Lemonade's hair is yellow. Let's not mix the hair when we wash it."

"The same with the horses I bought at Fort Smith. Biscuit and Promise both have completely black tails." Noah walked to Promise with Joy on his back. "It's going to take a long time to make this net, but we need to do it. We're spending too much time finding our animals every morning."

Eli severed a clump of mixed-colored hair from Ace. "We need to make two, so I'll help as well. We should all help."

As they traveled the following day, they sorted the cleaned hairs by length and color. After all the evening work, everybody started a braid using thin clumps of animal hair.

Sunday morning, Noah scanned the horizon. *It's always so hard to find the goats in this tall grass. What's that?* Noah stood up in his stirrups to get a better look at a white sparkle at the edge of his field of vision. He rode toward the strange apparition.

"Maaahhhh."

Well, at least I found the goats. Noah took them back to camp, but he wanted to find out what was on the horizon. "Ann, I saw something. Would you like to ride with me to see what it is?"

"All right. You carried Joy most of the day yesterday. Do you want to carry Chris this morning?"

"First, I'll saddle Zi for you. Then, I'll take Chris. Get the babies ready."

"Sure. Both of them love to see the countryside. They must get that from me. I do too. I'll get their sunhats on them."

Adahy and Ehawee came into camp with the two miniature donkeys. Noah told them, "Ann and I are going to search in that direction." He pointed. "Stephanie and Hattie are the only people still in camp. Will you stay here with them?"

"Of course. I'll help with the net." Ehawee climbed into the wagon. "Adahy, you can keep looking if you want." Hattie dozed as Stephanie and Ehawee tied the slender hair braids into loops with their spacers and threaders.

They drew closer to the white apparition. Noah looked with his spyglass. "It's a wagon."

Ann thought she knew what the wagon's owners were doing. "They must be looking for their animals."

Noah looked at a wide path of flattened grass. "A lot of animals went this way together."

"Maybe all the horses ran off, and they're chasing them."

Noah announced their intentions from a long way out, "Hello at the wagon! Do you need help?" They heard no reply. He repeated his statement as they drew closer. "All the horses left from here, but I see smaller trails coming in. People in the grass ambushed them."

"We better get back. Somebody might attack us or Stephanie and Ehawee."

"Let's quickly look in the wagon."

They circled to the back of the wagon. Ann exclaimed, "Lord, help us!" Several vultures picked bits of flesh off two sets of bones in the tall grass behind the wagon. Ann raced Zi through the birds, which landed only yards away. "What were these people doing out here all alone?"

"Probably coming down from the north. I read in Roscoe's journal that the mountain route through Raton Pass was treacherous. People may try to cut over to the Cimarron. Probably not many because of all the waterless miles between the rivers. Let's look in the wagon."

Ann pulled open the puckering strings. "A piano! And a dresser! Whoever took the horses and everything else must have left these because they're too heavy. We should hook up Eyanosa and Zi and take this wagon."

"And the bones too. Our shovels are back at camp. We'll bury them there."

Ann climbed into the wagon, took out a dresser drawer, and laid it on the wagon bed. She laid Joy in the drawer, then took Chris and put him with his sister. "You get the bones while I get the horses into the harness. It's still attached to the wagon." Ann noticed the driver's box as she took the saddles off their horses. *It's a waste of space to close in the area under the seat.*

Noah laid his shirt beside the wagon owners' remains. "I found part of a broken arrow." He gathered the arrowhead, with a few inches of the shaft still attached, along with all the clumps of hair, bits of clothes, and bones he could find. Last, he shook the feet out of the shoes. Noah placed the bundle and the shoes into the wagon, then got into the driver's seat beside Ann. "I think one of the babies needs a diaper change."

"I'll handle it."

Noah let out two short whistles. Eyanosa and Zi started walking. Ann checked. "Neither of them is even wet." She climbed out beside Noah. "Helen is going to be so happy. Several times I've heard her say she wished she could have brought her piano."

Five

At camp, when they had finally found all the animals, they had lost Noah, Ann, and their two horses. Roscoe peered across the prairie. "Which way did they say they were going?"

Adahy pointed. "That way. I see something. It looks like a wagon."

Since both Tom and Roscoe had previously been owners of stores, they had equipped everybody with a spyglass. Every one of them pulled theirs out and looked. When the wagon got close, they saw Noah and Ann in the driver's box. Tom exclaimed, "How in the Sam Hill did they get a wagon?!"

When the wagon arrived, everybody wanted an explanation. Noah jumped down and walked to the back. "Indian attack. Help me bury the victims."

Ann called out, "Helen, you should come look."

"I looked at poor Woodrow's body. I don't need to see another."

"Wait until they've removed the bones and then come over."

Helen walked to the back. "Why? If you've seen one wagon, you've... How can it be?!" She climbed in. The slightly off tones of "When we all get to Heaven" rang out across the prairie. "I do have a tuning fork. If only I had a bench," Helen commented.

Minus the arrow, its shaft, the hair that Ann wanted to use to make a memorial, and the shoes that fit Sally and Eli, they buried the couple. Each spoke words over the bones. Noah asked, "Do you think we should move some of the load from the other wagons?"

Tom cracked his whip in the air above his beloved horse. It was Spirit's day as the leader of the team pulling the wagon Tom stood on. "We've already lost the whole morning. Let's wait until tonight."

Ann remained the driver of the new wagon with her babies in the back in the dresser drawer. She sniffed the air. *This wagon does smell like ammonia. I'll give it a good cleaning tonight.*

Chris started to fuss. "Follow," Ann lay down the reins and climbed into the back. As they had been trained to do, Eyanosa and Zi continued walking between the other wagons. Ann picked up Chris, "Is my sweet baby boy awake?" Chris cooed at his mother. Ann turned toward the front to take Chris with her to the seat. *I don't remember seeing that hole under the seat.*

She held Chris on her lap, so he could see her face and thought no more about the hole until she heard a rustle. *Something's under this seat.* She held Chris tight, jumped out, and looked under the wagon. *More holes.* "Noah!" She dashed to the back of the wagon and snatched up Joy. Protecting both babies, she sprinted to Noah. "Something is under the seat. Don't say a word. Come look."

Ann pointed to the holes. Noah slowly stuck his finger into a hole. He motioned Ann away from the wagon. "There's cloth. Like a dust barrier. I'll bust it open."

"Don't. It might be a pet. You'll scare it, or you might hurt it. We need to open it carefully."

Since their new wagon's toolbox was locked with a padlock, and they didn't have the key, Noah got a hammer and a small pry bar from the jockey box of another of the wagons. Ann wanted to see what was under the seat but walked behind the wagon in case she had to run away with Chris and Joy.

Noah hammered the pry bar between the top backboard and the seat top.

A voice called out, "Halt!"

Noah immediately stopped. A jingling came from behind the boards. The right side of the backboards barely cracked open. A small boy with scared eyes peeked out.

"It's alright, child. We won't hurt you." Noah pointed to himself, "I'm Noah." He pointed to Ann. "That's Ann, my wife." He got Chris. "This is my son, Chris." Noah laid him in the drawer on the wagon bed and then took Joy. "My daughter, Joy." Noah held out his hand and helped Ann back into the wagon.

The boy still held the door mostly closed.

"Nikki." He opened the door more. "Adele." A baby about a year old dropped forward to her hands and started to crawl out.

Noah sat on the floor. He took Chris into his lap. "Come meet each other." The boy shrugged his shoulders. Noah held out his hand.

Ann sat beside Noah. Nikki pointed at Ann and then Adele. He dragged his sister to Ann and pointed at Ann's breast.

"She's hungry?" Ann took Adele, cradled her, and brought her to her breast. Adele nursed as Nikki stroked his sister's hair. "Do you know how to talk?" asked Ann. Nikki shrugged his shoulders. Ann said, "I think he doesn't speak English."

"Wo sind Mama und Papa?" Nikki looked out the front of the wagon. He ran to the back and peered out. "Wo sind Mama und Papa?"

Noah realized he was asking where his parents were. "I'm sorry. They died."

"Wo sind Mama und Papa?"

The boy is not very big. Probably around seven years old. I can catch him. Noah set Chris beside Ann. "Come." He jumped out and then held up his arms. Nikki leaned out into Noah's arms. Noah put him on his hip and then picked up the shovel from the back of the wagon. He put Nikki down before he dug out a shovelful of dirt and pointed into the hole. "Mama und Papa."

"Nein!" Nikki ran back in the direction from which they had come. Noah dropped the shovel and ran after him. He caught Nikki and picked him up.

Nikki screamed, "Nein! Nein! Nein!" and frantically tried to get out of Noah's arms.

Noah held him tight and rocked him. "I'm sorry." He hurried back. Grabbing the shovel, Noah got into the driver's seat, held Nikki, and let him cry.

Adele slept with a full belly, so Ann opened the door to the secret compartment and looked in. Nikki watched her. On the ceiling hung cloth pouches. On a raised platform stood a stack of diapers and a square wooden pail with a lid. The floor had a thick mattress, a blanket, and a pillow. A rack of bottles filled the left side. Holes had been bored into the bottom of the stands on both sides.

First, she felt in the holes. *More cloth to keep out dust.* She unbuttoned one of the pouches. "Dried apples, smoked sausage, hardtack, and raisins." Next, she pulled out one of the bottles, uncorked it, and smelled the liquid.

"Wasser."

Ann carefully placed a drop on her finger and then touched her tongue. "Water." She held the bottle toward Nikki. "Water," then repeated, "Wasser."

Nikki nodded. "Wasser. Water."

Ann smiled. "Wasser. Water." She held out a dried apple slice. "Apple."

"Es ist ein Apfel."

Ann repeated the sentence. "Es ist ein Apfel. Apple."

Nikki climbed into the wagon. Ann laid Adele and Joy inside the hidey-hole under the seat and then got in with Chris and Nikki. Ann and Nikki told each other the names of the objects inside. "Nikki, how did you feed Adele?" Ann put a raisin in her mouth, chewed, and then swallowed. She pointed. "Feed. How feed Adele?"

Nikki nodded his head, took a few raisins, chewed them up, and then spit them into his hand. "Feed." He ate the mash himself. Ann and Nikki ate raisins as they continued stating the names of the things they could see. Noah sat in the driver's box and listened.

Ann choked on a raisin. She pointed to the bottles of water. "Get wasser."

"Hol wasser," Nikki spoke the request as it should have been said and then handed her a bottle. "Bitte hol Mama und Papa." He pointed back the way from which they had come.

"I think he wants us to get his parents."

"I suppose I could get the bones and then catch up with you. Stay right beside the river. I'll get Rose."

Six

Noah returned with Rose, the mule he had saved from drowning in the Maumelle River, then tied on a large canvas bag and a shovel.

"Nimm mich."

Noah shrugged his shoulders. He pointed and told Eyanosa, "Follow." Noah mounted up and urged Rose forward.

"NOAH! Nimm mich!" Nikki held up his arms.

"Oh. You want to come. All right. Nimm mich."

Nikki correctly said I will take you. "Ich werde dich nehmen."

Noah attempted to repeat what he thought Nikki had said as he pulled the boy up in front of him. *This is going to be difficult until we both know the same language.*

At a slow canter, they retraced the mile they had traveled and were there in only minutes. Noah lowered Nikki to the ground beside the small grave.

"Sie können hier nicht passen." Nikki held his hands wide apart. "Papa." He had his hands very close. "Grab."

"They're just bones." Noah started to dig.

Nikki shrugged his shoulders. When he saw the bones, he was horrified. "Wie sind sie nur Knochen?"

Noah pointed to the sky, circled, and flapped his arms, then squatted beside the grave and acted as if he was pecking at the grave.

"Die Vögel haben sie gegessen?"

"Vultures ate them." Noah put something imaginary in his mouth, then chewed.

Nikki clenched his fists and shook them at the sky. "Ich hasse dich, vultures."

Noah put on his gloves before he started putting the bones into the bag. Nikki tried to help. Noah pushed his hands away. "You don't have gloves." Nikki tried to pick up another bone. Noah shoved his hands away again. "No."

Nikki pushed Noah's hands back. "Sie sind mein Papa und Mama."

I think he said, 'Me Papa and Mama.' They are his parents. Noah took off a glove and held it open.

Nikki slid in his hand. "Vielen Dank."

"You're welcome."

"Ihre Begrüßung." Nikki held the glove on with his other hand as he put his parent's bones into the bag.

"I think we've found all we can." Noah tied the bag shut.

"Vielen Dank." Nikki hugged Noah's neck.

"You're welcome." Noah secured the full bag behind the saddle, along with the shovel. He got on Rose and pulled Nikki up. Together, they silently traveled west.

Seven

Before the wagon train had stopped, Noah, Nikki, and Rose had caught up. Ann sat in the back with the three babies as Eyanosa and Zi continued to obey Noah's last command. Noah let Nikki down. Nikki ran and jumped up onto the end of the wagon. Inside it, he held his hands out for the bundle of bones. Noah kept ahold of it as Nikki lowered the heavy bundle into the wagon. Nikki said, "Mama und Papa."

I feel so badly for the boy. "I know," replied Ann.

After he had Rose back with the rest of the herd's unharnessed members, Noah walked between Eyanosa and Zi. He rubbed and scratched both of them behind the ears. "Good boy. Good girl. You did what I told you to do." Noah had been training Eyanosa since the horse had been given to him two years before. He had been training Zi just under a year since he had received the mare as payment for his medical care of two women in Maumelle.

The horses knew several spoken commands, whistle commands, hand signals, and all the usual bridle and legs pressure commands. Follow, stay, come, swim, forward, backward, right, left, run, stop, hide, kick, stomp, drink, and eat, as well as combinations of the commands were all well-known and followed by the two horses just like Noah's and Ann's other two horses, Biscuit and Promise, and their four mules, Honor, Justice, Starlight, and Glory.

Noah had become very attached to Rose and had been teaching her as well. He figured Roscoe wouldn't mind. After all, Stephanie had trained Redeemed; the mule Roscoe was going to put down because it was so contrary. She had slowly won the mule's confidence and then her obedience. Stephanie had then traded a smaller mule that was willing to obey Roscoe for the large mule that, at that time, was mostly only useful to her. Redeemed had since then become obedient to all of them.

Noah and Nikki had barely gotten back before Roscoe yelled, "HALT!" All the animals ceased walking. "The prairie is the same everywhere, but this looks like a good place for the animals to get to the river to drink."

Nikki jumped out of the wagon and ran to Rose to take her to the water. Sally turned her head and looked twice. "Who is that?!"

Noah helped Ann out of the wagon. "Nikki. We'll tell everybody everything in a minute."

Ann picked up Adele from the wagon. "And this is Adele." So they could both work and care for their babies, Ann got Chris and Joy into their cradleboards. "I don't know how we're going to carry three babies."

As he got Spirit out of the harness, Tom stroked the neck of the horse he loved. "Make me a cradleboard. I'll help."

Eli held out his hands to take the large baby. "Hello, Adele. Make it adjustable. We can all take turns."

Ehawee slipped on the cradleboard Adahy had made for when their baby arrived. "We can use this one while you make another. Put Adele in."

The family walked all the animals to the river. Sally held out her hand. "Hello, Nikki." Nikki turned and looked at her. "I'm glad to meet you. I'm Sally." She continued to hold out her hand. Nikki looked at Noah and shrugged his shoulders.

Noah put his hand on Sally's shoulder. "He doesn't speak English."

"He doesn't? What does he speak?"

"I'm not sure." Noah pointed to himself. "Noah." He pointed to Nikki. "Nikki." He pointed at Sally. "Sally."

Nikki said, "Sally," then pointed at Stephanie.

Stephanie tapped her chest. "Stephanie." The same procedure continued until everybody had told Nikki his or her name.

Ann wanted to know the heritage of the most recent children God had given her. "Nikki." Nikki trotted over. She pointed to herself, "Ann Williams," then touched Nikki.

"Nikki."

"Ann Williams. Nikki…" Ann circled her hands. Nikki shrugged. Ann put an angry expression on her face. "Nikki, come here now." She stomped her foot and pointed to the ground.

Nikki's eyes lit up with understanding. He laughed. "Nein, Nicholas Wolfgang Krüger, komm jetzt her."

Ann pointed to Adele. Nikki said, "Greta Adele Krüger."

Tom informed them, "Those are German names."

Roscoe started back to camp. "Let's jack up the wagons. I'll get the linseed oil troughs, so we can get them under tonight's wheels." He examined the wheels on Nikki's wagon. "We need to soak all the wheels on the new wagon. They're drying up. Some of the spokes are loose."

Tom removed the jack from the jockey box on the side of the wagon. "We also need to grease the wheel hubs on all the wagons tonight. I heard them squeaking."

"I'll get the grease, Pop." Eli leaned over and unhooked the bucket of grease from under the back end of one of their wagons.

As they did the evening chores, Nikki went to one person after the other. He tried to remember and then say each person's name. Later, even though Nikki didn't understand a word, he quietly sat while Sally read the evening's Bible verses. Eli played with Hattie. Noah lay on a blanket and entertained Chris, Joy, and Adele.

Eight

Every morning, Noah whistled for his horses and mules that then came galloping home to the wagons. Each day, more of the others came when called. So far, the sheep and goats had ignored the summons. The animals that returned to the wagons were rewarded with a handful of oats and then ridden to search quicker.

Once under way, they bumped along over the hard soil for most of the morning. Suddenly, an enormous hare sprung from a shallow depression, leaped over Hector, and then zipped under the animals tied to the lead line strung between the wagons. Mules, horses, and donkeys reared. Chaos ensued. The larger animals took off, jerked the goats, sheep, and miniature donkeys off their feet, and dragged them across the prairie.

The wagons lurched. The loose wheel spokes of the new hidey-hole cart snapped, the wagon leaned, twisted the falling tongue, and then sheered it off. Freed of their burden, Hector and his team flew across the prairie. Roscoe zoomed after them. "Halt!" he screamed.

None of the animals obeyed. The rope jerked the

slowing wagon. The twisted hemp snapped as the cart crashed onto its side. Eli, Noah, and Tom raced to catch the other teams.

Stephanie, who had been walking, aimed her rifle at the giant ears zigzagging through the grass.

BLAM! The retreating ears dropped from view.

"I'm going over to get it," she informed her fellow walkers.

"I see some of the little animals getting up over there. I will get them." Adahy looked at his wife. "Help me."

Still in view of the overturned wagon, Ehawee stood beside the carcass of a sheep. "We lost this one. Its head is smashed."

"It is a good thing the line broke close to the other wagon." Adahy handed Ehawee the lead rope tied to many of the animals. He hefted the sheep's remains onto his shoulders. "We should eat this."

Spirit raced beside Starlight's team. Tom reached for the reins. "Whoa!"

Not far to his left, Eli jumped off Ace onto the seat of a bouncing wagon and grabbed the reins. "Halt!"

Noah got ahold of the harness of June and brought the animals to a stop.

Roscoe still rode an all-out race to catch the free team. "Halt!" he hollered as he directed King to Hector's side. The mule didn't slow. King drew ahead and then ran in front of the charging team. Hector and the others followed the mule from which all the animals took their lead. Roscoe slightly drew back on the reins. He slowed the group to a stop, turned around, and saw nothing but open prairie. *How far have we come? It's not safe out here alone like this! I need to get back to the group.* At a canter, he led the team back along the swath of crushed grass.

Only minutes before the hare had wreaked havoc, Ann had been in the overturned wagon feeding Christopher. She looked at the wreck. "I could have been in there!" She hugged Christopher.

Beside her, Sally had Joy on her back. "Thank You, God, that Ann had already gotten out and that this isn't the wagon with the dynamite."

"We would have been blown to smithereens!" Helen loosened a wagon cover tie-down. "We might as well start salvaging what we can."

Stephanie draped the enormous white-tailed jackrabbit over her arms and carried it to the wagon. "This rabbit had nursing babies somewhere. It's no wonder that it scared our animals. She must be two-feet-long, and these legs have got to be every bit of seven inches."

"It has gigantic ears. Four inches at least. Do you want to search for the babies?" Sally asked.

"We need to deal with this mess first." Ann drew the canvas from the broken wagon bows. Minus the two drawers Ann had in her wagon and the one Stephanie was using as a baby bed, the dresser lay smashed at the bottom of the pile. Supplies spilled from broken crates. Cushioned by feather mattresses, the piano lay on top of it all. "Helen, the piano is all right. Let's set up camp. We'll cook the dead animals while we get this wagon back into traveling condition."

The days were getting hotter. The bones of Nikki and Adele's parents stank to the high heavens. "We should boil these bones." Helen set the bag aside.

Ann refused, "I won't put Nikki through watching us boil his parents."

Noah returned in time to hear the comment. *We have to do something. Nikki always sleeps close to them.* He got down beside Ann and whispered into her ear.

Helen had an idea. "Ehawee, do you think it would work if we wash the bones in the river, wrap them in clean duck cloth, and then weave horsehair around the bundle to secure it closed?"

"That's a wonderful plan. I'd like to help?"

Helen wrapped her arms around Ehawee. "Thank you."

Noah stated the conditions upon which he and Ann had just agreed. "Nikki needs to know that we honored his parents. We boil the bones and give the water with their flesh a proper burial. Everybody has to leave something in the grave that will help their souls get to heaven." Noah needed to know the exact names of Nikki's parents. "Nikki." He led his new son to the bag of bones and pointed to himself. "Noah." He pointed to Nikki. "Nikki." He pointed to the bones.

"Freda und Otto," Nikki replied.

Noah went down to his knee and hugged Nikki. "Danke."

"Bitte. Ich bin froh, dass du es wissen willst."

Noah shrugged his shoulders. Other than you're welcome, he had no idea what Nikki had said, but he had an idea. He got a shovel, dug a small hole, and then retrieved one of the bones and held it under his nose. He waved his hand and turned his head. Then, he picked off a piece of flesh, put the bone back in the tipped-over wagon, dropped the flesh into the hole, and covered it.

Nikki nodded his head.

Eli drove a wagon up to the overturned one. "Darling," Stephanie disemboweled the rabbit, "would you shear the sheep before you skin it? We should make yarn. Do you want to tan this rabbit fur?"

"Yes, and yes," Eli set the brakes.

Tom arrived. "We need to remove everything, so we can right the broken wagon." He climbed down and unharnessed the tired team.

Sally climbed into the wagon and got an axe. "I'll chop up the broken dresser. We can roast the rabbit over the wood. Maybe Roscoe will make his amazing barbeque with the sheep's ribs. I'll ask him when he gets here."

The animals' skins and strips of meat hung in the smoke as they boiled the flesh off Otto and Freda Krüger's bones. The men replaced two wheels, then lashed spokes from the ruined wheels to the broken bows. Roscoe had not yet returned.

"I'm worried about Roscoe." Sally gathered the ingredients Roscoe used to make the barbeque.

Standing outside the wagon, Helen took the

items Sally handed out. "I am too. Maybe somebody should go looking for him."

Tom searched the grass for the kingpin that had been thrown out of the breaking falling tongue. "As fast as those mules were running, they must have gone quite far. They'll be plum tuckered out. He'll have to come home slow. There's a clear path. He'll be fine. I don't think we'll find the kingpin. There's no telling where that went." He decided to get one of their spares to attach the replacement tongue.

While everybody else reloaded the hidey-hole wagon, Noah dug a pit several yards away.

The foamy sweat of running animals flung here and there as Roscoe pushed them hard to get back to the safety of the group. *Stupid animals. Why on earth did they take off like that? We're probably all dead now. I should have let them go!* An aroma reached Roscoe's nose. *I smell my barbeque sauce!* He pulled out his telescope and peered ahead. *I see them. Thank You, God, for getting us back!*

Eli took the reins from Roscoe. "I'll walk them until they've cooled and then rub them down with liniment. Sally and Helen cooked the sheep's ribs with your barbeque recipe. It's delicious. Get some."

"How many animals did we lose? What happened?"

"One sheep was killed. You can also eat some of what caused this wreck. They'll tell you what happened while I take care of these mules."

Nine

Just before nightfall, Noah twisted together a wand of sage. He put on his medicine man mink cape and tied his ceremonial medicine man bones in his hair.

Waving the smoldering sage, he spread the smoke of the burning plants, cleansed the path to the burial area, and removed anything that might hold the souls of Otto and Freda. Through the trail of smoke, Ann brought the water in which they had cleaned the bones. Nikki walked beside her. The other family members followed.

With great respect for the people who had been lost to the earth, Noah spoke, "Great Spirit, Father God in Heaven, we release to Mother Earth the flesh of these two who created Nikki and Adele. God, I ask that you send a guide to take Otto Krüger and Freda Krüger along the Milky Way to the center of the universe to dwell forever in Your presence." He turned to Ann. "Ann Williams, do you release Otto Krüger and Freda Krüger from the responsibility of raising Greta Adele Krüger and Nicholas Wolfgang Krüger from this day forward?"

"I release Otto Krüger and Freda Krüger and accept the responsibility to care for and love Greta Adele Krüger and Nicholas Wolfgang Krüger from this day forward."

Noah tossed the sage into the pit. "Mother Earth, accept this sage in exchange for the souls of Otto Krüger and Freda Krüger." He took the pot of water, poured it over the sage, and then pricked his finger and squeezed a few drops of blood into the watery hole. "Otto and Freda, accept my blood in exchange for Nikki and Adele Krüger. I also promise to love and care for them."

Ann dropped a clipping of her hair into the grave. "Otto Krüger and Freda Krüger, accept my hair in exchange for your hair, which I have kept." As agreed, Noah carefully pricked Ann's finger. She squeezed out drops of her blood. "Accept my blood in exchange for your children. Fly to God, in heaven."

Nikki hadn't known what the ceremony would entail. He held out his hand and motioned for Noah to prick it. Tears rolled down his face as his blood dripped into the grave. "Auf Wiedersehen Mama und Papa. Ich liebe dich und ich werde dich vermissen."

Each of the others gave their solemn promise to love and care for Adele and Nikki as they placed into the grave their gifts to help the souls of Otto and Freda.

Noah continued, "Mother Earth, take the fleshly remains of Otto and Freda Krüger back into the cycle

54

of life. God of the Bible, take the souls of Otto Krüger and Freda Krüger and use them in Your service in Heaven and use us who remain here on Earth in Your service as well." He shoveled a scoop of dirt into the pit. All of them took turns adding soil until the grave was full. "Their souls have been honored and released. We may return to the wagons."

Ten

They followed the Cimarron River west in the vast prairie of white Spring Beauty and Mountain Sweet flowers, yellow clusters of Wild Parsley and Star Grass, as well as purple Prairie Verbena, Vetch, and Violets. Helen took down the wagon cover and rode with Ehawee as they weaved the horsehair encasing around the bones. "I never knew that God had planted such an enormous garden of beautiful flowers."

"Thankfully, also full of buffalo chips," Sally unloaded her satchel of buffalo chips that she had found among the patches of vibrant colors.

That evening, not long after Sally had fallen asleep under the stars in that vast garden, a large drop of water struck her face. She woke and looked up. Water plopped into her eye. "Wake up! Get your bedding into a wagon." With their mattresses and pillows, everybody dashed to their prearranged sleeping areas inside the wagons.

The animal wagon had not had an animal in it for many days and was exceptionally clean. Since it was empty, and they didn't have to worry about throwing objects onto a baby, they quickly tossed everything else inside the animal wagon, then slept crammed in the other wagons instead of outside where they had plenty of space.

After the night of rain, the sun shone bright and hot in the cloudless sky. The air shimmered with evaporating water. Tom once again scouted ahead on Spirit. Far out in front, he saw what he had feared. "Oh, no! Maybe it's a mirage." He looked closely with his viewing glass. *It's real. They're not moving. It's too early for them to have stopped for a mid-day break. I don't know what's wrong. I don't want to ride into trouble.* He turned and galloped east.

When he was still a long way out, Roscoe saw Tom returning at full speed. "Circle the wagons! Get the animals together!" He jumped onto King.

Adahy dropped his armload of buffalo chips, dashed to his horse, and rode out with Roscoe.

Helen dropped the bone bag she was weaving and hurried to the driver's box. *I hope this prairie doesn't become our graves too.*

Ehawee sprinted to the front wagon as Ann, Stephanie, Noah, and Eli ran for the wagon with the hidey-hole. "Get the babies inside!" Noah quickly took off the cradleboard with Chris strapped in. The other three were already inside the wagon, getting Hattie, Joy, and Adele safely hidden. "Nikki, get in the hidey-hole. Eli, help me get the goats and sheep into the animal wagon." Noah jumped out the back. Nikki jumped out behind him. "Get in there!" Noah demanded.

Nikki ran to the animal wagon. "I help." He removed a backboard.

"Sally or Ann, drive the other wagon. I'm staying with the babies." Stephanie grabbed the reins.

"I'm not leaving them either." Ann prayed for protection, then crawled into the box under the seat and locked herself inside with four babies screaming their heads off.

For the first time, they executed their previously planned maneuver. The hidey-hole and animal wagons parked parallel. Roscoe's full wagon pulled in perpendicular to them. The fourth wagon was to complete the square.

Eli and Noah led all the goats and sheep up the ramp that Nikki had already gotten into position. "Danke, Nikki. Komm jetzt her." Noah picked him up as soon as Nikki had come to him. He put him into the wagon with Stephanie, Ann, and the babies. "Help Ann. Ann, let Nikki in—"

Nikki jumped out. "Help Noah."

Noah didn't have time to argue. "Komm." He mounted Eyanosa and pulled the boy up. They rode off to help Roscoe and Adahy herd the rest of the animals into the enclosure in the middle of the wagons. Eli replaced the backboards of the jam-packed animal wagon.

All the animals had been gathered before Tom screeched to a halt beside the configuration. "There's a wagon stopped ahead, and it's too early. It may be an ambush."

"How far?" Roscoe asked.

"An hour ahead. It's not even beside the river."

"How far away from the river?" Adahy continued to survey the land around them.

"Probably fifty yards."

Adahy looked at Noah. "If we go into the river, we could get close without being seen."

Noah also continued to examine the prairie through his spyglass. "I don't want to leave anybody. Somebody may be trying to draw us away. Did you notice any place where the river wasn't as slow as it usually is?"

"I stayed beside it going out. It looked slow and shallow the whole way."

Noah took the spyglass from his eye. "I think we should take down the wagon covers and bows and then drive the wagons in the river. If we stay close to the shore, the animals should be able to keep their feet on the riverbed. That way, we can stay together to defend ourselves and go find out what's wrong."

"That's the only plan that seems reasonable to me," Roscoe replied.

"Let's get at it." Eli loosened the tie-downs of the hidey-hole wagon cover. "We'll have to lay down the piano."

The heavy wagons showed only slightly above the water. To not make a wake or a sound as their four wagons and dozens of animals crept up the river, they moved very slowly. Helen, Ehawee, and Sally walked beside the animals that pulled the first three wagons. Ann and Stephanie stayed with the babies that were finally and blessedly all asleep at the same time. Eli walked in the river beside them. Noah pulled up plants and wove them into shaggy mats. Roscoe, Tom, and Adahy went before the procession and quietly cleared obstructions.

Hours later, and long after they normally would have stopped for dinner and rest, they finally approached the wagon still in the same place as Tom had initially seen it. They halted, then got all the women and children in one wagon with the rifles and pistols. Tom prayed, "God, for years, I thought You had deserted me and didn't care about me. I don't believe that any longer. You brought us here for a reason. Show us what You want us to do and make us brave, so we'll accomplish what You've called us to do. I know You have a plan to protect us. I trust You. In the name of my Savior, Jesus, I pray."

Everybody added, "Amen."

Covered by Noah's plant mats, the men slid a short way up the riverbank with their spyglasses, and most importantly, all four of their twenty-round Lefaucheux revolvers, along with four ammo belts holding a hundred bullets each. Eli, Noah, and Adahy also had their bows and arrows. For an hour, they lay on the riverbank hidden under the mats. Nothing moved in the vicinity of the wagon. There didn't appear to be an animal to draw it.

"The grass between us and the wagon is tall. I'm going to crawl over." Noah slithered up the bank. He moved a foot, then lay still under his camouflage. At less than a snail's pace, he sneaked closer and closer.

I don't think anybody is here. Nobody would do nothing for this long. He continued his slow, methodical approach until he saw the dead horse lying in the grass. He recognized it. *Roscoe told that stupid man he was going to do this. Maybe they're waiting for us to catch up.*

Noah didn't hear a sound as he lay close to the dead horse. Finally, he slithered to the wagon and peeked inside. *They're not here.* He searched the area. He found flattened grass where people had rolled on the ground. When he discovered a blood trail beside several bloodless paths, he waved for the others to come over.

Roscoe led the animals out of the river. He arrived first and looked at the horse. "Warren is an imbecile. We told him he had to let the horse have plenty of time to eat."

Noah watched the wagons come up from the river. "They must have become stranded and then been captured. It looks like he at least tried to protect his family. He was bleeding quite a bit when they were taken north."

Nikki realized the same thing that had happened to his family had occurred again. Shaking his fists in the air, he ran circles around the wagon, kicked it, the dead horse, and Noah's boot, and then started to sob. Noah picked up Nikki and held him as he cried.

Tom joined them. "Do you think they're dead?"

"They weren't when they were taken away."

"We need to rescue them," Tom replied.

Adahy heard the comment as he arrived with a wagon. "We could get ourselves killed."

Helen stood over the horse and shook her head. "We've used all the horsehair we already cut, and the net isn't long enough. Plus, we still need to make a third one. I'm going to take all of this one's tail and mane."

Already thinking the same, Ehawee arrived with two pairs of shears. "We shouldn't cut more from ours if we don't have to."

From the wagon seat, Ann said, "We need to let the animals eat. Should we set up camp here?"

Everybody looked at the two men who would know the most about the behavior of Indians. Noah replied, "There's no place that would be any safer, but let's set up defensively."

Eleven

In order to keep the animals confined but give them more grass, Ann drove her wagon behind the abandoned wagon. "We need to come up with a plan to protect ourselves."

"We can't protect ourselves. We need somebody to protect us." Sally added her wagon into what was now a wagon circle instead of a wagon square.

Helen continued to cut hair from the bloated horse that had probably been dead for several days. "It would be better if nobody knows we're here."

Tom, however, had Emily on his mind. "These people are going to know we're here one way or another because they pay attention to things. Besides that, I'm not leaving without trying to find Emily and Oscar no matter how ruffled anybody's feathers get." He looked at Ann.

Helen looked at her son. "And Warren."

"Of course!" Tom snapped back.

"I hope this horse doesn't pop." Noah worked the harness off the dead animal. "I could go far away from here, then signal that I want to trade. It would probably be the village that took them who came. I could say I want to trade in their village and then look for them."

"I'm going with you," Tom informed him.

Ann didn't like it. "Wait a minute. We didn't decide that Noah is going to risk his life."

Noah held Ann's hands. "It's safer to try to establish a good relationship than to just hope for the best." He didn't allow for more discussion because he knew that was what needed to happen. "Tom, gather up what you want to trade. I'll get some of our black cohosh, ginger, and ginseng to trade."

"But they have no reason to allow us to live. They've already killed two families. Please don't go," Ann begged.

"These people were not dead when they were taken away, and the fact that two families have been attacked means we need to give them a reason to not come after us. Before we go, I want you to pray for our safety and success."

Tom and Noah gathered their trade items while Eli got Eyanosa and Spirit ready to go. The family stood together as Ann spoke. "God, protect Noah, Tom, Warren, Emily, and Oscar. Let us help whoever has them, so they'll give us this family, and so they'll help us get safely across their land. Let us be a testimony of Your goodness, justice, and mercy to the people of this land. I pray in the name of Jesus. Amen."

Adahy watched the two men ride away. When they were almost out of view, he spoke up, "I don't think this is good. Let the animals graze for two hours, then leave the abandoned wagon where it is, go back into the river, and hide until we come back." He jumped onto his horse and galloped in the direction of his last glimpse of Tom and Noah. When Adahy caught up, he reported what he had told the family to do. The three men followed the trail away from the wagon.

"What's that?" Tom pointed to a strange formation. They trotted over and peered into a rocky pit in the earth.

"Looks like snakes in there." Adahy cocked his head. "They're shaking their rattles."

Noah pointed into the sidewinder pit. "That one is the biggest snake I've ever seen. I'm glad they're all down there."

They continued along the trail for an hour, then stopped and set up camp. An hour after that, they lit their fire and sent a smoke signal that they wanted to trade. A half-hour later, a group of twelve men approached their camp. Several wore an eagle feather in his long hair braided at each side and then tied with a deerskin strip. Other than the feathers, the Kiowa warriors wore only breech cloths and moccasins with ermine tails tied at the rear. They sat on prairie ponies they had tamed.

The warriors saw that the clothing of the men by the fire was not their style. They signaled using universal sign language. "You want trade?"

Noah replied the same way, "Rare medicine plants, white-man knives, fishing hooks, other useful things."

The one who appeared to be the leader signaled, "Show."

Tom opened the blanket around their trade goods. Noah displayed his plants. "You brought nothing. We trade in your village."

The warriors spoke to each other in their language, then signaled, "Come."

I hope this is the right group. Tom mounted Spirit. *I really hope so.*

The village, situated beside a stream, drew close. Tom saw the answer. A large wooden structure displayed two adult bodies. Emily's bright red, blistered naked body hung from the top bar by ropes around her wrists with her ankles tied to the uprights. A pool of blood congealed below Warren's suspended, clothed body. Both looked quite dead. Not only Tom but also Noah and Adahy struggled to appear indifferent.

Noah requested, "Mystery man look plants."

Two young men stepped forward. One of them spoke in a loud, abrasive voice. "I told you he was training me! You're not the one! Stand back!"

"He was training me! You stand back!" snapped the other.

The chief slapped his thigh to get their attention. He settled the argument. "Both of you look."

Noah listened to the men bicker as they looked over his plants. He made a guess. *Their mystery man must have died before he named his successor. This is how we get them to do what we want.* "The Great Spirit sent me. I, Tahatankohana, am Mystery Man. I come tell you who Mystery Man this village."

With their children, the women came out of their tipis. Their chief spoke, "No way prove you Mystery Man."

"You will know. Trade with these two. I come back." He swung up onto Eyanosa and rode away.

Tom spoke to Adahy in Quapaw. "Tell him I trade only for the two bodies and the boy."

Adahy passed the messages between the two.

Knowing the blond-haired child was well hidden, the chief replied, "There is no boy."

"I have a vision of a boy." Tom held his hand out at the height of Oscar. "This high." He put his hands into a circle the size of the boy. "This big with hair the color of the sun," Tom pointed up.

The chief glanced at a woman. "There is no boy."

Wearing a bright red shirt and tan breeches, Tom sat behind his trading blanket, opened up a sewing kit, picked up the scissors, and cut two corners from a piece of blue cloth. He unwound a length of yellow thread, which he cut off with the sharp shears. Next, he threaded a large needle and then bound the cloth pieces together with a few stitches in a flower's shape.

The women spoke to the chief aloud.

Tom opened a folded deerskin, unwound a section of the fishing line inside, attached a large fishing hook, and then threw it out. By God's design, the hook caught the corner of his blanket. He pulled it over.

Several of the men in the circle spoke to their leader.

When Tom removed the small whetstone from a knife sheath, sharped the knife, pulled a hair from his head, and cut it with the knife, the chief spoke. "Everything in the blanket for the two bodies."

"The two bodies and the boy."

"There is no boy."

Tom folded up the blanket containing many sewing kits, pieces of blue and red material, as well as many rolls of colored thread, knives with their small whetstone in their sheaves, and fishing kits. He stood up and tied it to Spirit. "All three."

"Sit. This one who speaks for you, show what you trade."

Faster than the Kiowas knew what he was doing, Adahy stood up, pulled his bow from his back, nocked, and then sunk two arrows deeply into one of the posts suspending the bodies. He unrolled a cloth and let his trade items spill out. "Twenty-four arrows."

All the warriors hurried over to see how far the metal arrowheads had gone into the wooden post. Rapid discussion commenced. The chief walked back to Tom and Adahy. "All three for the blanket, everything in the blanket, all the arrows, all the pale-face clothes, and the pale-face horse."

Adahy translated. Tom asked, "Will you add your arrows?"

"Of course." Adahy picked up the arrows.

"Two to each warrior." The chief held out his hand for his share of the arrows.

Tom removed the bridle and saddle from Spirit,

then undressed down to his full-body unmentionables. He held onto his clothes and the blanket with all the trading goods inside. "Bring me the boy, and then I'll hand it all over."

The woman who had spoken to the chief brought Oscar out of their tipi. Oscar ran to Tom and clung to his leg. Tom held out the two bundles. "I need a knife to cut them down."

Knowing full well that he had taken everything Tom had, the chief said, "Use your own."

Hoping Warren and Emily were not bodies but were still living people, Tom, Adahy, and Oscar hurried over. Unfortunately, Warren was dead. Oscar pinched his nose while his tears rolled. "He fought for us. He didn't win. He smells rotten."

"I'm sorry, Oscar. He said he was not well, and he was cut many times. It must have been too much for him. I know he loved you very much. I'm sure he tried his hardest."

Tom worked to untie Emily's hands, and Oscar tried to get her foot loose while Adahy dug his remaining two arrows out of the post. Emily moaned when she dropped into Tom's arms. "Oscar, come." Tom carried Emily to the stream. Facing the village to see what the villagers were doing, he lowered her into the water and then sat beside her. Tom wanted to protect the boy, as well. "Oscar, sit here in my lap. Help me dribble water into your mother's mouth."

Twelve

Noah galloped back to the abandoned wagon as fast as Eyanosa would run. He hollered, "They've got them! We're trading! I need to make something!" Noah gathered a bowl, drill, pry bar, saw, and the one six-foot-long strand of hemp rope that had remained after making the net.

"What are you making?" Ann asked.

"Just something to catch small animals. Somebody, swap my saddle and bridle to Zi." He pried a board off the abandoned wagon then sawed off a five-foot section. A few inches from one end, he drilled a hole just big enough for the rope to go through. A few inches up from that, he drilled another slightly larger hole and the last hole a few inches from the other end. "Everything is well. Take this wagon apart. Keep the spare parts, like the wheels, and axles, and such. We'll use the rest for firewood."

As Noah flew back to the snake pit, he tied a knot in one end of the rope then threaded it back and forth through the board. Noah peered into the sidewinder pit. *Where is that big one?* He lowered the board with the rope loop toward the small animal he wanted to capture. It rattled its tail as the board continued its slow approach. Lighting fast, the snake lunged at the board. Even though Noah repeatedly swung the board and jerked the rope, he caught nothing. The snake moved more quickly than he could react. Noah noticed that the rattler drew its head up and back just before it stuck. He opened the loop wide and waited. As soon as its head started up, he dipped the loop forward and then pulled the rope.

"Got you, you mean thing!" He drew out the snake with its head held securely against the board. He wrapped the rope around and around and fastened the snake to the board.

Holding the board just below the sidewinder's head, he hurried back to the Kiowa village. The chief rose at the report of Tahatankohana's approach. "Why you have snake?"

Holding the rattlesnake securely, Tahatankohana swung his leg over Zi and slid off the horse. "Where are my friends?"

The chief pointed. "Pale-face has woman and boy in creek. Young warrior stands guard. Doesn't need to. Pale-face traded for them."

Tahatankohana walked to the creek. "How are they? Why don't you have the man?"

"He's already gone." Adahy continued to hold his bow with a nocked arrow at the ready.

Tom looked up. "She's severely sunburned and dehydrated. The boy is fine."

Oscar added, "We're trying to get water into Mama. Can you save her?"

"You and Tom are doing the best thing. Cooling her and getting her to drink water."

"Why do you have a snake?" Oscar asked.

"You'll see." Tahatankohana signed to the chief. "Everybody gather around." He untied the snake from the board, making sure he held it firmly just behind its head. He lunged at a few of the warriors, thrusting the snake forward but keeping a tight grip on the instrument of death. Each of them jumped back. He drew the bowl from his medicine bag and handed it to the chief. "Is it empty? Pass it around." Everybody saw that the bowl was empty. He pushed the bowl under the snake's fangs and then darted his head at the creature. He commanded, "Release your poison!" Venom flowed from the fangs into the bowl. Tahatankohana spun a few times with the snake held high before he repeated the venom retrieval procedure. "Great Spirit, show these people that I am your Mystery Man. Allow me to drink this poison and be unharmed." He danced around the circle displaying the substance in the bowl.

The chief signed, "You will die. Then I will kill your friends because you are arrogant!"

"If I live, I will name your Mystery Man."

"If you live, it will be so. You won't live."

"He's not going to drink that. Is he?" Oscar whispered.

"It seems that he is." Tom thought, *Ann is going to kill me if these people don't.*

Tahatankohana raised the bowl high above his head. He opened his mouth and tipped the bowl. The stream of venom flowed into his mouth. He swallowed, then circled again with his mouth open.

The chief looked closely into Tahatankohana's mouth. "You have no sense!"

From his medicine bag, Tahatankohana drew the ceremonial knife Eli had made at Pine Bluff. He stabbed the bottom of the snake's throat and then ran the blade down its body, dumped out its innards, and then hung the skin around his neck. "Add to your gift if I live."

"I will give you my daughter."

"She is beautiful beyond compare, but give something different."

"You won't live. What you want?"

"You feed all my family and animals here in your village until that woman is healed." He pointed at the woman in the creek. "Then village send escort with me to end of Kiowa land."

"It will be so. You won't live."

Noah spoke in English, "Adahy, bring everybody, every animal, and everything, including the abandoned wagon. Don't tell anybody what I did."

"You better be alive when we get here!"

"I will be."

Thirteen

Two hours later, Adahy returned. He found Emily alive and conscious, sitting between Tom's legs with her back pressed against him, staring with fear at the villagers. Oscar sat in front of Emily, who had her arms tightly around her son. He did not see Noah. "Where is Tahatankohana?" Adahy signed.

The chief's wife set down a bowl of armadillo meat, then pointed at a tipi. "Tahatankohana test Mystery Man. You can't go there."

The villagers helped take all the animals to the creek to drink, then let them loose to graze. Ann kept the children hidden while Sally took Emily and Oscar into a wagon. Tom went into the other and put on clothes. Sally held out a shirt to Emily. "It will probably hurt to have anything touch your skin."

Emily took the shirt. "They killed Warren. He tried to fight the three of them who captured us. They cut him all over just like he wasn't even trying. I want to slit all their throats."

"We can't take on a whole village, and we're trying to get them to protect us to the end of their land, so control yourself."

"I hurt too much to do it anyway. Maybe I should just lie down without anything on."

"I'll bring you some food."

"And lots of water, please."

When Sally returned, Emily had on a shirt and trousers. "I'm on fire. I need to lie in the creek again. Ask Tom if he'll help me."

Sally handed Emily the glass of water, along with a bowl of cheese and bread, and then walked away. A minute later, Tom stood behind the wagon. "Of course, I'll help you."

"I'm so hot, but I'm afraid to be alone."

"I understand. You don't need to explain." Tom held Emily's hand. He helped her get out of the wagon, then sat in the creek with Emily laid out in the water with her head on his lap. Oscar sat with them. Every few minutes, Oscar handed his mother the glass refilled with water.

Because Tom appeared unable to sign, the villagers were surprised when all the women and other men signed to them. Ehawee, Adahy, and Tahatankohana were best, but the pale-faces weren't bad.

In the medicine man tent, Tahatankohana sat with the first potential mystery man.

"What is your name?"

The man signaled wind, "Gomda."

"Gomda, show me, tell me everything you know each object." Gomda relayed as much as came to his mind. "You know where get more everything?" Noah asked.

"Yes."

"Later, prove you know where. What you do for three captured?"

"They killed horse. Deserve death."

Tahatankohana released him, then went to his wagon and wrote as much as he could of what he had not already known and drew pictures of the items and the plants. He went into the tipi with the second man and asked his name.

The younger man, claiming to have been trained, signaled antelope, "Tapco." Tapco repeated most of the same information that the first man had. Tahatankohana asked him the same questions about where to get more plants and what to do for the captured people.

"Know plant helps burns. Long way, get some. Let boy stay with mother. Cut down, bury weak man."

"Get ready. We bury man. Tell Gomda." Tahatankohana returned to his papers, added the additional information he had learned, and altered some of his previously written notes. He spoke with Ann. "These people are supposed to feed our animals and us. You're safe here. They won't go against me."

"Why not?"

"They think I'm very powerful and connected to the Great Spirit. Here I am Swift Hawk. Call me, Tahatankohana." He kissed Ann while still inside the wagon. "I'll be just out of vision burying Warren. Fire the revolver if you need me to come back immediately."

Tahatankohana walked to the creek. "I don't want to leave Warren hanging. I want to bury him. Is that all right with you two?"

Emily continued to lie in the water. "I appreciate you respecting him, Noah."

"Call me Tahatankohana while we're here."

Oscar looked up with teary eyes. "He loved us very much. We were the people most important to him. He tried very hard to save us."

"I'm sure that's true. May I bury him, Oscar?"

"Yes."

"What is your last name?"

"Stringer," Emily replied.

Tahatankohana joined Gomda and Tapco. They untied Warren, draped him over Zi, and then rode away on their horses with three shovels and many duck cloth bags. Once out of view, Tahatankohana cut Warren open and showed Gomda and Tapco how to remove an appendix. They looked at Warren's organs and saw his enlarged heart. Tahatankohana stated what he suspected, "That is why he was weak." Even though Warren didn't have a uterus, Tahatankohana showed where one would be and explained how to open it to remove a breech baby. They practiced by sewing Warren back together, then dug a deep hole to bury Warren, and placed him in the pit. Noah signed as he spoke. "We should respect brave man. He gave his life trying to protect his family. Great Spirit, take the spirit of Warren Stringer. Comfort his wife and child. Thank you for allowing us to look at Warren to learn and be better Mystery men for the people You have called us to care for. In the name of Your son, Jesus, I pray."

Tapco asked, "Great Spirit has son?"

"Yes. Maybe no should tell you about Son."

"I want know Jesus." Tapco asked, "You drink snake poison because you know Jesus?"

Tahatankohana mounted Eyanosa. "Some secrets I won't tell. I might tell you about Jesus. Take me to medicine plants." All three gathered plants close enough to travel to and back in the remaining hours of daylight.

That evening, the village women served armadillo, prairie turnips, prickly pear cactus, berries, and pecans. They had also wrapped dough around sticks and then stuck the stakes into the ground beside the fire to bake it. Emily once again insisted that she sit with her back pressed against Tom with Oscar right in front of her where she could hold him.

Tapco sat beside Tahatankohana. "Me take you Pawnee land. Get burn plants tonight. You give me trade plants. Name Gomda Mystery Man. We have no food here. Tomorrow, Tapco take Tahatankohana across land. Tahatankohana teach Tapco. Tapco drink snake poison in village of girl."

"Why you think you can drink snake poison?"

"You teach me."

"Get ready. We get burn plants." Tahatankohana told his family the plan. He added, "Even though you are safe, stand guard." He left with Tapco.

Roscoe took the first guard shift. While the rest

of the family climbed into the wagons to sleep, he pried boards off the abandoned wagon.

Emily didn't know what to do. *I'm scared. It's one thing to ask Tom to let me sit with him. It's another to ask to sleep beside him.*

Tom watched Emily grow more and more agitated. "Emily, you and Oscar can sleep close to me, but you definitely don't have to. My mother will sleep in this wagon with us."

"Thank you. I'm sorry that I'm so afraid."

"Don't be sorry. I understand. I'm going to keep you and Oscar safe." Fully dressed, Tom lay on the feather mattresses on top of the water mattresses that covered the wagon bed. Emily lay down more afraid of having open space around her than the severe pain of pressing her burned skin tightly to Tom.

Oscar lay in Emily's arms. "This bed is very comfortable. We didn't have anything like this."

Helen squeezed in beside Oscar. "My son provides very well for those he loves."

Fourteen

Tahatankohana and Tapco rode through the night. Before the sun rose, they arrived at a dry, rocky hillside covered with clumps of two-foot-tall plants with long, thick, fleshy, grayish-green leaves. White spots covered the leaves' lower and upper surface and had small, sharp teeth at both edges. "Some people from village rip out plants. Pawnee know somebody stole plants. Pawnee attack us. Tonight, take so Pawnee not know."

"Many plants together. Take one, maybe two whole plants with roots. Fix soil."

"Agree."

Tahatankohana handed Tapco a spade and a few duck cloth bags. The two men slithered into the aloe stand and dug up small to medium-sized plants whose absence would not be noticed. They carefully repaired the broken soil and sprinkled pebbles over the removal sites.

Before the first rays of light shone over the hillside, Tapco heard a sound. He hoped that Tahatankohana had also heard it. He couldn't signal, or the approaching men would see him. With three large sacks of plants, he slid backward on his belly, pulling rocky soil over his exit path. Tapco looked at the patch of Aloe. He didn't see Tahatankohana. He watched the men look at the hillside and then walk back the way they had come. *They saw no difference.* He kept watching until he saw the top of a head on his side of the hill.

They joined at the horses. Tahatankohana tied his bags to Eyanosa. "They didn't know." The two men stealthily rode away with a large supply of stolen plants. *I'll be able to grow some of these and have plenty to treat Emily.*

Fifteen

Assuming he didn't know the sign language they were using, the villagers weren't careful as they signed around Tom. While Tahatankohana and Tapco rode home, Tom carefully observed. He looked for any indication that they were in danger. He quickly discovered that the villagers were not eating to give their little bit of food to fulfill the trade made by their chief. Tom spoke with his family in English. "They can't afford to give us this food. We should give them some of ours."

Adahy explained, "We eat their food because the chief must honor his agreement, or he will be disgraced."

Eli didn't like that Tom had lost Spirit. *I could trade pemmican for Spirit. I'll do it just before we go.* "Should we leave as soon as Noah returns?"

Adahy replied, "After Noah names their Mystery Man."

Nikki knew how Oscar felt. He had recently lost both parents and tried to mask his sadness in play. He stood beside Oscar and tried to signal play. "Wir spielen?"

Oscar asked Emily, "Can I play with Nikki?"

"You may, but stay close. I need to see you."

The tension was high for eight hours while the two groups waited for the return of the men gathering plants in Pawnee land. Only a few meaningless messages were signaled until Sally asked, "You show me how make bread on stick?"

Tapco's mother smiled. "I show you."

"Me get flour." Sally brought out a large sack of acorn flour. "I like each show how make. I decide how I like best." She gave each of the women a few pounds of flour.

Ann added, "I want learn how cook vegetables. I get some." She and Stephanie passed out vegetables that they had gathered and then dried in Noah's village.

Emily told them, "They killed Warren and almost killed me. Even with the painkiller tea you gave me, I can barely stand the pain. You're helping them because Noah is one of them."

Ehawee stopped weaving horsehairs around the Krüger's bones. "These people are Kiowa. We are Quapaw. We are completely different people. It is always better to be a friend than an enemy."

Sally added, "I told you we can put you to sleep, so you won't be in pain."

"They'll kill me while I'm unconscious. Oscar, Nikki, come with me." Emily walked to the creek. "Play here by the creek." She lay in the water with her eyes on the boys.

For dinner, both groups ate the bread and vegetable experiments along with grilled lizards.

83

While on their way home, Tahatankohana explained to Tapco how to prepare Black Cohosh to treat hot flashes, rheumatism, and depression. He also told him how to alleviate menstrual cramps and improve concentration with ginseng. Last, he explained how to use ginger to reduce nausea, fight infection, relieve joint and muscle pain, and flavor food.

Tahatankohana and Tapco returned. After his family updated Tahatankohana, he delivered his three trade items to Tapco. "Get ready to go."

Tapco gave half of the black cohosh, ginseng, and ginger to his mother and explained how to use them. He told them why he was going and assured them that he would come back and then take them to a different village. He took the other half of the trade plants to Gomda and described how to use them.

Sixteen

Tahatankohana prepared to name Gomda as the Mystery Man. Inside the Mystery Man tent, he put on his mink cape, tied his medicine man bones in his hair, and laid out the ceremonial blanket of the Kiowa tribe. Gomda and Tapco entered and sat with him on the blanket. "You both very knowledgeable. Both trained. Both able be Mystery Man. Great Spirit says, for this village, Gomda, is Mystery Man."

The edges of a smile touched Gomda's face. "Thank you, Great Spirit."

"You have concerned heart for your people and animals. You know how use everything here in tent. You cunning as coyote. He is first bringer of life. He is your spirit guide." Tahatankohana wrapped Gomda's shoulders with the hide of one of the coyotes Tahatankohana had killed while escaping Little Rock. "You young enough serve long time. Beyond silliness of youth. You have wife, family in this village." On each of Gomda's wrists, Noah put a wide gold bracelet from Hank Butterfield's jewelry booty that his family had found. "Serve Great Spirit well."

Gomda gave Tahatankohana the highly decorated turtle rattle he had made for the day he became a Mystery Man; he thought by choice of the village's previous Mystery Man. "Thank you, Tahatankohana."

Gomda exited the tipi wearing his spirit guide's hide. The sunlight sparkled from the gold bracelets up in the air on his arms.

During the celebration of stewed skunk and more prickly pear cactus, Eli approached Gomda. Eli signed, "I want my father's horse. I own things."

Maybe I can get food for my people as first act of Mystery Man. "Horse belong village. We eat horse. You want horse. You give village other food."

"Pemmican for horse."

We have twelve families. "Two parfleches and more vegetables like today. Times two. Leave tonight when give horse."

"Bring horse. I get pemmican and vegetables." Eli had already laid out the two parfleches of dried antelope, tallow, and chokecherries that belonged to him. He gathered dried apricots and other dried vegetables that he and Tom had brought from their store in Harmony.

Gomda spoke with the chief. "I get pemmican and vegetables for pale-face horse."

"How much?"

"Vegetables two times today. Two parfleches pemmican. They leave now."

"Do it."

Gomda walked to the wagons with Spirit. "You ready go?"

86

Tahatankohana and his family had horses, mules, and donkeys all harnessed with one spot open. All the other animals were tied in strings behind their five wagons. Tapco sat on his horse beside them with his small pack tied behind him. Covered in Aloe juice beneath her clothes, Emily remained close to Tom with her son's hand in hers. Eli, Stephanie, Ann, and Sally handed the food to Gomda, the chief, and their wives. "You shrewd men," Eli signed.

Much to the happiness of Tom, Eli secured Spirit as the lead horse of the last wagon. They left with Emily, Oscar, and a guide who would provide safety to the edge of Kiowa land.

The village had all their unacknowledged food, the hidden items they had taken from Emily's wagon, the food they had traded for the pale-face's horse, a lot of aloes safely taken from Pawnee land, and a new Mystery Man. Most importantly, there was peace in the village because Gomda and Tapco's conflict ended when Tapco departed.

Seventeen

So Emily and Oscar could say goodbye, they rode past Warren's grave. Tom asked, "Would you like to have a service?"

"Yes," Emily replied.

Tom read Psalm 23, "The LORD is my shepherd, I lack nothing. He makes me lie down in green pastures. He leads me beside quiet waters. He refreshes my soul. He guides me along the right paths for his name's sake. Even though I walk through the darkest valley, I will fear no evil, for You are with me; your rod and your staff, they comfort me. You prepare a table before me in the presence of my enemies. You anoint my head with oil; my cup overflows. Surely your goodness and love will follow me all the days of my life, and I will dwell in the house of the LORD forever."

Emily cried over Warren's grave. "You weren't perfect, but you loved us. You were a good father and a good man who gave his life trying to protect us. I love you, and I'll miss you. Be at peace and healthy in heaven."

88

"Pa, thank you for saving me in the river and for thinking me and Ma are the most important people. I love you too. I'll miss your hugs and your stories."

For this purpose, Noah had secretly kept something of Warren. "When I buried him, I cut this from Warren's head." He gave both Emily and Oscar a lock of hair.

They each asked God to take Warren's spirit and then left him behind. They traveled a few miles before the sun went down, then a few more by the light of the full moon. As the distance between her and the village grew, Emily's anxiety lessened. Even so, she remained close to Tom. Ann wanted to help. "Emily, I don't think I told you about the Butterfield Gang."

"Who are they?"

"The first time I saw Noah, he was unconscious and bleeding to death because of Gus and the rest of the Butterfield Gang. Gus got the gang to shoot up my house, and later, he burned our farm to the ground. I lost everything except our rifles, a few pieces of clothes, a picture, and two candlesticks. Gus was the worst of people. One of his own gang killed him. I hated him with everything in me. I still despise him, but I learned that hating him was hurting me and hurting the people I love. I try to think about all the wonderful things that I now have that I wouldn't have if he hadn't done what he did. I don't know what good things will come to you, but I'm sure they will. Anyway, if you ever want to talk about anything, I'm here for you."

"Thank you, Ann. Right now, I'm hurting too much in every way possible. My skin is on fire, my heart feels like murder, and I'm weary to the depths of my soul."

"I haven't felt that my skin is on fire; the other two I'm intimately familiar with."

At midnight, they stopped. Everybody wanted to leave quickly in the morning for the sake of Emily and Oscar, so they circled the wagons with the two nets between them to keep the animals confined. Emily covered herself with aloe, then lay beside Tom and Oscar and attempted to sleep.

After the sun came up, Tapco tried to make himself scarce. Even though he hadn't been one of the men who had captured or tortured the Stringers, he thought he was reminding Emily and Oscar of what had happened. As a future Mystery Man, he wanted to help, but he didn't know how. "Tahatankohana, how I help? How I not upset Emily and Oscar?"

"First, call me Noah. Second, be kind, be helpful. Don't push yourself on them. Allow them to be angry."

Tapco tried to do as suggested. He kept to himself and looked for medicinal plants and things to eat. He saw wild potatoes. "We dig these. Catch up after get them."

Noah and Tapco always carried spades and sacks, but Noah decided it would be good to take shovels as well. Nikki saw Noah toss them out the back of a wagon, then walk toward Rose. He ran over. "Take me."

"We're just digging up plants, but you can come."

Noah and Tapco stomped the shovel into the ground and pried. Nikki removed the potatoes from the loosened soil with a spade. As they searched for more plants, Tapco felt a vibration through his moccasins. He put his ear to the ground. "Large herd antelope coming. We need get to wagons."

They tossed all the tubers into their sacks and swung up onto their horses. Noah pulled up Nikki, then expanded the telescoping parts of his spyglass. He examined the flat prairie. "Something has stampeded them. We need to hurry."

They galloped as fast as they could. Several yards back, they screamed, "Tie up all the animals! Get them into the wagon!"

Everybody turned and saw the growing cloud of dust. The family flew into action. Noah lowered Nikki into the empty wagon. "Get the backboards off."

Nikki knew what to do. He jerked up the removable top board. Noah quickly rode behind the sheep and herded them to the wagon. Tapco herded mules. Eli, Tom, and Adahy rounded up the other animals.

Ann issued orders to the women. "Get all the babies into the hidey-hole. Let them scream if they want to. Turn the wagons. If we tie the canvas up a foot or so, we can shoot from under it." She ran with Chris on her back. Sally, Ehawee, and Stephanie arrived as Ann climbed into the wagon. She took the cradleboards off the backs of her three sisters.

"Get the wagons ready." Stephanie jumped into the driver's box and yanked the reins.

Helen and Emily screeched to a halt. Emily still hurt something awful. "Oscar, get in here." Unable to help, she scrunched into the wagon corner to stay out of the way.

Helen jumped in and grabbed a rifle. *Roscoe showed me how. I guess I'll find out if I'm any good.* She tied up the canvas.

Sally ran to another of the wagons and maneuvered it into position.

"Ehaw!" Tom cracked his whip behind six mules and ram-rodded them to the wagon cluster. In only minutes, mules, horses, and donkeys had all been run into the space between the wagons.

Ehawee jumped into the fray. Sally frantically handed her a cluster of lead ropes. "You tie your end to the wagon. I'll hook it to their halters."

The antelope herd covered the land as far as they could see. Oscar and Nikki looked out the back of the wagon. Their eyes grew large as the mass of moving animals approached. Noah ran the last baby goat into the wagon. "Boys, jump out! Get in the hidey-hole wagon!"

Sally snapped the ropes to animal halters. Since they didn't do as told but had decided to help, the two boys tied the ropes to the wagon as fast as they could. Sally picked up Nikki and put him on the floorboard. "Come on, Oscar." She climbed inside right after Nikki.

The pounding hooves vibrated the ground.

Tapco stood beside the wagon. "Oscar, get in now!" The leading edge of the stampeding herd split to round the obstacle in the way. Tapco grabbed Oscar and tossed him into the wagon. A horn stabbed into Tapco's arm. He jammed his knife into the animal's neck, jerked free, and jumped into the wagon.

Thousands of bounding animals passed. The family's animals, crammed into the small space between the wagons, jostled with agitation. The instinct to go with the herd told them to run free. They bumped and bumped against the wagons.

Everybody had joined in the hidey-hole wagon, unaware of Tapco's injury. The barrels of several rifles protruded from the wagon. Noah remembered what had happened to his father when he had hunted antelope in Cherokee land. "Shoot only those directly in front of the wagon, or they'll be trampled into nothing."

Carcasses piled in front of them. Antelopes ran past in what seemed to be a never-ending stream of fur, thundering hooves, choking dust, and long horns. Behind the herd, the silence was overpowering.

Tapco jumped out of the wagon. Roscoe took the rifle from Helen. "Great shooting. I saw you kill several."

"It wasn't like it was possible to miss."

"We need to move the wagons apart slowly. I'm sure the animal ropes are tangled." Roscoe exited through the driver's box. "I'll separate them. I'll need some help."

"Maybe we should unhook them first." Sally followed.

Ann walked toward the back of the wagon, "Better yet; I'll crawl under the wagon and untie the ropes on the safe side of the wheels."

Sally saw blood on the wagon floor. "Somebody is hurt! Who is it?"

"Small hurt," Tapco said from outside.

Sally saw Tapco's arm dripping blood. "It is not."

Noah heard and got the supplies he needed. He moved past Sally. He signed, "You should have told us."

"Need kill all we could."

"Let me see," Noah demanded.

Tapco held out his left arm.

Noah looked at the perfect circle a few inches above his wrist. "If you hadn't thrown Oscar inside, this hole would be in his chest. You saved him."

Emily hurried out of the wagon and hugged Tapco. "Your people killed my husband, but you saved my son. Maybe I don't hate you anymore."

"I don't either." Oscar also wrapped his arms around Tapco.

Not one of their animals was lost. However, several in the group had been kicked. Sally made a cedar poultice for Tapco and the animals. She also made the sedative because she could see how much Emily was suffering from sunburn blisters. The others removed skins and scooped out the insides of dead antelopes. Tapco found the carcass with his knife in its neck. After Sally had wrapped bandages full of cooked cedar around the mule, horse, and donkey injuries, she explained to Emily how the liquid from the cooked cedar would keep her rupturing blisters from becoming infected. She also offered the sedative again.

"I don't think Tapco will try to kill me. I can't take the pain. Watch over Oscar." She held out her hand for the cup of liquid oblivion.

All the antelope carcasses lay side by side. Nikki walked down the long row. "Eins, zwei, drei, vier, fünf, sechs... siebenundsechzig."

"Sixty-seven," Oscar ended right after him.

Eighteen

Several days later, Adahy, Tapco, and Noah, with Nikki riding in front of him on Eyanosa, returned to camp with several prairie chickens. Adele stood beside Ann next to the campfire. Adele saw Noah get down and walk toward them. She turned, held up her arms, and took her first step. "Did you see that?" Noah exclaimed as Adele fell.

"What?" Nikki stepped out from behind Noah.

"Adele took a step." Noah knelt and held out his hands. Ann put Adele back on her feet. She took an additional step into Noah's arms. He swooped her up and twirled her around, which was one of Adele's favorite things. "Good girl." He put his hand on Nikki's head. "Nikki shot an arrow today. He pulled the string and let it go, and he didn't even hit his elbow, Eli."

Eli informed his new nephew, "You did better than I did."

Nikki clapped, "I did better!"

The three smaller babies lay on a quilt on the ground. Noah bounced Adele on his knee and then put her beside the other children. She took off at a fast crawl toward Chris, Joy, and Hattie. Before they knew it, she had plowed over Chris. He rolled over and watched her go. "Girl, you are fast. We better keep a close watch on you, and you, my son, you rolled over." He picked up Chris and hugged him.

Chris responded with, "P."

"He's trying to say, 'Pa'."

Ann informed her husband, "He can't talk, Noah."

Joy rewarded her parents by raising on her hands. Several times Hattie raised her head. Stephanie picked her up. "These children are going to be all grown up before we know it."

"Especially me. Look how well I'm making this braid." Oscar held up the new horsehair rope he was braiding for the third net.

Nikki darted over to look. "I make one."

"Get some hair." Oscar pointed. "I'll show you."

After days of pain, the itching was about to make Emily lose her mind. She pulled dead, peeling skin from her arm, but looked at the contentment around her. She thought about what Ann had said. *I do have something good.* The frown on her face left for the first time since the Kiowa had taken her. "I'm glad Oscar and I are traveling with such a nice family."

"We're thrilled that you're with us." Tom flashed his most charming smile.

Helen and Roscoe brought over the pot of antelope stew they had prepared. Emily slid over to Sally. "I think I'm not too afraid anymore. Maybe I can sleep between you and Helen."

"Of course. Is everything all right?"

"I think I like sleeping beside Tom too much."

Emily lay on the ground between Sally and Helen. "Don't we want to sleep on the soft mattress?" Oscar asked his mother.

"We can't push ourselves on anybody."

Tom carried over the feather mattress. "I'd rather you have this. Your skin is still very tender."

"You saved our lives. I don't want to repay you by taking your mattress."

"Please, I won't be able to sleep knowing you're on the hard ground. I'll lay in the wagon on the water mattress."

"It's cold without the feather mattress."

"I have a buffalo hide. I'll be fine."

"I'll lie on the cool water mattress in the wagon with Oscar."

Tom laid the feather mattress on the ground. *I wonder what I did wrong.*

As the days passed, every sharp sound startled Emily and sent her into Tom's shadow. He liked having her close. Oscar remained stuck to Tom too, and he liked that as well. He frequently took Oscar riding on Spirit. He, Noah, and the two boys practiced archery and worked on the net together. Oscar helped Tom grease the wheel hubs and jack up the wagon to put the linseed oil under the wheels to soak them. Tom explained, "So the wood doesn't shrink and break from the dry soil."

Tom felt confused. Sometimes, Emily smiled at him and walked with him all day. Then she would retreat into her mind someplace a thousand miles away and stare at the ground. Tom sat beside his mother. *Emily must think she owes me for saving her life. She doesn't like me. I'm nine years older than she is. There's no reason to think she might like me.* He stared into his plate.

Helen patted her son's knee. "Give it time, son."

"Give what time?"

"I know why you're sulking. It's been very traumatic for her. I know she's interested in you."

"I'm not thinking about her!"

"Yes, you are. Be patient."

Tom jammed his fork into a hunk of antelope back strap that Roscoe had made into a savory roast. He chewed much harder than the meat required. After the meal, he rode Spirit into the prairie, knelt under the stars, and prayed. "God, first You took Hattie from me, and I hated You for years. Now, I've come back to You. I'll take whatever pain You give me, but can't You find it in Your plans to not put a woman like Emily in front of me when she doesn't like me? Help me let Emily live her life with whomever she wants and be happy that she's happy."

Emily watched Tom ride away. *If only I knew whether or not he only feels obligated to take care of me. Sometimes he seems so upset. I don't want to push myself on him, but we can't make it across the prairie alone.*

Ann walked to Noah with Chris on one hip and Joy on the other. "Please hold our babies for a few minutes." She strolled over to Emily. "He's a wonderful man."

"I know... It's just... I don't know. That horse died just like Roscoe said it would. We thought we'd wait there for you to catch up, and then we'd stay with you. After a few days, those Indians rode up. They looked at our horse stinking to the high heavens. Before Warren even knew it, they'd knocked his rifle from his hands and slashed him all over his arms and chest. For several minutes, he fought them. He stayed between them and Oscar and me. They just kept slicing tiny cuts on him. I was too afraid to try to help. I begged them to stop. Then Warren went down to his knees, panting.

"They tied his hands and then mine and Oscar's. They made us walk all the way to their village. Those vile people tied Warren and me, and they took Oscar away. I screamed, "Don't hurt him!" I begged them to give Warren water. Warren hung beside me with his blood dripping into the dirt. He apologized for not being able to defend us. He thanked me for loving him and giving him Oscar. I watched him bleed to death right there beside me, and I hadn't done anything to try to save him when he was trying to save us. He was dead before the day ended.

"I hung there for two days beside him with no water. I begged to see Oscar and know that he wasn't hurt. Then it poured rain. I kept my mouth open and drank rain all night. In the morning, they stripped me. I guess I was taking too long to die, and they thought the sun would kill me. All morning, the sun cooked me. I felt my skin blistering before I passed out.

"I woke in the creek with Tom and Oscar looking down at me. I've never seen anything more reassuring. Tom had me. I knew I was safe, and Oscar was too. How could I think that? How could I feel glad that Tom was there? Warren died for me, but I wanted Tom to be there. I'm a horrible person."

"You are not horrible. Yes, Warren did something remarkable. Knowing they were killing him, he did everything he could. Few people are that brave. I'm not. I'm so far from brave that I can hardly stand it when Noah is his usual brave self. If you had tried to fight, you would have lost, and Oscar wouldn't have either parent. You did the right thing. And there is nothing wrong with wanting to feel safe. Tom makes me feel safe too."

Emily turned to Ann and let Ann wrap her arms around her. "Thank you for listening. I feel a little better. I still don't know about Tom. I don't want him to feel that he's responsible for me. I don't want to be a burden hung around his neck."

"I'm sure he doesn't think you're a burden. Give yourselves time. You went through something horrible and traumatic."

Nineteen

The village of Tapco's girl drew near. "Noah, teach how drink snake poison. Need be Mystery Man P'ahy village."

"Nothing to teach. Poison in blood. Poison in stomach. You die. Venom in blood. You die. Venom in stomach. You live. Snakes make venom. Make big show. Not boring. Scare people with snake. Get venom in bowl. Make sure everybody knows venom in bowl. Make sure everybody knows you drink. Nothing more to it."

"That is all?!" Tapco felt astounded.

"Much is Mystery Man show. Medicine real. Make people believe is real with show and ceremonies. People must believe. Must feel what you want, just like war make enemy feel fear. You win. Mystery Men make people feel happy, healed, afraid, loved. You make them feel and believe what you want."

"Need find viper."

"Only have skin last one. Hard to find. Ask Great Spirit son, Jesus, help you find."

"Jesus, son of Great Spirit. I need be Mystery

Man, so P'ahy be wife. I drink snake venom. Make them believe I Mystery Man. Help me find viper."

Noah signed; let it be so. "Amen."

Tapco repeated, "Amen." He explained his travel plan. "Tomorrow, me and you ride north," he held up one finger, "day. Drink venom. Make P'ahy wife. P'ahy come with Tapco and Noah."

Noah didn't want to feed two people, but it was a small price to be safe from attack. "If you don't find snake, what you do?"

"You tell me something."

"Mystery Man must think for self."

Noah and Ann had taken to sleeping with their four children in the hidey-hole wagon. The babies couldn't get away while sleeping in dresser drawers, and nothing could easily get to the children. If they needed to, they could hide the children in the hidey-hole. Stephanie, Eli, and Hattie slept in the wagon they had bought in Harmony.

In the privacy of the wagon, before the sun came up, Noah loved on Ann, then lay beside her, and held her tight. "I'll only be gone a few days. It was part of my agreement with Tapco. Help him become the Mystery Man of the village just north of here, so he can marry the woman he wants."

"I know. You already told me three times. Tapco and P'ahy are coming with us."

"I guess it's more that I'm telling myself that I have to do this because I don't want to leave you or the children."

"I'm going to miss you too. We'll be fine. We'll stay right here until you come back."

"No. I decided. Everybody goes together. You wait only a little bit away from the village."

A day later, they set up camp just beyond the area surveilled by the village's men. When the sun came up, Tahatankohana and Tapco put together a large bundle of Yarrow, Echinacea, Wild Mandrake, and Evening Primrose that they had gathered as they traveled. They rode to the village, still searching desperately for a rattler. They were escorted in without a snake. In Kiowa, Tapco informed their escort, "I want to speak with Guipago." They walked toward a tipi. The loud, irritated voice of a woman issued from inside. Guipago came out of the tipi so quickly that he bumped into Tapco. "Tapco. Why are you here?"

"I come to ask for P'ahy."

"This is not a good time to ask. Ankímä is always so unhappy and mad around this time of the month."

"I heard that!" said a voice inside the tent. "Bring Tapco in here!"

Tapco turned toward Tahatankohana. "I have a friend with me."

"Bring him," said the voice inside the tipi.

P'ahy had heard the whole conversation. She sweetly smiled at Tapco but remained silent behind her mother, as instructed. Guipago stood behind Tapco and Tahatankohana for shelter from the unhappiness of his wife. Ankímä stirred the pot over the fire in the center of the tipi and rubbed her belly. "Why are you not waiting until the Sundance to ask for P'ahy?"

Tapco remembered what Tahatankohana had told him. *What should I make this family believe and feel? They are important. I will love them all. I will make life better if they give me P'ahy.* Tapco noticed that Ankímä continued to rub her belly. *Guipago said Ankímä is always upset this time of month.* "The Great Spirit sent me to bring these plants to Ankímä."

"He did?" Ankímä and Guipago asked together.

"She is important. He wants her to have them now. I make you something to help your stomach."

"It does feel bad." Ankímä put both hands against her abdomen.

Tapco took off his pack. "This man is Tahatankohana. He is great Mystery Man from rising sun." Tapco had already learned how to prepare the Echinacea to calm the stomach and the Evening Primrose to reduce bloating, irritability, and depression during a menstrual cycle. "Tahatankohana bring me message. P'ahy's family, whole village need Mystery Man. Tahatankohana say that man is me. Great Spirit say, 'Get P'ahy. Take Tahatankohana across land. Become Mystery Man. Live in Ankímä's tipi with P'ahy'."

Tapco chanted unknown words over the pot as he made the tea, then informed them, "We must use a cup never touched by blood."

"I have one." Ankímä searched and then handed Tapco a wooden cup.

"We also need a cloth that has touched your hair only."

"Get the blue one. The one you wear at the Sundance," Guipago suggested.

Tapco poured the tea through the cloth into the cup. "Great Spirit, take away what makes Ankímä feel uncomfortable." He served her the tea.

Twenty minutes later, Ankímä's face brightened. "I feel better. What else do you know?"

"I know I love P'ahy and this family. Will you give your blessing for P'ahy to be my wife?"

Ankímä put her daughter's hand in Tapco's hand. "Tomorrow, you bring horses to Guipago. You take P'ahy. Come back Mystery Man. Help this village."

Guipago took the two newly arrived men to the meeting lodge. All the men of the village sat on ceremonial buffalo hides. The village chief said, "We have no Mystery Man to offer the peace pipe."

Guipago sat beside the chief. "Tahatankohana great Mystery Man from rising sun."

"You offer peace pipe," the chief commanded.

Tapco wondered if Tahatankohana had a Calumet or even kinnikinnick. Tahatankohana reached into this medicine bag and drew out a pipe stem. He stood up and raised it to the east. "The pipe is the male principal." He touched the turkey feathers and the eagle feather he had added since they had left Pine Bluff. He flapped his arms and circled the group. "The feathers are all the winged ones."

He touched the bundle of hair fastened to the pipe stem, bent toward the earth, and brought the pipe toward Mother Earth. "The horsehair is all the four-legged ones that walk on Mother Earth."

After touching the alligator hide wrapped around the wooden tube, he continued his dance. He brought his hands together then spread them apart as if swimming and parting the water. "The alligator skin is all the swimming ones. The wood is everything that grows." He raised the pipe stem to the south. "Together with the two-legged ones, all are one."

Tahatankohana retrieved the bowl from his bag and raised it in the west. "The bowl is the female principle and the sun. Both bring life."

He inserted the stem into the bowl. "All things join with us who smoke the pipe."

Tahatankohana brought forth his pouch filled with the herbs of power: sage, cedar, tobacco, and sweetgrass. He filled the bowl as he twirled and circled. "With the Calumet, we send prayers to the Great Spirit in Father Sky."

He used small tongs from his bag and drew an ember from the fire in the lodge's center. He lit the pipe, drew in smoke, and then blew it out. "Great Spirit, we send our prayers to you on this fragrant smoke. Hear our prayers. Aho."

He offered the Calumet to the chief.

Tapco had never seen a Calumet Dance performed more elegantly. Once again, he thought about Tahatankohana, saying much of being a Mystery Man is about the showiness of the ceremonies so that the people believe and feel what he wants. *What do I believe and feel? That Tahatankohana is a real and worthy Mystery Man. That I am part of something sacred. That the chief has been*

107

honored and respected, as well as all of us. That I am one of the men of this village.

The chief spoke, "Great Spirit, receive my gratitude. You have sent this Mystery Man to make our village whole. Hear my prayer. Aho."

Tahatankohana realized something he needed to clarify. Each of the men smoked the pipe. Tahatankohana added more kinnikinnick to the bowl when needed. They sent their many prayers to the Great Spirit. Tahatankohana spoke last, "Great Spirit, you heard the words spoken many days ago. You answered the prayers of the worthy people of this village. You sent me to polish the person you want to be the Mystery Man in this village. Hold them steady for a short time more, and Tapco will return to them with power. Aho."

Tahatankohana hadn't officially named Tapco as a Mystery Man, but he had declared his intention to do so. All the men said, "Aho."

Tapco was as good as accepted into that position. Tapco smiled to himself. *We did it without a snake. That will be something for when it is needed.*

After the pipe ceremony, Guipago announced, "Tomorrow, Tapco will marry P'ahy. They will travel with Tahatankohana, then Tapco and P'ahy will return.

Tahatankohana stood. "Tapco, hunt for seven steps ceremony. P'ahy, prepare marriage dishes. Village, prepare gifts. I will purify the marriage lodge shortly after sunrise. Be ready."

Twenty

Tahatankohana and Tapco returned to the wagons. Tapco didn't have to hunt for new meat. He had killed so much that they had plenty, but he wanted his offering to be entirely for P'ahy, so he took his bow and arrows and left the camp.

Noah told the family what had happened. Stephanie hadn't been at Ann and Noah's Indian marriage. She had never seen one. "May we come?"

"It's best not to. I don't think this family in any way changes who I am as a Mystery Man. The people of P'ahy's village might think so. I don't want to jeopardize Tapco's future."

P'ahy had something she had to tell Tapco, and she couldn't do it in her tipi. She followed them away from the village. When she arrived at the wagons, she was very surprised and alarmed. It was Ann who noticed her. "Noah, a girl from the village is hiding in the grass."

Noah climbed into the wagon and peered through his spyglass from under the cover. He got out of the wagon and faced the field. "P'ahy." He signaled, "Come."

This Mystery Man has the power to see hidden things. She slowly stood up.

Noah signed to her, "Tapco hunting. Meet family. Tomorrow you come with all." He put his hand on Ann's shoulder. "Wife, Ann." He touched Nikki, "Son, Nikki." He pointed to the four children on a blanket with a net around them. "Son: Chris also named Wambleeska, white eagle. Daughters: Joy and Adele. Niece: Hattie." He walked to each person and stated his or her name and how they were related.

"So many," P'ahy replied. "I need tell Tapco something important."

"Don't know how long Tapco be gone. I tell him for you."

"Maybe he should hear from me."

"You might wait until morning."

"Have to get back. Get ready." P'ahy fidgeted, then explained her dilemma. "Tell him I hiding sister, Akea. She not want man father picked." She balled up her fist, stuck the air, and then pointed at her face. "He hit eye." She drew a big bubble in front of her stomach. "Hit baby inside. Not his. Baby from Sundance. Must take sister with us."

That makes three people to feed. Although Tapco certainly has found enough food for three. "Can you bring sister here now?"

P'ahy smiled and nodded. "Yes. Maybe Tapco marry sister too."

Tahatankohana said, "For now. We only bring her."

P'ahy nodded and ran away. Thirty minutes

later, she returned with her sister. "This Akea. I go home." She dashed back in the direction of her village.

Noah again named everybody. The girl retreated to a wagon wheel and tried to scrunch herself into as small a space as possible. Ehawee, also clearly soon to be giving birth, sat beside her. "Give hand." She placed the girl's hand where the baby inside her was kicking. "Baby." She pointed. "Growing babies same time."

The girl smiled. "Growing babies together. Many babies." She pointed but remained pressed against the wheel as she looked from behind a black eye. "Many everything."

As the sun went down, Tapco returned with twelve prairie chickens. "Hard find..." He noticed the girl sitting beside the wagon's wheel. "Akea! Why are you here?"

"P'ahy brought me. Said I go with you. I have big trouble." She stood up. "Husband no good. I hiding."

Tapco saw her eye. "Who did this?"

"Not tell you who husband."

"Who is he?" Tapco demanded.

Noah spoke up, "P'ahy wants you to marry both of them."

"I am not! I take you home right now. You show father!" He seized Akea's hand and started to drag her.

Noah interfered, "Tapco, leave her here. Tomorrow, marry P'ahy. Later, decide about Akea. Talk long with P'ahy and Akea. Think much."

Tapco stopped. "I wait."

Later, Noah also told Tapco, "Other thing about Mystery Man. Many things make angry. Shock you. Must not show feelings. Must think long. Like friends on rack. Noah, Tom, Adahy not show angry, worried. Not easy. Found out everything first. Got Emily and Oscar back. Got new friend, Tapco. No more people hurt."

Twenty One

Tapco returned to his original thought. "Found only small game. Not good enough. Have only one horse. Not good enough. P'ahy worth more."

Akea spoke, "Steal P'ahy tonight. Bring father many horses when return."

"Maybe cannot be Mystery Man if I steal P'ahy."

Noah felt led to intervene. "Tahatankohana will go tell Ankímä and Guipago, Great Spirit says must leave now. Pay whole village bride price later."

Akea nodded her head and shooed Noah toward the village.

Tapco agreed, "Get her."

Noah walked away because he didn't want to decide between leaving a horse or leaving P'ahy. He returned at midnight, wiping away the trail left by him and the girl. "I gave message. Best we leave now."

Tapco asked, "You want stay this side river? You want cross? Save…" he held up ten fingers, "days. Cut straight across bend?"

Roscoe saw the question. He signed back, "One hundred twenty miles with no water. Cannot do it."

"I know where water. Cross here. Drink much at pit houses. Fill everything water. Walk one day. No break. Drink half water. Walk one day. No break. Drink half water. Walk one day. No break. At waterhole. Drink much. Fill everything. Rest. Walk one day. No break. Drink half. Walk one day. No break. Drink half. Walk one day. No break. Back at river. Drink much. Rest."

"You sure?" Noah asked.

"Tapco sure. Tapco done it."

"How far to bend?"

He held up one hand of fingers. "Days."

The decision was unanimous. They had left late and had already lost over a week of days along the way. They broke camp, rode south, and then forded the shallow, slow-moving river. All the animals walked across the broad stream. Along with Tapco, Noah brought up the rear. "I never would have guessed such a wide section of the river would be so shallow all the way across."

"Most of summer, no water here."

They didn't stop until it was time for the dinner break the following day. Noah and Nikki rode beside the river. They heard a frantic scramble of animal noises. Nikki looked through the spyglass he was holding. "Kuh. Die Hunde versuchen es zu essen."

"What?" Noah took the spyglass and looked across the river. "Hyenas!" He put Nikki on the ground and handed him the spyglass. "Stay." He drew his Lefaucheux revolvers and swam Eyanosa into the river. Nikki watched the cow kick at and try to run the hyenas away from the calf they had already killed.

Noah shot a dog that he could take out with a clean shot as soon as he was close enough. Nikki screamed, "Tötet sie!" The rest of the family noticed the commotion and hurried over.

Two of the wild dogs swam into the river to attack the creature that had just killed one of their pack. The others continued their attempt to take down the cow. The hyenas in the water didn't have a chance. Noah shot them as they swam toward him. As he came out on the far side, he killed another. The hyenas turned tail and ran. Noah and Eyanosa ran down the hyenas trying to escape for two reasons: he wanted the cow, and the hyenas might swim the river and attack them.

Except for the two that were slowly floating away with the current, he dragged together all the carcasses and tied them to one end of his rope. He lassoed the cow with the other end of the line, then swam his horse into the river, towing the unhappy cow trying to get back to the shore where the hyenas had attacked it. The river wasn't more than fifty feet across, so Noah let the rope feed out behind him.

It wasn't the first time they had towed an animal out of the water. Roscoe and Eli hitched up King and Ace. They expected to meet Noah at the river's edge but had to wade out because the rope didn't quite make it with the cow standing on the land across the river and the group of tied-on dead hyenas floating downstream behind the two loose carcasses. Roscoe tied the rope to the two-mule harness and turned back toward camp. "Pull, King. Pull, Ace."

As the mules pulled the cow toward the water, its hooves dug into the soil. Even so, it wasn't able to hold itself back. When it couldn't touch the bottom of the river, it swam because it had no way to resist the force. In only minutes, the dead hyenas and calf lay on the riverbank, and the cow grudgingly came up out of the river. Sally walked toward it with a bucket of grain. "Stop," Ann ordered. "That's a mad cow. Put the bucket beside our camp where it can reach it and let it calm down."

Even though they had separated at Fort Smith due to Warren's health, Emily had previously been with the wagon train. "The doctor with the wagon train brought a whole herd of cattle. This one must have become lost and left behind. It sure is courageous."

"Courageous is a milk cow, and she's ours now." Sally started back toward the wagon with the bucket full of grain. She hoped it was close enough for the cow to smell.

Emily contemplated. "They can't be far ahead of us." *I wonder if Tom will try to get rid of me when we catch up.*

So that they wouldn't be pulling the cow against its will for the remainder of the day, they remained where they had set up for dinner. The new cow quickly found the cow the family already had and then the grain. Sally made willow water for the pain of the hyena bites, then left a bucketful of it beside

116

their new cow while she made a poultice of cooked cedar. "I won't try to put it on her if she's not happy to let me."

Ann told her sister, "I'm the one deciding if she's happy to let you or not."

"All right, Ann."

Eli looked at the five hyenas. "Anybody willing to help me skin these and tan the hides?"

Nikki and Oscar both ran over. Nikki hadn't understood the question, but Oscar looked excited. Tom, Adahy, Tapco, and Noah joined them. Oscar worked with Tom. Nikki worked with Noah. The other three men each skinned one on their own.

At the end of the day, the cow that Sally had decided to name Courageous was full of grain, happy to no longer be on its own, almost pain-free due to the willow painkiller, and wearing bandages of cedar poultice. It was also unaware that Roscoe and Helen were cooking its baby.

Oscar held the nicked skin he and Tom had removed. "Are we going to eat the hyenas?"

Adahy shook his head. "They have bugs inside. Best not to."

"Why did we cut off their skin?" Oscar asked.

Eli still carefully worked to remove the skin from his. "We'll make the hides into rugs."

"Really? Can I make this one into my very own rug?"

Emily called out from across the camp. "*May* I make this one into my very own rug?"

Oscar replied, "I want it."

117

Tom whispered into Oscar's ear. Oscar repeated the question, "Noah, MAY I make this one into my very own rug?"

"If it's all right with your mother, then you may do so."

Emily had walked over and stood directly behind her son. "You may."

Oscar jumped. "Jeez, Ma. You shouldn't sneak up like that."

Nikki laughed.

Oscar pushed him. "It's not funny. You didn't just watch your father be killed."

Nikki hadn't understood what had been said. He pushed back. With tears in his eyes, Oscar knocked Nikki over. Noah picked Nikki up. Emily stepped between them. "Oscar, Nikki doesn't know what you're saying. His parents are bones. He's suffering too."

Oscar held out his hand. "I'm sorry."

Nikki realized he hadn't understood and had done something wrong. "Don't talk good. Tut mir Leid."

"It's all right. I know you're sad too. Sie spielen möchten?" Oscar had been learning Nikki's language along with the rest of them.

"Ja." They crawled under the wagon and made dirt tracks, then pushed rock wagons around their newly built roads.

A few days later, they saw the wagon train that had stayed in Fort Arbuckle with them. Tom stopped his wagon opposite them but on his side of the river.

It happened to be narrow enough that they could wave at each other and holler loud enough that they thought they might have understood what the people on the other side of the river had said. After a rest, grazing, and drinking plenty, they left behind those on the other side of the river.

Emily commented, "As Warren said, they spend a long time resting every day."

Tom walked beside her. "They're not likely to get to the mountains early enough to cross over. They sure have a lot of cattle. Do you think they noticed that one of them is with us now?"

Evening approached. Vehement barking stopped them. "What is that?" Stephanie asked.

Tapco looked at the ground. "Must stop now. Keep all animals at wagons tonight."

"Why?" Eli walked to the lead wagon.

"Horse step in hole, break leg. Spend night where safe. Tomorrow go around."

Through his spyglass, Oscar peered at what seemed to be thousands of dark brown animals sitting on their hind ends with their front legs hanging down before them. "The prairie is full of puppies. How did they get here?"

"Prairie dog colony."

"Can we eat them?" Noah asked.

Tapco stated the difficulty. "Go into hole very fast. Not easy get close."

Stephanie examined the land ahead. "Maybe we can carefully pass through before we stop."

"Best go around."

Roscoe pulled out his rifle. "If they taste good, we can all shoot at the same time and get several from here."

P'ahy told them, "Can eat. Not that good."

Sally remembered how bad she had felt when she and her friends had killed dozens of snow geese only for target practice. "It would be good target practice, but we shouldn't kill them unless we eat them. Maybe we can make them into jambalaya."

Ann reminded Sally, "Noah told you target practice is important. You and Roscoe are excellent cooks. You can make them into something we can eat."

"Then, I want to practice with my bow." Sally walked away.

"I want to practice," Oscar informed everybody.

"No kill. I want hund." Nikki wasn't sure what they were saying but guessed they planned to shoot the very loud animals barking their warning.

Noah knelt beside him. "Not hund for people. Not pet."

"Why?" Nikki asked as if he would be able to understand what he was told.

"They're wild and not dogs. Not hund." Noah left him with Ann but asked, "Ann, do you want to see if you can shoot one?"

"I know I can with my rifle. Bring that, please."

In a line, all except Nikki held a weapon. Tom explained to Oscar how to hold and fire the pistol that didn't have much recoil. Tom held a second pistol. "Nikki, are you sure?"

Nikki yelled, "Run!" The prairie dogs didn't feel threatened enough to dash to their escape tunnels.

"That's the one I'm aiming for." Ann pointed the rifle her father had used to teach her years earlier. It was one of the few things that had survived the destruction of her farm. Nikki saw which one Ann wanted.

Rifles, pistols, revolvers, and bows released their projectiles. A thousand disappeared before anybody blinked, but eight prairie dogs lay dead on the ground. "Where did they go?" Oscar was sure he had missed and wanted to try again.

"Into their holes. Going downfield," Sally informed the group, so nobody would accidentally shoot her. She picked up her arrow. "They were too far away. Noah, how did you get yours?"

"I've had much more time to build up my strength."

Nikki had never seen Ann shoot. He picked up the dead animal she had shot. "My Ann's one!" He looked at it closely. "Not dog."

They set up camp and then let the prairie dogs come out again. Nikki let Noah show him how to shoot with a pistol. When the animals again covered the ground, they shot more. After the third round, the prairie dogs stayed in their boroughs. Nikki complained, "I wanted one."

Noah hugged him, "We'll practice, just like we do with the bow and arrow."

"All right," Nikki sulked as he ate prairie dog jambalaya.

When the sun rose, they made their way around the ten-acre complex of prairie dog tunnels and holes, taking potshots when an animal popped its head above ground. When somebody was successful, he or she pulled the body out, gutted the animal, and put it with the others.

Twenty Two

When the Cimarron started its vast curve north, they came upon the pit houses. Tapco walked to a low mound of earth with an extended covered ramp dug from the east down to the below-ground pit's floor. He pulled open the uncovered door constructed of sturdy branches.

Eli hated to bring up the problem. Sally had been so upset with him when he had suggested that they crawl through the tiny crevasse under the Boston Mountains and had then lost her lantern all alone in complete blackness. He wasn't sure if the pit house would bring out her subsequent fear of caves. "What do you think, Sally? It's just a pit on the surface. It's not like the cave back home. Will you be able to go in?"

Sally looked at the narrow dirt-covered entrance. "I went into the cave at Noah's village to find Kimimela." She walked to the opening, holding Eli's hand. "Catch me if I faint again."

"All right. Don't breathe fast."

Sally didn't even have to duck her head, and

123

plenty of light filled the passage. She purposefully focused on breathing slowly and thought about the kiss she had shared with Melvin and how much she had liked it. In only a few seconds, she had traveled the constrictive tunnel with the help of Eli. They stood inside a large room. "I made it. That wasn't even bad."

Tapco moved a ladder, leaned it against one of the large lodge poles that lay ten feet up across the top of the fifteen-foot-wide pit. He climbed up and pushed open the hatch with deer-hide sides that hinged on the west side. In the center of the twenty-five-foot-long room was a rock-lined fire pit. Wooden shelves, stacked beds, and ladders hugged the walls.

"I show where take animals." Tapco walked to the southern side of the rectangular pit to a covered door. Except for Sally and Eli, who remained with her because he still felt responsible for her fear, they traveled a long, underground tunnel supported at the sides and topped with interconnected logs. They arrived at the enormous central chamber with many additional exits from the circular room. He pointed at the doors. "More family units. This meeting area."

Noah counted. Twelve doors. "Are they all as big?"

"No. One very big. Fit all animals."

They followed another long, dark tunnel into the animal quarters. Boxes constructed of wooden boards stood close beside two of the walls. A stone-lined channel hugged the other two. Tapco pushed down a lever and raised a flat stone fitted into a stone slot. Water flowed into the trench. "Animals go river and eat grass outside, or animals eat grass we bring here and drink water here."

Roscoe didn't see any sense in cutting grass to bring it in. "They can eat and drink outside. Let's make a corral between here and the river. We can bring them in tonight if we need to." The men and the boys took the animals to the river to drink, maneuvered the wagons into position, hung the nets, and performed the nightly maintenance on the wagons. They decided that they would examine the animals the following day before going into the waterless land.

P'ahy returned to the pit house. She started a fire in the first dwelling they had entered. "Hope not eat prairie dogs tonight."

"Let's cook dried vegetables with pemmican," Sally suggested.

"I get vegetables." Akea went to the wagon.

"Everybody, help. We'll bring in lanterns and bedding." Ann followed her with Adele on her back

Soon, their beds had been made with feather mattresses, blankets, and pillows. Supper cooked while the men filled the water mattresses in the wagons. The baby corral stood in the center of the room beside the fire. Chris got up on his hands and knees and rocked. Repeatedly, Hattie rolled from her belly to her back, then returned to her stomach. Joy batted at buffalo fur stuffed shapes that Sally held suspended above her. Ann placed Adele inside with the other babies. "I want to explore this complex. Would you watch the children, Sally?"

"I'd love to. The children might decide they love me best while you're gone."

"They love us all, and I'm very happy about it." Ann took a lantern into the dark tunnel. She noticed holders on the walls. *Must be for torches.* She looked at the large central fire pit in the meeting room and all the torch holders on the walls. Next, she examined the many support posts, roof logs, and boards that held up the sod ceiling above. Water had leaked in and exposed the side of a support post. She stuck her lantern into the gap. *There's a big hollow back there. I wonder if they know how big this is.*

Next, Ann traveled a different tunnel into a living area almost identical to the one they were occupying. She walked out the tunnel to the outside. *Also, going east. That's strange.* To her right was another entrance, once again heading due east. She went over, entered, found the same type of pit, and then followed the other passage back into the meeting area. Ann went into and out of each house. They were all configured the same. Every entrance faced the east and all the roof hatches hinged on the west. However, the tunnels to the meeting area left the dwellings at different angles in order to converge at the central hall.

She found only one animal unit. It looked large enough to hold all fifty-nine of their animals. *After supper, we should cut grass and fill the food bins for tonight.* She tasted the water that filled the stone trough. *Not bad.* She went out and tried to determine the size of the whole complex. *Must be at least a hundred feet long and wide.*

She returned to the family through the entrance from the outside. "We should cover the door with a buffalo hide. When we push it shut, the fur should seal it up." She looked up and saw the smoke from the fire going out the hatch Tapco had opened. "This place must be cool in the summer and warm in the winter." She put a hand on the shoulders of P'ahy and Akea. "Your people very clever."

She walked over and saw that all four of the babies had fallen asleep. "Stephanie, let's enjoy some time away from the children. Help me cut grass." Sally and Helen remained inside to cook and watch the babies. The six other women went out to cut grass.

When the men and boys returned, Stephanie informed them, "The bins are full of grass."

"With our three nets and four wagons, we made a corral all the way to the river. Let's leave them out. We won't have to shovel manure in the morning."

P'ahy snuggled beside Tapco in one of the beds. "Do you want to decide about Akea?"

"No. Right now, I want to enjoy you. Let's see what life brings and decide when we have to."

Twenty Three

Ann woke in a sweat. *We can't leave tomorrow. Why do I think that?* Her hair stood on end. *I'm being silly.* She tried to go back to sleep. She stared at Noah's handsome face.

"I feel you looking at me." Noah opened his eyes.

"We need to stay here for a few days."

"The whole point of cutting across the land is to recover time. Why would we want to waste time?"

"I don't know. I have a strong feeling that we need to stay here."

"We're not staying here. Go back to sleep."

We can't leave. Ann waited until Noah once again slept, then put her empty canteen over her shoulder. She filled a pack with diapers, dried meat, dried fruit, and a loaf of the bread they had cooked that afternoon. *I'm sorry, Adele, you're big enough that you don't need to nurse.* She took Joy and Chris and slipped away into the dark tunnel. She got a buffalo hide from a wagon then filled her canteen in the empty animal quarters before she quietly made her way back into the meeting hall.

At the support post, she placed the pack and canteen behind it and then pushed the buffalo hide into the hole before she laid the babies inside. She turned sideways and wedged herself through the space between the posts and the dirt wall.

Noah felt cold. He rolled over to get closer to Ann and then sat up. He looked around. The morning light was dim, but he saw that Ann wasn't in the room. Noah pulled on his buckskin pants and had his shirt on before his feet were on the floor. He slipped his feet into his boots without putting on socks, and then hurried to a lantern, lit it, and held it high. Chris and Joy were not in the dresser drawers they were using as baby beds. He stepped over to the entrance. The door was securely wedged in place with a buffalo hide. "Where is she? God, please let Ann and the babies be all right." Noah dashed into the tunnel to the meeting room. His commotion woke the others.

"What's happening?" Sally asked.

Tom sat up. "It sounded like Noah said, 'Please let Ann and the babies be all right.'"

Everybody joined the search. Ann heard their concern and fear. *I'm upsetting Noah, but he's determined to go, and I'm sure we have to stay.*

They examined what they thought was every inch of the complex and the surrounding land. Noah screamed, "Ann!" Everybody joined him. All morning they diligently searched. Tears rolled from Noah's eyes. "I can't lose her."

Tapco remembered what Noah had said about

keeping emotions under control. At the moment, Noah was practically hysterical. *He must love Ann very much. Why is she doing this to him?* He voiced his question, "Why would she hide?"

Noah hit his forehead with the heel of his hand. "That's what it is! She's hiding. Last night, she told me we couldn't leave. She said we have to stay here. I told her no. Everybody, take a different room. Holler that we won't leave today." They all hurried down the tunnel into the meeting hall and then scurried into different passageways. Noah stood in the center of the meeting room. "Ann, forgive me. After you heard God tell you to run to Fort Arbuckle, and we found Joy, I should have believed you last night. I believe you now. Please come back to me."

In her hiding place, Ann heard Noah. "I forgive you."

Noah dashed to the post that had spoken. He saw the slender opening then held his lantern to the slit. "Ann, I should tan you. You've scared me about to death!"

"You just asked me to forgive you."

"I know. I'm sorry. We'll stay here."

"Then forgive me for worrying you and everybody else. It's just that I'm sure something terrible is going to happen if we leave. Do you believe me?"

"I do. Pass me the babies." He yelled, "I found her!"

Sally ran into the room. Noah held out a baby. "Take Chris." He reached back into the hollow and retrieved his red-haired girl. Tom stepped over and took Joy. He handed the pack, canteen, and buffalo hide to the family as they arrived. Last, he helped Ann get through the narrow opening. "How did you find this place?"

"I was looking at how the support structure was built. I stood where you are to see how the logs joined, noticed the erosion, and then looked closer. There's a big hole back there. Too bad we can't leave a note telling them to fix it."

Sally hugged her sister. "I'm so glad you aren't hurt."

Akea leaned closer to her sister. "I guess we have to wait for her permission to leave."

Twenty Four

The following day, Ann still refused to leave. Roscoe told Noah, "Force her to go. We left a month late, and we've lost time twice since then. We can't just sit here because Ann is afraid of some mysterious something that might happen."

"She knew we had to get to Fort Arbuckle when there was no way she could have known that Joy's parents had died or even that Joy existed. She knew something that could break us up was coming the day before Russell and Arnold showed up at your trading post. I think God is telling her to stay."

After two days, they voted, packed up, and left the pit houses. Ann protested continually, "We can't do this." Two hours out, she called Nikki, Sally, and Stephanie over. "Get in the wagon." She turned the wagon carrying the children and her sisters. "I am NOT allowing our children to die. We have to get back to the underground houses as fast as we can. Forward run." She repeatedly cracked the whip and screamed, "Run!"

For a minute, Noah watched Ann disappear

with several animals tied to the rear. He knew they weren't going to catch her.

Akea felt the static in the air. "Give me your looking tube." She looked west. "She is right! Run!"

Everybody looked west. A thin line of tan sat on the horizon. "What is it?" Roscoe asked.

"The widest dust storm I have ever seen," Akea informed them.

Noah jumped off Eyanosa. "I hate to leave the dynamite, but I'm sure bouncing it that hard would set it off. I need somebody to help me."

Roscoe hurried over. "I will. The rest of you get the little animals into the wagon."

Everybody else grabbed a goat or a sheep and dragged it to the animal wagon. Tom ran to the men wrapping the dynamite in a tarp. "We can't fit Little Jack or Little Jenny."

Roscoe gently set down the last crate. "They're my animals. I'll come with them as fast as they can go."

"I'm not leaving you alone." Noah swung up on Eyanosa as Roscoe mounted King. "The rest of you fly as fast as you can."

An all-out-race to the underground facility commenced. They flew east, praying they'd get there before the storm overtook them.

Sally sat in the back of the wagon and watched the monstrous dust cloud draw closer. "We should have listened to you."

"Get all the animals into their quarters and start moving food into ours. Stephanie and I need to get the children and all their things before we help move the food."

Nikki clutched the wrapped-up bones of his parents. "Nikki take Mama und Papa."

"All right," Ann replied. They screeched to a halt. Ann maneuvered the wagon behind the slight dome of the pit house. Everybody jumped down and hurried to do as instructed.

Eli, Helen, Emily, Oscar, and Tom arrived with a plan. Tom parked behind another dome. Helen, Emily, and Oscar jumped out with the nets and stakes made from Emily's disassembled wagon. Tom and Eli untied one side of the wagon cover and started pulling out the bows. Stephanie joined those stringing the net from the pit house entrance to the river. Sally and Nikki got the second batch of animals into the appropriate pit. Inside, Ann set up the baby net to keep them, especially Adele, contained while they hurried to get ready.

Adahy and Ehawee rounded the roof mounds in the third wagon with all the goats and sheep. They saw what the others were doing. Ehawee led the animals into their dormitory with the mules and donkeys already inside. Adahy pulled out wagon bows.

He had half of them flat on top of the wagon when Tom hollered, "Bring your jacks!" Adahy hurried over. Tom had one side of the wagon up and the wheels off. "Help me get these wheels on top. Then we'll take off the others."

When the fourth wagon arrived with Tapco,

P'ahy, and Akea, all four wheels and the wagon bows lay on top of the first wagon with the cover pulled tight over everything. They lowered the jacks and then moved on to the next wagon.

"You have enough food inside?" Akea signed to Ann.

"No."

"I help."

Ann placed a ninety-pound parfleche of pemmican into her arms and dragged two fifty-pound bags of flour to the back of the wagon. She and Akea took turns carrying food inside while the second wagon was made secure and as low as possible. "Where's Noah?" Ann asked.

"Noah and Roscoe bring tiny donkeys," Tapco informed her.

Ann looked through the spyglass to see if they were close enough. "I don't see them. I told you we had to stay! But would any of you believe me? No! If Noah dies, I'm never going to forgive you!" she told nobody in particular.

Enough food for a week sat inside the pit house. All the animals except the two miniature donkeys and the two animals Roscoe and Noah rode were in their quarters eating the grass Ann and Stephanie had cut and brought in days before. Outside, the net ran from the pit house door to the river.

Eli, Tom, Tapco, and Adahy, took down the third wagon, then the empty animal wagon. Stephanie stayed with the children while the rest of them wrapped buffalo hides around the outer door to the animal quarters and the doors inside the meeting room to close the other ten tunnels.

Tapco went into their two chambers, climbed up to the hatch, pulled it closed, and secured the tie-down. "Barely had time. Storm be here soon."

Twenty Five

"We're not going to make it. We have to prepare." Roscoe halted King. He slid off and opened his packsaddle. "It'll be hot." He handed Noah his scarf, goggles, and point-blanket coat. "We have to protect ourselves first." Noah donned the clothing they hoped would protect them from the coming sandblasting.

While Roscoe did the same, Noah pulled out the blanket pieces they had sewn to protect the mules and donkeys during the blizzard the year before. They tied the protective material on with the same red ribbons and then tied the six of them together. However, this time, they completely wrapped all four animals' heads with the red trade material. "We'll have to lead them." Noah tied a silk handkerchief over his mouth, put on the goggles, and then wrapped the scarf around his head. He tied it tight and tucked the ends into the front of his coat. "Let's run while we can still see."

Ann, Ehawee, and Nikki watched the horizon. Sally hurried out the entry tunnel with her spyglass.

137

"Do you see them?" She joined those scanning the horizon. *If they're still too far away to see, they won't get here before the storm.*

Roscoe saw the four people ahead. "We're almost there."

"Ich sehe Sie!" Nikki pointed far to the right.

Ann, Sally, Ehawee, and Nikki saw the giant storm swallow the two tiny men with their four animals.

The wind whipped Noah and Roscoe's clothes. The dust swept over them and obscured their vision. Roscoe yelled, "I hope we don't miss it!"

Noah barely heard Roscoe over the screaming wind that battered them from behind. To remain on his feet, Noah held onto Eyanosa. Roscoe held King. Not only were Little Jack and Little Jenny tied to their waists, but the men also tightly held their halters. They ran to stay in the thinner dust at the leading edge of the storm as long as they could. The dust grew denser. Roscoe ran blindly through the howling wind. "We're not going to make it. I'm such a fool." Even through the cloth, the smell of dirt gagged him.

Noah thought about Ann's beautiful green eyes. To look into them again, he struggled through the deadly dust the wind whipped into a frenzy. It became impossible to run. They had no idea how they would know when they were at the pit houses. They didn't even know if they were still headed east. Roscoe feared that they had shifted south. He waved to Noah and pointed to the left. "Better to aim toward the river. We can't go too far north. We can go too far south."

Even though Noah hadn't heard what Roscoe had said, he turned slightly left across the wind. Fifteen minutes inside the storm, Noah thought they should have been at the river or the pit houses. *We aren't going to last much longer.* "God, once again, I'm admitting that I need You desperately. Get us to our family quickly." His horse stopped walking. "You can do it, Eyanosa. It can't be much farther." Then, Noah also ran into the net. "Thank you, God, and thank you, family." They followed the net to a door covered with soft buffalo fur. *I'm home.* As he pushed the door in, he realized why all the exterior doors opened inwards. *The wind would blow this door clean off its hinges.* "Go in, Roscoe." He shoved Eyanosa and Little Jenny behind King and Little Jack, then pushed the door back into place and secured it tightly shut.

Twenty Six

The roaring wind prevented the people kneeling in a prayer circle from hearing the door open. They didn't hear Noah and Roscoe enter the room as Ann spoke, "God, how many people are You going to take from me?"

"Not this one, at least."

Ann's eyes flew open. "Thank You, God." She jumped to her feet, tripped over Sally, scrambled up, and ran into Noah's arms. Dust billowed from his clothes as she pulled down the silk scarf and found his lips.

Eli walked over and took Noah's hand off the tiny donkey's halter. "Enjoy the welcome home. I'll take the animals." He started away and pulled Noah out of Ann's arms.

Noah stepped back to stay on his feet. "We're tied together."

"Sorry."

"That's all right." Noah untied. "We should take off our coats and the animal blankets in the meeting room. I don't want to dump all this dust in here. We'll come right back."

In the central room, they dropped the blankets and coats. All six just in from the storm were covered with fine dust. Roscoe and Noah wiped off as much as they could, then reunited the animals with the rest of the herd. The four animals sucked down gallons of water. In the meeting room, with their mouths once again covered, the men shook out their coats and scarfs and beat the dust from their clothes. As dust-free as he could get, Roscoe walked into the living compartment. "Putting up that net saved our lives. We would have gone right past if it hadn't caught us."

"That was Gram's idea," Eli informed them.

"Thank you for your marvelous idea, Helen." Roscoe hugged her tightly.

She whispered into his ear, "I didn't want to lose you."

The storm raged through the night. They tried, but none of them slept. Instead, they feared that the storm would suck the hatch off and then bury them alive. They feared that the same thing might happen to their animals, and they feared that the wagons would blow away with everything they owned.

Emily thought about the people she had been with at the beginning of her adventure into the west. "I don't know what the people in the other wagon train are doing. I'm worried about them."

Tom put his hand on hers. "We'll look for them as soon as the storm has passed."

Twenty Seven

The pouring rain came with the morning. Noah went to see if their wagons still existed. "I hope we still have our medical supplies. I'm sure there'll be injured people and animals at the other wagon train."

Eli braved the rain beside Noah. "Oh, no! We tied the empty animal wagon to the heavy ones, but it's gone! It must have whipped at the end of the rope, been smashed to pieces, and blown away."

"The other wagons look fine. Tying the covers down like that was smart." They went back inside. Noah took a cup of hot coffee. "The animal wagon is gone. The others are fine. After the rain stops, we should open them and make sure everything is dry."

Once breakfast had been cooked and eaten, the heavy rain had passed. Across the river, Emily saw the remains of the other caravan and cried, "If we had known they were right there, we could have gotten them inside."

"Start making the willow tea, antiseptic wash, antiseptic paste, and the sedative. Make a lot. It's going to be bad. And remember; don't say anybody's name."

Emily asked, "Why?"

Noah explained, "I'm sure you've figured out that some of us are Indians. I'm one."

Oscar said, "Indians have brown eyes."

"I'm half. Ann is completely white. We are married. Judge Daniel Hall of Arkansas knows we are not the same, and he doesn't like it. He says he wants to whip us and make us serve a second hard labor sentence, but I think he'd rather kill us. He was furious when he saw us together. He's sent people to find us more than once. We don't want to give him any way to track us."

"All right. We won't use anybody's names," Emily agreed.

Noah got the buffalo hide boat they had repaired, the ropes with the pulleys, all the medical books, and all the medical supplies they had. With one end of the line, a pulley, an iron stake, and a sledgehammer, Noah swam Eyanosa into the river.

The leader of the wagon train, Jedidiah, stood on the bank. "I hope you're able to help. Most of them are dead, but some can be saved if you know anything about medicine."

"I do, and so do some of the others, but we don't have many supplies. As soon as I get this pulley set up, they'll send over what we have."

"Do you only need to hammer that stake into the ground and attach the pulley?"

"Yes."

"I'll get somebody. The sooner you can look at these people, the better. After the people, I also have a horse with a broken leg. I've owned her for a long time. I'm hoping to save her somehow."

"I thought you had a doctor."

"He was one of those who didn't make it."

Noah approached the destruction. The wailing of heartbroken men, women, and children filled his ears. The two westernmost wagons both lay on their sides. The flying departure of two others had left voids in the circle, and the two easternmost sheared off just below the top of the wagon beds. Wagons sat at odd angles with ripped covers, broken axles, smashed wheels, and other damaged parts. Noah stepped into the space in the center. Cows, mules, horses, and donkeys lay in a jumble of carcasses. Ten mules and two steers stood beside a living horse lying on the ground.

"We got the close ones under the covers of the wagons that blew over. We tied shirts over their heads. I think dust got in the lungs of the rest and suffocated them." Jedidiah stepped over cow legs. "The man in this wagon is the worst."

Noah climbed into the cock-eyed wagon, struggled through the jumble of supplies that had slid to the lowest point, removed a heavy crate off a barely breathing man, and unbuttoned his bloody shirt. *His chest is completely smashed!* He rebuttoned the clothes.

"Save him," a woman demanded.

"I can't. Hold his hand, look into his eyes, and tell him how much you love him." Noah raised the edge of the cover no longer secured to the broken wagon bow. He slipped out and left the woman to say her goodbyes.

"That's what I thought." Jedidiah climbed over animal bodies. "There's probably nothing you can do for Nell either."

Noah looked into the wagon. The woman appeared to be enough in her body to think, but she struggled to breathe. With the amount of dust she had inhaled, it wouldn't be long before she wasn't there. "Your lungs are full of dust. Are you at peace with your maker?" She shook her head, signifying that she was not. "Do you want to ask God to come into your heart and be your master?" She nodded. "Do you acknowledge that you are a sinner, that Jesus died so that you are forgiven, and do you accept the gift of His pardon?" She nodded in the affirmative. "Then, He forgives you. You are now a child of God. He will send His messengers to take you into Heaven. Peace be with you."

Noah heard the next man before they entered the wagon. "I'm in too much pain. I'm not going to make it. Shoot me or give me the gun. Please. I'm suffering."

"Ruben, I will not. I love you. The children love you, and we need you."

"I'm dying, just slowly. Give me the gun, then walk away."

Noah saw an arm across the wagon. "Ma'am, don't give it to him. I'm sure he is hurting badly, but he can live without an arm. I have people coming

145

who will put him to sleep. He won't feel the pain much longer." Noah climbed in. "Get me a rope. We need to stop this bleeding. Get as much water into him as you can."

Tapco and Sally got into the buffalo hide boat. They carried canteens with red, yellow, or green ribbons tied to them. They also had the surgical kit that Noah had purchased in Perryville and all the extra tourniquets, sutures, clamps, scalpels, forceps, and their two stethoscopes. A man with a thick shock of black hair and a beard twice as big as his head that curled out at the sides into points by his ears pulled them over. "Howdy."

Sally told him, "This man can care for your wounded. Take us to whoever needs our help the most."

"He may not be hurt the most, but his shoulder has a piece of wood through it, and he's my son."

"Take us."

Sally poured liquid from a canteen with a red ribbon. She held the cup to the boy's lips. "Drink all of this." Sally handed the father three canteens. "Take these to the first man who came over." She didn't see the boy's mother. "Then come right back to your son. We'll be back after he's gone to sleep."

"Thank you for helping Cleo. I'm Ken."

Jedidiah hurried over to the new group. "Leave the boy. There are people in worse shape." Jedidiah led them to a woman speared with multiple pieces of flying debris. He left them and ran to the river to escort Roscoe and Helen to their patients.

Tapco signed to Sally, "Make sleep. Come back and stitch up. Tell child give mother water."

Sally issued the instructions. "Get me a cup." She filled it from the red ribbon canteen. "First, your Ma must drink all of this, then help her drink at least ten cups of clean water." Sally handed Helen a set of canteens as she went past with Roscoe and Jedidiah.

Tapco thought about the bride gift he owed the village. "You need more horses. You have plenty animal bodies. Wife bring village. Trade dead animals for live horses."

Sally told Jedidiah what Tapco had suggested. Jedidiah didn't hesitate. "Tell her to bring as many horses as they can."

P'ahy and Akea arrived. Sally signed, "P'ahy, get horse. Go home fast. Come back fast with all horses can trade." She swept her hand toward the pile of carcasses. "Food."

Roscoe and Helen got into the wagon with a teenage girl. Jedidiah held the girl's hand. "Both her parents are gone now. Henrietta has pain in her stomach. Show them where."

The girl pointed a hand's width to the right from her bellybutton. As he felt her abdominal area, the girl told Roscoe, "It started before the storm."

"Sedative, but Doc should do this one. Who next?" They left the girl with her three siblings weeping over the bodies of their parents.

"Grandma Elliot."

Sally started into the wagon. "Stop right there, young lady. I'm an old woman, and I've had a good life. I'll be going to my Blessed Savior. Go help those sinners, so they can have more time to come to Jesus."

"You're the last one."

"All right then. I think I only broke my arm."

Sally poured willow tea out of the canteen with the green ribbon. "This is a painkiller. We made it strong. We'll return to set your arm." Several yards from the wagon, she asked, "Who is next?"

Eli, Tom, and Adahy arrived with the large animal tent. Several times, Noah had read the book How to set up and run a Field Hospital that he had gotten from the doctor at Fort Smith. He had asked his two brothers-in-law to set up the tent. After they had it up, the three men tried to figure out how to make beds.

The people attempting to give medical help continued from wagon to wagon. Everybody who needed surgery or who had been in extreme pain had drunk the sedative. The patients were then carried, along with their bedding, and lain on broken wagons that had been turned upside down and had all the undercarriage removed by Tom, Eli, Adahy, and the uninjured people of Jedidiah's wagon train.

Ehawee and Akea set up the tipi acquired when Noah's family had to escape the latest man Judge Hall had sent, which had forced them to flee their village in the extreme cold of the previous winter. Ann and Stephanie planned to use the tipi to keep the children contained and out of the sun as they boiled water to clean wounds and make more medications. Once the tipi was up, Ehawee and Akea took their scissors and sacks to the dead animals to cut clumps of tail hair from every horse and mule.

Jedidiah walked past the pile of animal bodies. "Some able person from my wagon train, butcher one of these cows. Cook it for everybody, along with whatever else you want to prepare."

Eli volunteered, "I'll skin it for you and get it cooking on a spit if I can have the hide."

"By all means, go ahead." Jedidiah looked at three young men of his group, who were brothers. "We also need a big hole to bury the dead."

Noah walked into the hospital behind the two carrying in the last patient. "Tell me what you've got. We need to prioritize." He remembered that the book had said, 'If you have many wounded, quickly calculate how many doctors and nurses and the amount of time to save each individual. Leave for later care those who do not have a time constraint. For those beyond hope, provide pain relief and non-essential personnel to help them pass to the blessed afterlife. Don't try to save a life if the loss of time would cost several other lives. Ruthlessly save the most lives.'

Noah listened to the reports. *That book is referring to a group of young soldiers. How am I going to prioritize this group?* He didn't waste time deciding. He pointed at Tapco. "Care for the man missing his arm. Get second wife to help you."

"She's not my wife," Tapco signed.

Noah signed back, "I know." He pointed at

Roscoe. "You and wife," he pointed at Helen, "clean and stitch all the injuries on that lady," he pointed to a woman with many pieces of wood in her body, "and then anybody else who needs stitches. Make sure you wash your hands well with the antiseptic before and after and also clean the wounds well. Jedidiah, do you know how to set bones?"

"I do."

"Get started. Let me see the first one. All the others who don't have life-threatening injuries, if we haven't already, somebody put them to sleep. They don't need to suffer. I'll operate on the girl."

Oscar went into the tent. "Doc, what can we do?"

Jedidiah saw him. "Howdy, Oscar. Where are your parents?"

"Those Indians back there killed Pa and they tried to kill Ma too. They wanted to keep me, but these people rescued Ma and me."

"Oscar, tell your mother to speak with me. Doc, I'm sorry for interrupting. Go on and tell Oscar what he can do to help."

"Bring hot water, get bandages, and whatever else anybody asks you to do. Hol wasser, son. Before you touch anything, wash your hands in clean water. Like this." He demonstrated. The boys nodded. They each washed in a separate bucket, then ran to the tipi.

Surgery began. Sally passed Noah the scalpel. When Noah opened the girl, as he expected, he found the appendix inflamed. "Just like Kangee. Forceps." He held out his hand. Sally placed the requested implement in his hand. Noah called out, "Hey!" Tapco looked. Noah signaled, "Come see when can."

Tapco clamped the last bleeding vessel in the armless shoulder then went over to look.

Noah showed him the appendix. "This what I told you when we look at other body." He demonstrated where to cut. "Must close completely. Very important. When you finished fix man—"

"Yes."

"Take wood out woman. Close up bleeders."

Noah carefully and tightly sewed the colon shut, then closed up all the layers of Henrietta. When he finished the final layer of skin, he looked at Nikki. "Antiseptic wasser." Nikki, already with clean hands, brought a bucket of the warm water Ann had used to cook cedar branch tips and then poured off to use as a germ-killing wash. Noah cleaned the girl then dressed the wound. He went to look at the man Tapco had treated. "Couldn't have done better myself." Noah told Sally, "Sister, clean and dress this arm just like I did for the girl." He examined the wood in the boy's shoulder and decided it was shorter to pull it out than to push it through. "I'm going to need bandages."

Oscar ran to the new wash bucket, cleaned up, and went to the bandage box. "How many?"

"Two hands full for now."

Sally called out, "One of these is bleeding."

Tapco hurried over. "I put two more stitches." He reached for a suture.

Nikki saw him. "Stop!" He signaled wash and

took Tapco the bucket of water he had just brought from the tipi. "Very important," he signed.

Tapco did as reminded. He added the extra stitches and double-checked the others. "Better now. Sister, wash and bandage. Bandage that man next." Tapco pointed at a man with stitches he had just put under the man's eye.

This arm needs blood. I wish we had leeches. Noah sewed together the ends of the severed artery that ran into the boy's arm. He tied off the last tiny stitch and then opened the forceps. He watched the blood expand the artery as it flowed down the arm. In a few seconds, the color of the boy's arm looked much better. *I think that worked. Three more to go.* "Sutures."

Nikki was at the tent, getting water, so Oscar went to the suture box. "There aren't any more."

Noah looked around. "We need a lot more."

Jedidiah spoke up, "Dr. Pennyworth had supplies. Emily could get them for us."

"Which one was his wagon?" Noah asked.

"The one with the top knocked off that's closest to the river."

"Look for boxes with these same words." Noah handed Oscar the empty box.

Nikki put a fresh bucket on the wash bench. Oscar waved him over. "Come."

Since a sizeable cast-iron stove blocked the wagon's back end, the boys climbed onto the wagon seat and looked in. It was full of dirt. "We can scoop it out with cups." Oscar returned with two tin cups. They had flung several cupfuls of sand over the edge before they heard something. They crawled on top of the dirt to the muffled sound's location and dug away. As a cloth-covered crate became visible, they heard the sound more clearly.

"Es ist eine Katze!" Nikki dug furiously. Oscar helped just as intently. They found handles on the sides but couldn't pull it out of the dirt.

"We need help!" Oscar called out.

Sally went to the wagon, expecting to receive a box of sutures.

"Get it out," Nikki told her.

Sally reached into the wagon and pulled up the crate.

"Meow."

"What in the Sam Hill?" Sally pulled off the cover. "There's a cat in here."

"Meow. Meow. Meow." The cat rubbed its body against the inside of the cage closest to Sally.

"We need to give it some water. Being under that cover must have saved it." Sally looked into the wagon. The surrounding dirt had collapsed into the hole and exposed another crate. She pulled it out and removed the cover. "A chicken! And there's another crate!" As the dirt fell into the emptiness, it exposed the medical supplies. Sally carried the medical crate into the tent. "Anybody have a pry bar?"

One of the brothers spoke up, "Howdy, I'll get it open for you." He returned with a long metal bar. He smiled at the beautiful young woman.

Sally recognized the symptoms and didn't want another heartache. "Just give it to me. I don't need any help," she practically snarled.

"All right. Geeze." The young man handed her the tool and walked away, shaking his head.

Maybe I was too short, but I don't need anybody fawning all over me. Sally jammed the metal bar so hard into the top of the crate that it flew off without any prying.

Emily went to the wagon to see what the boys had found. She pulled out a dozen hens and one rooster. "I'll get some string." She hurried away.

Jedidiah called out for her. "Emily, come here." Emily saw that he had all the rolls of string beside him and went over. "I'm sorry about Warren. Oscar told me. Are you all right?"

"We're as well as we can be, given the circumstances." Emily didn't want to talk about it. It was already hard enough not to think about what had happened. She grabbed a ball of string and hurried away. She opened a chicken cage only a little, then reached inside and tied the end of the twine to a leg. She unrolled several feet of line. "Do the same with the others." Before she opened the cages, Emily checked every knot to be sure they didn't lose any chickens. She brought one out and tied the long piece of string to the wagon wheel. The chicken scratched at the wet ground then gulped a worm that had come up to breathe. They secured all the chicken's strings to the wagon and let them out of their cages to have a worm feast. Last, she tied a line to the collar around the cat's neck. "The cat might try to eat the chickens. We should tie it to the other side."

Nikki carried the mostly white cat with an orange head, black ears, and large orange and black spots on the rest of its body. Its tail started white, then faded into orange but became black at the tip. The most striking feature was the long black whiskers growing out of its white face. Nikki held the animal tightly while Emily tied it to the wheel. Oscar set out bowls he had taken out of the wagon. He ran to the tipi then returned with Ann, Stephanie, Akea, all the babies, and a water bucket. "Can we keep them?"

"They belong to the owner of this wagon," Ann informed him.

Jedidiah came over. He noticed something the others hadn't seen. His previous belief had been that the owners of the wagon had been blown away in the storm. Now, he knew that wasn't entirely true. "Tie the animals to your tipi. They're in the way. I'll get the rest of the medical supplies."

There are bodies in so many wagons. The boys shouldn't be allowed to go into any of them. I wish nobody had to see this. Jedidiah respectfully pulled a crate from behind half a body. After he had removed a few containers that looked like they held the supplies they needed, he pulled a canvas off one of the other wagons and used it to hide the human remains.

It was a long morning. Except for the already dead, everybody received medical care and were all expected to live. After the mass grave had been dug, the two groups gathered to eat the mid-day meal.

Jedidiah looked at the damaged wagons whose owners had passed. "To pay you three doctors for your services, each of you may have one un-owned wagon. You can have it and everything inside, except money. We'll keep that."

Ann quickly spoke up, "Husband, pick the one with the cast iron stove."

Oscar added, "We'll own the cat and chickens."

"My family decided which one they want, but you don't have to let me have that one, but I do want to replace my medical supplies."

"Take that wagon and all the medical supplies, except we'll keep enough for the rest of the journey. Dr. Pennyworth had planned to start a practice on the west coast. I'm guessing that he has a large supply packed into that big Conestoga wagon. Doc, if you'll help my horse, I'll give you two of these dead animals. Although your family will have to butcher them."

Roscoe spoke to Helen, "Let's look at the wagons and decide which one we want."

Tom heard the comment. He had already realized that his mother and Roscoe were becoming a couple. "Mother, I think that's a good idea."

"You do?"

"Yes. Be happy."

Helen hugged Tom. "I was afraid you'd think I wasn't being respectful of your father's memory."

"I know you loved Pop, but he's gone. It's all right for you to love somebody else. And you were right. I was thinking about Emily. Maybe love will come back to me too."

Twenty Eight

Sally served the injured. "Take another dose of sleeping potion, eat quickly, and then drink as much water as you can while you're awake."

Ruben asked, "Can you put my arm back on?"

"If the arm had been in ice, maybe we could have tried, but we may not have gotten everything reattached correctly. In your case, it's been off too long, and it would make your chance of getting an infection much higher. I won't try."

"I don't know how I'm going to be able to farm with only one arm."

"Find something different to do. You and your family can still have long, happy lives."

Tapco had been watching for his wife's return. He signaled, "Village comes. Chief is Haungooah." Tapco turned to Akea. "Hide, so husband does not see you."

The village chief rode into camp with his warriors and P'ahy. Guipago signed to Tapco, "Must be very good trade for P'ahy."

P'ahy secretly signed to Ann, "Offer food."

Haungooah looked at the injured. "Tapco, you fix people?"

"Some of them," Tapco replied. "This man." He touched the bandaged, armless shoulder. "This woman. Many injuries under clothes." He walked to a woman with splints bound to her bandaged arm. "This one." Then Tapco stood behind a man and two children with lacerations that he had stitched. "These."

Haungooah looked at the one he knew was a powerful Medicine Man. "Tahatankohana, Tapco fix people?"

Noah answered, "Yes. All he said. Did very good."

Ann didn't have to pass on P'ahy's message. Jedidiah spoke up. "Join us." He pointed at the steer sizzling over the fire.

Haungooah dismounted. "We will eat. Then trade."

All the men sat together. Led by P'ahy, the women of Noah's family and those of Jedidiah's wagon train who were able, served the newly arrived men. After everybody had plenty, the women took all the children and ate in the tipi away from men.

P'ahy sat beside Ann. "I sent friend to her village. Bring trade horses. They send one person to other village. Bring horses. Get many villages bring horses."

"Excellent thinking." Ann praised P'ahy.

P'ahy smiled.

Sally wanted to stay away from all the unattached men. She sat with the other women and decided to leave the tipi as little as possible.

Haungooah looked at the pile of carcasses. "Four food body. One horse."

Noah wanted the trade to be good for everybody. He told Jedidiah, "He wants four dead animals for one live horse. How many bodies are there?"

"We had a hundred. Thirteen are still alive. We ate one. I gave you two. We need to keep more to eat the rest of the way. Eighty."

"How many wagons are you going to fix?"

Jedidiah counted on his fingers. "Probably six Conestoga Wagons. We need two teams of six horses to pull each of them. We have ten, so we need sixty-two more. Four for each live horse would take two hundred and forty-eight. I can't trade more than one for each."

"That's not enough. You'll have to have less than two teams. Go slower and let the horses rest more."

"At two, I can get six teams of six plus four extras. Offer two."

Noah signaled, "Two for one. Don't have any holes. Died from can't breathe. You get perfect hide. You pick the best."

Guipago spoke to his chief in his language, "Must be three. Must be very good trade for Tapco's bride price to village. Tahatankohana told me."

"Must be." Haungooah held up three fingers.

Noah knew he had promised P'ahy's father what

Guipago had just reported to Haungooah. Noah told Jedidiah, "He agreed to three. They get to pick which ones they want. They won't come lower."

"Agreed." Jedidiah held out his hand.

Noah gently pushed it down. "They will smoke the peace pipe to confirm the trade. Will you and your men smoke?"

"Of course."

Noah spoke and signed. "I get Calumet." He went into the tipi to get his medicine bag. Ann told him what P'ahy had done and that Akea was hiding from her husband, who had come into the camp. This time, Noah filled the bowl and only raised the pipe to Father Sky, lowered it Mother Earth, and then raised it to the four directions. "Father Sky, Mother Earth, East, South, West, and North, see that we have agreed to trade three carcasses to the people for food in exchange for one tame living horse to the men of this wagon train. We seal this agreement with the sharing of this pipe." He lit the pipe and passed it first to the chief. All the men smoked the tobacco that Noah fed into the Calumet.

The last man to smoke was Tom. He had an idea. Once the village people started moving cow, horse, and mule bodies, he spoke with Noah. "We could use more horses too. We don't need all the pots and pans and such from these three wagons. Maybe we should go through them. We take across the river what we want to keep. We can trade what we don't want and get some of the animal bodies back."

Noah pulled a cow out of the pile. "More

villages should be coming to trade. I'll get my wife to look through our wagon. Talk to your mother about theirs. Leave Tapco's alone."

Inside the tipi, Ann listened to Noah while Tom spoke with Roscoe. "Sally, will you watch the babies for me?"

Sally picked up Chris. "Come to Aunt Sally."

Ann found Nikki. "Help me."

Jedidiah saw Ann and Nikki walking toward the wagon, dropped the leg of the mule he was pulling, and ran. He stood in front of them. "Don't look in there right now."

"My husband asked me to do so, and you gave the wagon to him."

Jedidiah had realized that the boy didn't speak much English. He still worried that he might understand. "There is at least one partial body in there. I didn't want you or the children to have to see that. I was going to remove them."

"Jedidiah, that is very thoughtful. I will send my son to the tipi. I have seen vultures eating bodies and bodies lying in pools of blood. I will help you."

Ann told Nikki to return to the tipi. He asked, "I heard vultures. Vultures eat people in wagon?"

"No, vultures did not eat them, but they are dead and cut." Ann acted as if she cut her waist with her hand. "I don't want you to see." She shook her head from side to side, then pointed at Nikki's eyes.

"Geschlossene Augen." He squeezed his eyes shut. "I help."

"Promise you'll geschlossene Augen."

"I promise."

Jedidiah dashed over to Doc and explained. Noah went over. "Jedidiah and I will get them out. We'll tell you when the wagon is ready. Please."

"All right. We'll help move animals."

Noah informed Jedidiah, "We're going to offer other trades. You might want to offer things that no longer have owners. We should move everything not for trade across the river."

"I'll speak with the others." The two men removed the five adults and three children who had been instantly divided in two when the wagon lifted by the storm had sheared off half their wagon.

Jedidiah stuffed the money bag he found deep into his pocket. After he and Doc had removed the body pieces, Jedidiah and his men searched for money and removed the bodies from other wagons without owners. Jedidiah permitted the families still crying over their dead to keep the bodies until they were ready. Ann, Ehawee, and Nikki removed dirt from Noah's wagon and decided what they wanted to keep. Helen and Oscar worked in the wagon from which she and Roscoe had already removed the previous owners.

Oscar tied a scarf over his ears. "I wish I didn't have to hear the crying. It makes me remember how much I miss my Pa."

Helen hugged him. "I understand. I miss Woodrow." Even though it didn't help, she tied on a scarf as well.

P'ahy cleaned the dirt out of the wagon that Tapco had selected.

Twenty Nine

Noah returned to the animal pile. Cow, mule, and horse bodies already covered a large amount of the land surrounding the wagon circle. Near the bottom, Noah heard, "Moo."

"Alive." Adahy came over. "I help you. Maybe not dying. Under here, might have good air."

They uncovered the cow. "Moooooooo."

Noah examined the animal. "She's a milk cow with a broken leg. I can splint it and sedate it as I did for Jedidiah's horse, but it will take a long time for their legs to heal enough to walk. It's not like my sister's mule. It only needed to be carried for a few days. They shouldn't try to haul either of them for months."

Adahy stood up. "I get sedative, bandages, splints, and rawhide strings. They decide what to do later."

After the cow slept, Noah, Eli, Adahy, and Tapco set its rear leg. Roscoe watched Noah bind it up. "Some of these wagons are too damaged to fix. I can use the parts to build a small mobile forge. I could make a cage from the wheel rims that we could

163

secure around its leg and support its body. If I made it with wheels, it could walk, maybe."

"Go ask Jedidiah. He might want you to do that."

Roscoe made the deal. He would build the forge and make cages for the cow and Jedidiah's horse. Roscoe would keep the forge.

Jedidiah had plenty of wagons without owners. The people in his group had decided to keep the six best and largest wagons. "Sir, do you think your family could fix some of these wagons? I'll give you another wagon if you fix those we want to keep."

"I'll ask."

Eli returned. "For a wagon with everything inside and one horse body, my father and I will fix the wagons."

"Wonderful. I'll show you which to repair."

Tom got the carpenter's tools Roscoe had brought when the family had left Bacon's Trading Post. Eli told Stephanie to pick a wagon and look through it for what she wanted.

Tapco neared the bottom of the animal pile. "Found living horse with front leg broken just above hoof." He turned to a man from P'ahy's village. "Settan, help me fix it." Helped by the man P'ahy had identified as Akea's husband, Tapco set the leg.

Settan pulled on the horse's hoof. "Did P'ahy speak about her sister?"

"She asked me if I would marry her too."

"Do you want to?"

"I told her no. She has a husband."

"I'm asking because maybe P'ahy knows the father of that baby. Maybe you can go there and tell him he can have her for two horses."

"You're saying you want to get rid of her!?"

"Maybe."

"I could buy her and then try to find the father. I don't have horses. What else would you take?"

"I'll think about it."

Across the camp, Ann scooped dirt out of the large wagon. She saw a wooden handle. *I wonder if that's…* "A butter churn."

Ehawee dug beside her. "The bouncing wagon turns the cream into butter without us doing anything. We don't need it."

"We will once we get wherever we're going." Ann put it in the things she wanted to keep section of the wagon. "Here's a silver tea and coffee service." She relocated the crate that also contained a set of china dishes for eight.

"What these?" Nikki asked.

"Milk Cans. When I was growing up, we kept all our milk in containers like these. Mama always added copper coins to make it last longer. I wonder why they've driven nails through the lid." She lifted the lid to look inside and heard clanking. Strings hung from the nails into the milk. "What in tarnation!" She raised the cover higher and higher until she had exposed the makers of the clanging. "Silverware? Maybe silver does the same thing copper does. I guess when you have as much money as these people did, you use silver."

Ehawee held up a silk sheet. "There are so many nice things. We should just clean out the dirt."

Nikki plopped a hat with an ostrich feather onto his head. "Put on." He handed Ehawee and Ann hatboxes. They did as requested.

Ann opened her hat container, "Wonderful! We didn't have any small goggles. Here are three." Nikki put on a pair as Ann picked up another hatbox. She laughed at Nikki wearing a set of blue glass goggles under the big purple hat with its plum-colored feather jetting into the air. "You're gorgeous." Wearing an emerald-green hat, Ann hugged him before she searched the other hat containers for more goggles.

The wagon had only lost its previous owners, the wooden bows, and the cover. They kept everything except the cooking items that duplicated what they already owned. They removed those from the wagon and set them in a pile on the ground.

Stephanie, Emily, and Oscar kept the food, a rug, a tarp, all the tools, and the broken Conestoga wagon with its cover to replace the lost animal wagon. They also kept all the clothes and shoes because Emily and Oscar had lost theirs when the Kiowa had captured them. Most of the rest of the contents sat in a pile with Oscar perched on top.

Helen kept the wagon cover, tools, food, fiddle and bow, and all the music books from the wagon they had picked because they had found the music. P'ahy only removed the dirt from Tapco's wagon.

Noah walked over and hugged Ann. "Tapco and

I are leaving to look for the wagons that blew away. There may be more people who need help. Guipago is coming with us."

Ann prayed, "God, help them find whoever needs our help, and bring everybody safely back."

Adahy and Roscoe removed spare parts from Roscoe's new wagon to fix Eli's and Noah's. "What these for?" Adahy examined the brackets on the side of Roscoe's wagon.

Roscoe looked at them, then poked through the pile of items he had removed from the wagon. He pulled out a bundle of longboards rolled up in ropes. "Help me. Let's see if these fit in the brackets." They slid the first board through the metal bracket near the top of the sideboards, then into the frame at the lower edge of the wagon bed. Four feet above the wagon bed at the other end of the boards, two sets of ropes ran from holes that had been bored through the boards. They unrolled the bundle and slid a board into each group of brackets to the other end of the wagon. Roscoe stepped back. "Clotheslines for drying your clothes. I'll get the other bundle. We have to replace the top set of boards on Noah's wagon. We'll use these boards with the clothesline and wagon bow brackets."

"We make clotheslines for all our wagons," Adahy removed a board from Roscoe's wagon.

Meanwhile, Eli and Tom fixed the wagons Jedidiah wanted. Weeping and wailing, Jedidiah's people lowered into the mass grave the last of the twenty-seven bodies of the men, women, and children who had not survived the storm.

Afterward, Helen laid out the canvas they had kept from Roscoe's new wagon. Jedidiah brought the canvas he had used to conceal the bodies of Dr. Pennyworth's family. All the able women took turns inside the tipi caring for the small children and then outside, skinning and butchering Noah's and Jedidiah's cows.

Tom had discussed his plans with the family. He had the authority to trade everything in their piles of unwanted items as well as the bowless, bracket-free remains of Roscoe's shortened wagon that still had a jockey box full of tools. Tom put his plan into action. He went to each Indian warrior. "How you get meat back to village?"

"Women come tomorrow. Pull with travois."

"Trade wagon for twelve cow carcasses."

"Don't need it."

"I also give you six dutch ovens," Tom took them out of his pile of trade goods, "and six cast iron pots," Tom added them to the items for P'ahy's village.

The warriors looked at Tom's pile. Haungooah pointed at the spit, roasting the cow. He held up all ten fingers, then two more. He had also watched the women use the matches from the bottles. He picked up a bottle and again signaled twelve. "And blankets." He picked up a butcher knife. "And knives."

Tom didn't have enough knives and spits in his pile. Across the river, he had the items he had brought from Yates Mercantile. He also didn't want to give twelve full bottles of matches. "Be back." With six of the bottles, he got in the buffalo hide boat and crossed the river. A short time later, he returned and added twelve bottles of twenty-five matches, along with the additional butcher knives and spits.

"Don't tell wives ever had more meat."

"Agreed." Tom held out a folded piece of deerskin. He opened it. Inside were six small rolls of colored thread, a metal awl, folded pieces of paper, a pair of scissors, two bundles of fishing line, and one hunting knife with the whetstone to sharpen it.

Haungooah touched a paper packet. "What inside?"

Tom handed the bundle to Haungooah, unfolded the paper containing twelve large needles, and then the other with an equal amount of large fishing hooks. "One for each man. You take inside out of all." He swept his hand over all the carcasses.

"Only take out insides?"

"That is all."

Thirty

Four of Jedidiah's mules pulled a small undamaged farm wagon east. Two hours into the ride, Noah stopped and again peered through his spyglass. "We can't go any further and get back to camp before sundown." Tapco turned the wagon. The change in the angle sent a flash into Noah's eye. "Wait. I might see something." He pointed north. "Go that way."

Not much farther ahead, they found and followed a path of broken wood, pots, smashed crates, and other objects that had fallen from a wagon as it had blown along. They gathered everything as they went.

Half a mile of gathering later, they arrived at a wagon lying on its side. The canvas from the sheared-off wagon still clung to the broken wagon bows that had speared it. Noah tugged at the ripped canvas that had belonged to the wagon given to him. "The people must have fallen out along the way. I don't see any blood or tracks. Help me get this cover. I need it."

"What should we do with everything else?" Guipago asked.

Noah had already decided what they should do if they found a wagon either with or without the owners. "Tapco owns this one. Ask him." He climbed the wagon to detach the oiled cloth he wanted. While up there, Noah looked for the other wagon from the higher elevation.

Guipago looked at his son-in-law. Tapco said, "I give it all to Guipago as part of bride price for P'ahy. We take it back to camp."

"I need fix wagon. Use to take everything to village."

Tapco pulled an unbroken wheel off the damaged wagon. "We'll figure out later. Start loading."

"Somebody is coming this way. I'm going to take a mule and ride out. When you have everything, come get us." Noah unhitched a mule, slung two canteens and his box of medical supplies onto the animal, then mounted up and hurried away.

He drew nearer to the approaching lone traveler. The figure stumbled, rose, and struggled on. Noah called out, "I'm coming! Wait where you are!"

The figure looked up and then dropped. Noah urged the mule into a gallop. He jumped down beside a body, lying face down in the prairie grass with a shoulder that poked up at an odd angle above her blood-soaked dress. She whispered, "You have to help my husband."

"I have water." He rolled the woman over and

held a canteen to her cracked lips. With one arm secured with a piece of unidentifiable material wrapped around her body, the woman barely had the strength to take the water and swallow.

"Where is he? If I put you on the mule, can you show me where?"

She pointed. "I've been walking all day."

"It will hurt for a second when I get your shoulder back into place. It will feel better after. I have something that will make you sleep, but first, you have to help me find your husband."

"We have to hurry. Just fix my shoulder. I'll take the pain."

Noah unwrapped the cloth around the woman. He stretched the woman out on the ground and held her arm up and out. "What's your name?"

"Abigail."

Noah rapidly and forcefully pushed Abigail's shoulder into the ground. The woman screamed as the arm popped into the socket. "I'm sorry," Noah told her.

"Help me onto your mule. Josiah needs help."

Noah assisted the woman onto the mule then got on behind her. "We can travel faster with the mule running than if I'm walking." Also, Noah assumed he would have to keep the exhausted and weak woman from falling off.

With all haste, they followed the woman's tracks. Trying to get help, she had walked many miles from the wagon in extreme pain.

Unfortunately, they were much too late to help

Josiah. Abigail lay beside her husband and sobbed. "I tried, my love."

Noah commented, "Much harder and longer and better than most people would have or could have, but I wish we had gotten here in time to have saved him." Noah looked around. Blood soaked a wagon wheel. *Abigail must have used it to help tie the sheet she used to secure her arm. With only one usable arm, it was the only way she could have done it.* "Do you have a shovel? I'll bury Josiah."

"It's in the jockey box. The key is attached to Josiah's belt." She moved away so Noah could get the key, then rolled back to her position beside Josiah. She held him as long as she could before they laid him to rest in the vast, lonely prairie.

Noah pulled loose a long board and then propped it up with a white shirt attached to make a beacon. He dug the grave and then laid Josiah in the bottom of the pit. "Heavenly Father, take this good man, Josiah, to Your side. I know he was good because of how much his wife loved him. Help her to be strong and to feel Your comfort as she goes on without him. Is there anything you want to say, Abigail?"

"Josiah, thank you for loving me. I know you would have made us a beautiful home. I'm still going to do just what we planned because it's what you wanted. I love you beyond compare. Lord, take and keep Josiah. Amen."

Noah shoveled dirt over the body. "What do you want to do with everything?"

"I'd like to take all of it."

He poured liquid from the other canteen. "Drink all this straight down, then put whatever you can in the canvas. I'll get what you can't after I get done." Noah started to remove the canvas from the wagon.

Abigail drank the bitter liquid. As weak as she was, she moved only two items before she slept. The wagon arrived with the previous salvage. Noah put the mule back into the harness. "Help me get," he pointed, "on wagon." The three men lifted the canvas containing everything Abigail owned. It sat on top of the already full wagon.

Guipago looked at the wood. "Leave flag. I come back later."

Noah got into the wagon seat and held out his arms. "Give me Abigail." Tapco and Guipago picked up the unconscious woman and raised her to Noah. They started west as the sun touched the horizon.

Thirty One

While Noah, Tapco, Guipago, and Abigail rode toward the demolished wagon train camp, ten men from a second Kiowa village joined the camp with ten more horses.

Jedidiah gave twenty carcasses that the warriors could pick themselves and the wagon that Adahy and Roscoe repaired in exchange for two wagon wheels, four wagon bows, and an axel, all undamaged. Jedidiah received ten living tamed horses.

Except for the very young children and the babies, everybody cut meat until long after the sun had gone down. The fire used to roast the cow still burned to smoke the cow, horse, and mule meat strips. The fire also made an excellent beacon for the men out in the dark, looking for other survivors.

Nikki ran to the returning wagon. "Noah, I happy you home." He immediately realized what he had done. "I sorry." Nikki hung his head and kicked the ground.

"Nobody was close. Don't worry. Just be careful." Noah called out, "Jedidiah."

"Did you find anybody?"

"Yes. Take this woman into the hospital tent." Noah lowered Abigail into Jedidiah's arms.

"Where is Josiah?" Jedidiah asked.

Noah got down. "He had already passed when we got there. We found the other wagon too, but nobody was in it." Noah picked up Nikki and hugged him. "I love you, and I'm glad to see you too. Where are Mama and the babies?"

"I show."

Noah put Nikki down and then followed him. Ann stood up. "I saw that you found somebody. Will she be all right?"

"I already did some surgery on her shoulder and arm. She needs more cleaning on her chest. Will you do that if I stay here with our children?"

"I will. I'll warm some antiseptic wash." Ann kissed Noah's cheek. "More of that later," she whispered.

By the small hours of the morning, everybody had stopped processing dead animals and slept either in a wagon, a tipi, or under the stars. Shortly after the morning sun rose, a group of men from the third village arrived with horses to trade. "Have fourteen horses. Sent message other village."

Jedidiah had another wagon fixed by Roscoe and Adahy for all the broken wheels with their metal rims. Jedidiah also had all the pots, knives, matches, blankets, and such that he needed from un-owned wagons. His problem was that he had only twenty-four carcasses. He strolled over to Tom. "I need four more bodies. What will you trade for four of yours?"

"Another wagon with everything inside. I get to pick the wagon. Those men can pick whichever carcasses they want."

"I'll make the trade."

Four of the warriors from village three joined Tom. Tom signaled. "Pick the," he held four fingers, "you want."

The men of village three got started. The men from village one still worked on their meat because it had taken them a long time to gut all the dead animals. Tapco went to each man of P'ahy's village. "Is the bride price paid?" He went to Settan last. "Is the bride price for P'ahy paid?"

"For P'ahy, yes. For Akea, no. I know Akea in your tipi. You took her. You must pay."

"It's not my tipi, and I didn't take your wife. That's Tahatankohana's tipi. He took her."

"We go ask him." The two men walked across the camp. Settan stood in front of the Mystery Man who was able to drink rattlesnake venom. He wasn't sure how much power the man possessed but went ahead and pursued what he wanted. "Akea in your tipi. Tapco say you took Akea."

Tahatankohana looked up from the fire where he sat beside Ann. He knew Ann understood what was being signed. Noah thought about it. *I am the one who decided to take her.* "I said she could come with us."

Settan had thought Tapco was lying and that the Mystery Man would deny it. Now, he was even less sure if he should try to be rid of Akea. "She my wife. You must buy her."

He's not even trying to get her back. I could say, try to take her. He won't, but that would probably make bad feelings against Tapco. Plus, Akea needs to know that she's valuable. "What is her price?"

Tapco answered because Settan had named the price earlier. "Two horses."

"For P'ahy, Tapco paid the wagon recovered from the prairie. Tapco gave it all to Guipago. Everything else has been trading with the people. I buy Akea for one wagon with everything inside. She will not be my wife. She will be free."

"I agree. Which wagon?"

"I will go. When I come back, I tell you." Noah spoke to Ann in English. "I love you only. Do you understand what I'm doing?"

"Completely. Thank you for helping Akea."

Noah found Jedidiah in a wagon. "Jedidiah, I need to buy a wagon with everything inside."

"I sold one to your friend for four mule carcasses. For four more, I could get two more horses. I'd have all six teams plus two extra and still have the first four cow carcasses for meat for my people."

"I also want those cows," Noah pointed at the living animals.

"One has a broken leg. It'll be nothing but a problem, and you can't do anything with only three oxen."

"I'll care for your people for three more days for the cows."

"Which wagon do you want?"

"I'll tell you soon." Noah went to speak with Tom.

"I need four of your carcasses. What will you trade?"

"May I decide when I know what I'll need? You know I'll be fair."

"Yes." Noah walked across the camp again. "Jedidiah, get the carcasses from my friend. I want the wagon you're in."

"This isn't the best one."

"It's the one I want, but I'll also take that four ox harness I see over there."

Jedidiah climbed out. "They're yours."

Noah took a broken rocking chair with spiral rods of cherry wood out of his newly acquired wagon. He placed it in the tipi and then got Settan. "This one is yours. Akea is not yours. You will leave her alone. If you touch her, or scare her, or bother her in any way, you will not like what happens to you."

"She is yours." Settan got into the wagon to see what he owned.

"She belongs to herself." Tahatankohana, the Mystery Man, hadn't needed any special powers to solve the problem. He had only needed to be observant. He gathered the family in the tipi. "Akea, you are not married to Settan. He has traded, but only for an entire wagon with every single thing inside. He will not bother you. You belong to yourself."

Before the day ended, the families of P'ahy's village arrived. They set up their tipis. With the wood they had brought, they started fires to preserve their meat. Not long afterward, the fourth village arrived with twelve horses. For ten of the horses, Tom traded the wagon he had bought for the four animal carcasses and then stripped to its bare bones. However, instead of fresh meat, he exchanged the already smoked meat of thirty antelope along with their untanned hides rolled in salt, their horns, and hooves.

For the other two of village four's horses, Jedidiah traded the carcasses Noah had given him for Settan's wagon.

Noah went to each village's Mystery Man and traded ginseng, mugwort, and tobacco for chunks of red catlinite, one of which he planned to carve into a pipe bowl immediately.

The strips of cow meat belonging to Jedidiah, Noah, and Tom hung in the billows of Kiowa fire smoke. Adahy, Tom, Roscoe, Jedidiah, and Ken herded their newly acquired living horses across the river. Once across, Roscoe and Tom left to recover the dynamite.

Noah went into the tipi. "We should make leather. Will you remove the hair from my two hides and hang them in the smoke?"

"I'd be glad to," Sally replied.

Noah set off to the hospital tent to wake the injured people to eat and drink.

Thirty Two

Oscar and Nikki watched the trading. The two boys saw that Jedidiah had done nothing with the meatless parts of his three cows. Oscar went to Jedidiah. "Nikki and I can take all of that away for you."

"Thank you, boys. That's very helpful."

Eli had rubbed salt into his horsehide. The rest of the thing remained untouched. Oscar and Nikki believed he didn't want it. Oscar did the same as he had with Jedidiah. "We can get rid of that for you."

"I don't want to throw it away. Somebody might want the meat."

"We want," Nikki informed Eli.

Eli assumed they were up to something, but he saw no harm in giving it to them. "Take it."

Next, the boys went to Tom. "We'll get rid of the skin and bones for you," Oscar offered.

Tom had seen the boys gathering parts. "Thank you. You can take everything except the skins."

Oscar and Nikki lay a cowhide over the horse and then pushed and pulled on its legs until they had flipped it over, which wrapped it in the hide. They went to Ehawee. "Help us trade."

"What do you have to trade?"

Oscar spoke for them, "We have one horse inside a cow skin. We have two more cow skins with everything of five cows except the meat. We want buckskin clothes like yours and moccasins with tails. Trade with a family that has boys our size."

"You can probably each get a set of clothes for the two cow skins with the parts. You would still have the horse with the third cow skin to trade for something more valuable."

"Will you help us?"

"I will. Let's go."

Meanwhile, Jedidiah casually visited each adult member of his wagon train. "I found all the money from the wagons of those who have passed. I divided it equally between all the adults." He handed each of them sixty-seven dollars.

Ehawee and the boys returned to the skins and bones with two women. Ehawee pointed, "You can divide those two skins with all those parts."

Each woman handed a boy a set of soft deerskin clothes and a pair of moccasins. One of the women asked. "What you do with that?" She pointed at the carcass.

Ehawee explained, "They not decided what they want. It cow skin but horse inside."

"Come back to tipi. See what I have. I will take this now."

Ehawee refused, "Not until they decide."

The boys returned with a soft fuzzy buffalo hide with many spear holes. The woman pulled the carcass and skin onto a travois. Once they had taken it away, the boys carried their buffalo hide and clothes into the tipi.

Emily asked, "Oscar, how did you get that? Take it back right now. You can't steal from these people. They'll kill you and us too."

"I didn't steal. We traded."

"You have nothing to trade. Don't lie to me."

"We did trade. I'm not lying. Ask Ehawee."

"Ann, don't let them leave this tipi. I'm going to find Ehawee." Emily dipped her head and went out the door.

"Honest. We got the parts from Tom, Eli, and Jedidiah. We took the parts as clearing away their mess. They gave them to us. We traded for these."

"Very resourceful. Nothing ended up wasted. You, and whoever you traded with, all got things you wanted. May I see what you have?"

"Yes!" Oscar and Nikki laid out their treasures.

Ann picked up the buffalo fur. "Very well done."

Emily came back into the tipi. "I'm sorry that I didn't believe you. I spoke with all those involved. They all assured me that everything was just as you said. Show me what you have."

Oscar held his new buckskin shirt in front of him. Emily pulled it around to his sides. "It looks a little too big. Put them on." The boys stood in clothes two sizes too large. Emily rolled up Oscar's sleeves and pant legs. "You'll grow into them."

Wearing their too-large new clothes, Nikki and

Oscar laid on their new buffalo hide with the cat. "We should call her Whiskers." Oscar pointed to the thick black hairs by the cat's mouth. "Whiskers."

Nikki rubbed its orange head and spoke a word he had learned. "Howdy, Whiskers."

Thirty Three

The families of the other villages arrived the following day. The field around the camp filled with tipis and drying meat. Everybody socialized. Noah cared for the injured in the hospital tent. Except for two short times each day to allow them to eat, drink, and relieve themselves, Noah kept the wounded people and animals sedated. Akea walked the camp openly.

Men, now without wives, flocked around Emily, Sally, and the newly widowed women. Neither Sally nor Emily appeared to want the attention. Tom didn't like it, but those men were much closer to Emily's age, and he wanted her to choose for herself who she wanted.

Roscoe built his forge. He made a removable firebox with boards from broken wagons, pressed four large flat river stones against the sides into clay from the riverbank, wedged a thick rock at the bottom to hold the vertical stones in place, and then packed the spaces with more clay. He used broken wheels and their metal rims to build smaller wheels and mounted them with broken axles he cut shorter. He attached the wheels and axles to a wooden box into which the firebox could be placed and then rolled away from the wagons.

On the last day that Noah was contracted to care for the injured, Tapco left with P'ahy's father and brothers. It wasn't long before they galloped full speed back to camp. Tapco informed the tribe. "We saw hundreds of wild ponies."

Guipago slid off his horse. "They're not far from the canyon. All women and children go into side canyon and close off with wagons. We run herd into far end and block in with more wagons. We camp while tame ponies."

Thirty Four

The Kiowa tribe packed. Noah told his family, "We made arrangements with the people to help them catch a herd of mustangs. We should move the injured people into the pit houses while we're gone. They don't need anything except their painkiller, food, and water. Maybe you women would also wash the tent in the river and set it up to dry. We should only be gone a day or two. To get around a herd this big, we need all the animals and all the people who can ride. We'll need to take everybody except Ann, Stephanie, Ehawee, and Akea. Only because you—"

Ann cut him off, "We know why we should stay. What about the three animals with the broken legs?"

Roscoe jumped into the conversation with a status update. "I've made the cages. We can drag the animals into the river on canvas. In the river, they can get their legs under them, and we can get the braces on. We'll bring them out on their feet and take them into the animal quarters in the pit complex."

Ehawee spoke up, "Get it done. Everybody else, help cut grass and bring it in."

Before the hour was out, the Kiowa tribe was ready to move to the canyon. The two horses and the cow with broken legs stood with the four healthy cows, the goats, the sheep, and the miniature donkeys in a section of grass roped off with all the nets and all the wagons they had moved to the south side of the river. The animal food troughs were full even though the animals remained outside. Tied to the wagons, the cleaned hospital tent flapped in the breeze. The hospital bed wagons sat beside the pit houses to use as firewood. All the patients lay in beds in the pit house. Roscoe took several of the boards and squirreled them away in his wagon. Ann placed a few aside in the pit house.

Noah hugged Ann. "Be home soon. I love you."

Nikki said, "I'm ready."

"I didn't know you were taking Nikki. Is it safe for him to be running down wild horses?"

Noah knelt in front of Nikki. "All the young children are staying here."

"Nikki go with Noah."

Noah hugged him. "I have to be fair. Do exactly what Ann tells you." Noah picked up and hugged Chris, then Joy and Adele. "Love you all."

Nikki shrugged his shoulders. He wasn't sure what Noah had told him. He only knew that he wasn't allowed to catch horses. Noah turned, waved, and then rode away with Tom, Emily, Eli, Helen, Adahy, Sally, Roscoe, Tapco, and P'ahy. They crossed the Cimarron back to the north. With Jedidiah, his able-bodied people, and the Kiowa, they left the prairie of tall grass empty except for the grave below the sod filled with half the wagon train.

Ann wanted to extend their ability to trade spools of yellow, red, green, blue, white, and black thread. She thought they could make smaller spools from the wagon boards and then divide the two hundred-yard spools of thread in halves and make twice as many spools. She took boards to the two men who had broken legs. "If you would chop these into pieces about this long," she held her fingers three inches apart, "and this wide," she narrowed the space to just over an inch, "I'll pay you two pennies for each spool."

Thirty Five

At the small side canyon, the Kiowa families unloaded everything and set up for the summer. Two of their six wagons blocked the way in. They strung a buffalo hide tipi from the top of a wagon bow of one wagon to one at the far end of another. They parked a wagon far enough away from the cliff to allow other wagons to pass in or out. They hoped, to horses charging past, that it would appear as an impenetrable barrier. They left the other four wagons hitched to teams.

Those not remaining with the children attached a tin cup and a spoon or a fork to string, which they tied at their waists before they rode out. The scouts who had followed the horses saw the signal that the tribe was ready. Sixty men, women, and teenagers hurried toward the large herd.

Lying tight on top of their rides, they flanked the wild ponies that paid no attention to the horses, mules, and donkeys joining them. The people saw to it that the only way to run was toward the canyon. Suddenly, the shouting of people and the clanging of eating utensils on tin cups rang out.

Wild horses tried to escape the unknown danger

and charged off in the open direction. A few tried to break off. Sally wheeled Beauty and raced to the perimeter of the mustang herd while loudly banging her cup. Heath, the young man who had given her the pry bar, helped her. The wild animals attempted to escape the irritating noise. The people forced the fleeing group tighter together.

Helen blocked the lead stallion that didn't want to go the way its rivals were forcing it. Helen held tight as the spotted stallion slammed into Lemonade. "They're all going the way you go. I'm not letting you out." Still holding the reins tightly, Helen gripped her saddle's pommel. The stallion slammed her again. Helen refused to give way to the aggressive leader of the herd. Emily charged to Helen's rescue. She beat and banged on her cup until she had scared the beast away from Helen.

The herd moved closer to the canyon. Individuals broke through the gaps and escaped. Slamming their cups, Noah and Adahy dashed after an escaping mare and her colt.

Even though the recent rain had moistened the ground, the relentless pounding of hundreds of hooves created a cloud of dust that threatened to choke Tom and Eli, bringing up the rear. Tom pulled his silk scarf over his nose and tucked the bottom into his collar. He continued the pursuit. Eli did the same.

All the Kiowa whooped and hollered as they galloped beside the mass of moving horseflesh. They drove the mustangs toward their capture. The lookout on the canyon cliff saw their approach. "They're coming!" Four women ran to the designated wagons poised behind the barrier.

Sally and Heath veered off at the leading edge as the mustangs thundered into the canyon's mouth. Behind them, others did the same as the horses charged into the trap.

The scout on the cliff saw Tom and Eli, bringing up the rear. "Now!" he signaled from the clifftop. Below, an Indian boy, not quite old enough to have run down the horses with the others, ran to a carefully positioned wagon and jerked the rope holding up the wagon cover that blocked the side canyon. The canvas dropped.

The lead wagon sailed through the opening as if flung from a sling. Three wagons followed, hot on its rear. At the high cliff wall, the first wagon screeched to a halt in the narrowest part of the gap. "Get the boards up!" The women in the rear, with babies in cradleboards on their backs, raised the wooden walls they had built from the wagon boards Guipago had recovered from the prairie.

The lead mustang ran full out to the end of the canyon, ran a wide arc, and then turned back toward those attempting to block the way out. The people in the wagons quickly lowered the wooden walls into position. The herd thundered toward them. Rapidly, the women tied the walls to the wagons. The spotted stallion made a tighter turn and tried to run up the rubble at the foot of the cliff. It slid down, then again ran for the far end of the canyon.

The towering rocks still blocked the stallion's way out. It snorted its anger and frustration, turned, and flew back toward the wooden wall. Those in the wagon saw him coming. They desperately tried to secure the final ropes. The spotted stallion didn't slow.

"Get out!" screamed one of the women. Everybody jumped from the wagons and ran for the side canyon.

Just before impact, the stallion turned and slammed sideways into the boards. The wall stood. The furious mustang reared. It pummeled the wall with its hooves. Members of its herd joined the assault. They kicked with their hind legs and slammed the wall. Boards cracked, but no hole large enough to escape opened. Finally out of steam, the captured horses only snorted and pawed the ground.

Thirty Six

Helen ran to Roscoe. "I've never felt so alive." She threw her arms around his neck and kissed him. He kissed her back. She enjoyed the return for a moment then drew back. She whispered, "I shouldn't have done that. I didn't have your permission."

"You may kiss me any time you want," Roscoe assured her.

"Your kiss makes me feel even more alive." Helen kissed him again.

After Roscoe had lost the woman he had wanted when he was fifteen, he had never tried to keep a woman in his life. That is, until he had met Helen. "Helen, I want you to be my wife." He remembered that Ann and her sisters had needed to hear that they were loved. "I love you. You are the only woman I have truly loved for a very long time."

"It has to be a real marriage. Not absconding and then giving somebody a few horses."

"Captains on ships can marry people. Maybe Jedidiah, as the wagon train leader, has that authority. Do you want me to find out?"

"Please do." Helen held out her hand, so Roscoe could help her navigate the small opening through the wagon barricade into the side canyon.

Tom stood beside the wagons with a scowl on his face. At one of the fires, Ken sat beside Emily and Sally and told them what had happened the night of the storm. "I told Caroline not to leave the wagon. She said, 'Cleo needs help. If you won't get the doctor, I'm going.' I told her the storm was too strong and that he would be all right until it passed, but she wouldn't listen to me. She climbed out the back, let go of it, and was gone. I didn't even have time to grab her. The wind just sucked her away."

"I'm so sorry, Ken." Emily patted his hand.

"I am too, but now I need somebody to help me raise Cleo. Emily, I've always thought you are a fine woman the way you put up with Warren. It would please me very much if you became my wife."

Emily looked across the camp. Tom had avoided her ever since they had joined Jedidiah's wagon train. Ken was a good man, but she had no feelings for him. "I'm not ready to marry again."

"You can rejoin us. Maybe, when we find a place to make a home, you'll be ready."

Emily saw Helen come into the camp. "I'll think about it. Would you excuse me?" Emily escaped. Besides, she honestly did want to find out if the spotted stallion had injured Helen.

Sally immediately stood and followed her. *I'm glad he's after her and not me.* She hurried to Noah and Eli. "May I sit between you?"

"Sit a spell." Eli scooted over.

Sally lowered herself into her chosen position. "Much obliged. I should have stayed with Ann. All the men looking for new wives, keep looking at me."

"Maybe you should talk with them. They're already going west, and that one hasn't stopped mooning over you since he gave you the pry bar."

"I practically snapped his head off. You'd think he'd lose his interest." Sally put her arm through Eli's. "How do I make it clear that I'm not interested?"

Thirty Seven

At the pit houses, Ehawee went out to check on the animals. *What's that?* She went back inside and got her spyglass. A black mass expanded across the southern horizon. *Maybe it's buffalo.* She watched for a long time before she returned to the others. "I'm afraid they went after the wrong herd. The real herd is just now coming up from the south."

Those who could walk went to look. The massive group of animals expanded as far as they could see from the east to the west. Ehawee continued to look. "They'll probably be here by sundown. We need to get all of ours inside."

Ann contemplated. *Thousands of horses are going to walk right past us.* She had an idea. "Get all the ten-gallon tubs into the other pits and fill them with water. Boys, get as much cut grass into the pits as you can. We also need to rearrange the wagons and nets."

Nikki, Oscar, and Cleo scurried off to cut grass. Late in the afternoon, they were ready. Oscar asked, "You sure this will work?"

Ann took Chris out of his cradleboard in the pit house in which the injured people had moved. "I don't see how it can fail." She bounced and cooed at her baby. "My sweet, sweet baby boy. How I love you."

A portion of the horses walked between the rows of wagons and nets that Ruben, Ann, and Stephanie had set up. Nikki ran down the ramp, across the pit house, into the tunnel to the meeting room, across the meeting room, then into the pit where everybody waited. "They're here."

Ann looked at Ehawee. "Do you still want to do it?"

"I do." She exited through the tunnel out of their living area.

The horses funneled between the nets. The crush of more animals at the rear forced them down the ramp into the pit house and then out the other side through the tunnel into the meeting room. Ehawee counted as they followed the net across the room into the third tunnel where she stood hidden behind a buffalo hide. The horses went into the second room with the outer door securely closed. The room contained grass and water. After six adults with some foals, she closed the interior wooden door and backed to the next exit from the meeting room, pulling the net with her. The first set of animals had been peacefully trapped and remained content.

Ehawee directed the following six into the next corridor and repeated the procedure until all eight pits contained six adult horses and their offspring.

When the meeting room had ten plus a few baby horses, she pushed the entry door closed, slipped into the tunnel to the people's house, and pulled that door closed as well.

Outside, laying on top of the corridor into their area, Oscar, Cleo, and Nikki had been counting as well. At fifty-eight, they had pulled the rope and released the net that had forced the animals into the pits. Abigail put on her backpack and slipped from her hiding place behind the entry tunnel. She followed the last horse into the tunnel and pulled the door closed. Once the horses had all entered the pit, she closed the inner door and set up camp in the tunnel where she would stay until the herd passed.

Cleo and Oscar watched the field between the pit houses that they had enclosed with their wagons. When it looked full, they pulled up the net and trapped the animals inside. At the same time, Nikki lowered the net at the side of the corridor that had funneled the animals. The rest of the horses went out the side and continued to the north. In the twilight, the boys counted again before they slid into the hole in the top of the tunnel. Oscar informed the others. "We got nineteen more, not including the babies." Horses came up from the south, crossed the river, and continued north throughout the night.

Thirty Eight

In the morning, Jedidiah negotiated the exchange of thirty-six more tamed horses for most of the food that had been in the wagons the Kiowa now owned. The Kiowa would then have more than enough food to spend the summer breaking the hundreds of horses in the canyon. They hitched up the two wagons at the side canyon and rode to the main canyon's mouth to go get the food. Horses blocked the way out. Noah, Eli, and Adahy climbed to the top of the cliff. The herd spread as far as they could see. Adahy put his spyglass into his pocket. "I don't like this. Ehawee may need me."

"I don't like it either," Eli remarked.

Noah turned toward the path down. "I'm not happy, but there's nothing we can do about it, and they're intelligent women. I'm sure they're safely inside the pit houses." They went back to the camp to wait out the passing herd.

Thirty Nine

Halfway down the tunnel at the pit houses, one torch burned. Nikki and Ann stood in the tunnel and looked at the beautiful animals in the meeting room. A pregnant mare seemed quite distressed. Nikki pointed, "Krank."

It does look sick. Ann looked closer. *I see a hoof coming out! Her baby is breech, but I doubt she'll let me help.* Ann took a step into the room. The horse sidled away. She retreated into the tunnel when the others snorted and pawed the ground. "We have to get her away from the others, then let her become exhausted."

Attached to the tunnel's doorframe, Ann saw the net Ehawee had used to direct the horses. She attempted to hold the other end and toss the net over the pregnant mare. It landed short. Ann pulled it back and threw harder. The net landed on the horse's back, then slide to the floor on the wrong side. Crammed inside the room, the horse couldn't move away from the harassment. Ann pulled the net back and tried again.

After several attempts, it landed on the far side of the horse. Ann slowly drew the mare into the tunnel. She closed the door to separate it from those crowded in the meeting room.

After the horse became too tired to stand and lay on its side, Ann replaced the sputtering torch with a new one. She knelt away from the mare's feet behind its head, cupped her hand around the mother horse's nose, and then gently blew into the horse's nostrils. The horse calmed. "Nikki, you do this." She waved him forward. Nikki approached and then edged around between the animal and the wall. He got on his knees and did as he had seen Ann do while he rubbed the horse's head and neck.

Ann had watched her father help a cow. She pushed her arm and the foal back up the birth canal, forced the baby's leg out of the way, seized the mane, and pulled its head toward the way out. With its hoof and leg no longer preventing its exit, the baby slid out the birth canal. The mare lay exhausted. "She must lick her clean." Ann pretended to lick her arm. "Mama must lick her."

With hands that smelled of the birth fluids, Ann pushed the baby to the mare's head. Ann took Nikki's hand. "Let's move away." They backed to the far end of the tunnel. For several minutes, the mare lay unmoving, then sat up and started cleaning the baby.

Nikki silently clapped and then held his hands clasped together by his chest. "Good now?"

"I hope so."

A couple of hours and several torches later, the mare returned to her feet. Ann and Nikki watched the baby make its first faltering attempts to stand in the dim light of the tunnel. With its wobbly legs spread wide, the foal stood on its own four feet. Its mother moved beside it. The baby took the first drink of its mother's milk.

"They'll be alright now. Let's leave." Ann opened the door into their chambers.

Sally looked at Ann covered in horse blood and birth fluids. "Are you all right!?"

Nikki took Ann's hand. "We make baby horse."

"What happened?" Oscar asked.

"Let me clean up, then I'll explain." After the story, they put water and oats in the tunnel. Everybody who could walk looked at the horses in the tunnel.

Late in the day, Abigail thought she no longer heard the sound of passing horses. She peeked out. The tail end of the herd rounded the pit house. She walked to the people's quarters not far behind them. "They've all passed."

Forty

At the canyon, Noah, Eli, and Adahy again stood at the top of the cliff. The herd still spread across the land, but Adahy saw the enormous herd of mustangs' southern edge. "Maybe in the morning."

Noah, however, noticed a golden eagle flying into the southwest. "Maybe the three of us should ride through the herd. The rest can come later."

Forty One

The fifth group of warriors arrived at the pit houses where they had been told others had gathered to trade for meat. They saw no field of cow, mule, and horse bodies. Across the river by the pit houses were a few sheep and goats, two horses with something strange around a leg, and a few live cattle, along with wagons. They had not seen the mustang herd that had passed east of them.

Oscar slid into the hole in the tunnel roof. "Another group of Indians is on the other side of the river."

With Akea and Ehawee, Ruben went out the door holding a broken arrow in the air. Akea spoke to the men in their language. One shifted on his horse, furrowed his brow, and stared intently at Akea. Akea purposefully looked only at the village chief. "We have wild horses to trade for tame horses. Two for one."

"We heard there was much food to trade," said the village chief.

"You are the fifth group. All the meat is taken. We have wild horses to trade."

"I don't see horses."

"Come."

Fifteen men rode across the river. Horses in the netted area between the pit houses came into view. Even including the babies, there weren't thirty horses. "Not enough."

"That's not all." Akea led the men to one of the tunnels. "Six plus little ones." She opened the door and went inside with Ruben and the chief. At the far end, she opened the second door.

The chief looked at the six horses eating grass. "Mostly mares. Two pregnant. Trade one tame horse two wild horse, pregnant or not."

Akea signed to Ehawee. Ehawee passed the message to Ruben, "He will trade one for two adults. A pregnant mother or a mare with a baby counts as one."

Ruben remembered how they had sealed the previous trades. "I'll smoke to confirm the deal. Somebody else will have to lead the ceremony."

Ehawee translated to Akea. Akea turned back to the chief. "You give fifteen tame horses. You take out of this and next four houses what is inside. You can look first. The white man will smoke with you. Ruben gives a gift of tobacco to the people. He can't lead the ceremony."

The chief nodded his agreement. They exited. As they walked to the next tunnel, the young warrior, who had not stopped eyeing Akea, strode toward her. Ruben stepped in front of her and held up his only hand. Akea touched Ruben's arm. "Adoeette won't hurt me. I know him."

The young warrior looked at the one-armed man who clearly could not defend himself or Akea. The man had still attempted to protect a Kiowa woman. *Maybe it's not what I thought. Maybe the white man is the father.* He looked at Akea and pointed to her large belly. "Is it mine?"

Does he want it to be? He looks upset. "Yes."

"Is he your husband?" The young Indian nodded his head in the direction of Ruben.

"No."

"Why he want to protect you?"

"He is friend."

"He has only one arm. He cannot win. He must know."

"He is good man." They arrived at the next tunnel. Akea left the father of her child standing outside and went in.

After the chief had looked into five pit houses, he said, "We smoke." The men followed Akea, Ehawee, and Ruben into the quarters where women cooked a roast. Injured men, women, and children spun thread onto small spools, cut bright red material, worked on braids of horsehair hanging from the top of a bunkbed, sewed large sheets of heavy cloth, or lay in beds. Everybody looked white except Akea and the other woman translating.

"Why you with these pale-faces?" the chief asked in Kiowa.

"They are helping me, my sister, and her husband."

"Tell him get his gift." The chief left with his warriors.

Akea passed on the message. "You have to give them tobacco." She went to continue her conversation with Adoeette. Ruben spoke to Ann, "I've gotten us fifteen more horses. I need a plug of tobacco. You must have some. What will you trade?"

"Don't charge me for all the thread you've respooled."

"Deal."

"I'll get some." Ann went to the appropriate wagon and found one of the Indian warriors inside. "Get out!" He immediately exited through the other end of the wagon. Ann hid the tobacco in her pocket. Openly she carried cakes of raisins.

Ruben left with the tobacco. He smoked with the chief and the other warriors. After the deal was sealed, Adoeette again spoke with Akea and then spoke with his chief before he went back to Akea. Akea signed to Ehawee. "They have families not far away. They have fifteen more horses. They will send one warrior to get families and horses to come here. Trade for thirty more horses. Keep wild horses in pits. Stay here. Break them."

"I'll speak with my sisters."

The sisters agreed to the trade. Ehawee added, "I don't like the way some of the men were looking us over. I want them to promise over the pipe that they won't hurt us or try to take anything except what we freely trade or give. We need all the men to smoke with us."

Ann informed her sisters, "I found one of them in our wagon."

Ehawee went out alone. Frowning, she returned with Akea, Adoeette, and the chief. "These two will smoke with us. The others will not."

Ann looked directly at the chief. Even though he hadn't, Ann believed he could sign. She did so. "The other horses are ours." She pointed to Stephanie and Ehawee. "If the others will not share the Calumet, you cannot have our horses or bring your families. You must leave here now with the horses you have already bought."

The chief signed to Ann, "Why are the horses hers?" He pointed to Ehawee.

"She is my sister."

"She Kiowa. You not."

"I marry Tahatankohana, her brother."

"Who is Tahatankohana?"

Akea spoke up, "Powerful Mystery Man. He drink rattlesnake poison."

Ann's brow momentarily furrowed. That was something she had not known. However, she did know what was agreed to over a peace pipe would not be broken. "He is very powerful. You must all smoke with," —telling one's name gave the other power— "us. All must agree you will not harm anyone here or steal from us. Then you bring wives. I trade things with wives too." Ann picked up some of the pieces of cloth and spools of thread. She put them down. She retrieved and opened a sewing kit then handed the chief one of the knives with the sharpening stone. "You think wives like these, you all smoke."

The chief pointed to himself. "Dohosan say they

no hurt the people. Not take anything not traded. You feed us too. Then they smoke."

"We smoke first."

"Agreed." Dohosan motioned to Adoeette. They left the pit house.

Ehawee notified Akea. "I tell you when let warriors in." She jammed a spit through another big hunk of cow leg and placed it over the fire. "Hang the tipi across the middle of the room. Everybody, go to my sister's hiding hole. No lights or sound." Ehawee turned to her sisters. "Put on your beaded doeskin dresses, beaded moccasins, and your medicine bags. Get a twist of sage, your Calumet, the pouch of kinnikinnick, the smudge bowl, and the tongs."

Ann dug in Noah's pack. "The things we need must be in the wagon."

"Get them, the revolvers, and some tobacco before you change clothes." Ehawee drew a circle on the floor with the sacred tobacco that Ann handed her upon her return.

Ann handed the revolvers to Ruben. "Twenty bullets each, and there are only fifteen of them, but only shoot if you have to." Ruben and Akea took the people to safety.

All fifteen warriors came in. With the sage, Ann smudged them as they entered. She signed, "You honor me with your presence." The men sat in the ring of tobacco. Ann stood in the east and drew the two halves of the pipe from her medicine bag. With her right hand, she raised the pipe to the east.

Ehawee translated Ann's words into sign. "The wooden pipe symbolizes all plants, the male, and his straightforwardness of thought and his cunning."

She touched the hanging turkey feathers. "The feathers are all the winged ones and the love of the first kiss my husband gave me."

Ann stroked the attached horsehair. "The hair of the horse given to my husband for saving a man's life. It is all the four-legged ones.

"The skin of the alligator," she pointed at Stephanie, "my sister killed because it tried to eat her husband. It is all swimming ones." Ann held out the bowl, shaped like an eagle's claw holding the earth. "The bowl is the earth, the female, and the eagle the Great Spirit has directed to watch over us." She attached the bowl to the stem. "Together, all are one. The smoke connects us to the Great Spirit."

Ann raised the bowl in the east. "Thunderbirds, you helped Tahatankohana go to the spirit world to get the message from the ancestors and took him there again to bring the spirit of his child back into my body. See the agreement made between us and these men. Cause powerful punishment if agreement is broken." Ann tossed a handful of red beads into the air. The color of war descended over the warriors.

Dohosan stiffened. *She couldn't know.*

Ann put a pinch of the mixture of sage, cedar, tobacco, sweetgrass, and red willow bark into the pipe bowl and then stepped to the south. "Spirit of the wolf, bring happy and peaceful trading. Give keen sight to see what must be seen and courage to do what is needed." A handful of white beads flew up. The possibility of peace rained over them and joined the alternative around them. Adoeette looked at his chief.

A pinch of kinnikinnick went into the bowl as Ann moved into the west. "Great Spirit who is called Jehovah, rip out the souls of any who make themselves our enemy. Send them into the black coffin where the serpent coils above them." In a great spin, Ann flung beads at the feet of the warriors and warned of the end of life.

Dohosan's eyes became pits as black as the beads Ann had flung at his feet. *She has no power to summon the spirits.*

Adoeette saw the chief's expression and realized the man's intentions. *I have seen what the Medicine woman called me to see. Give me the power she summoned.*

Ann moved on to the north and flung blue beads. "Fat Buffalo, sense the troubles, hardships, and sadness that comes. Provide the layers of fat for those who remain, so they can survive the coming cold." *Jehovah, I pray that sadness will not come, but let it be their families and not those who love us if it comes to a choice.* Ann reached into the fire with the tongs, drew out an ember, and lit the pipe. "I smoke for peaceful trading." She looked into the eyes of Dohosan and held out the pipe.

Dohosan smacked it from her hand. A warrior jumped to his feet and clamped his hand over Ann's mouth. Others silenced Ehawee and Stephanie. The women struggled as the warriors pulled them toward the door. Adoeette knocked Ann free from her captor. "They offer peace and good trading. You call down death!"

"She has no power." Dohosan grabbed Ann. "She is a pale-face woman; nothing. All this will be ours. Stay with us, or I will send YOU to the black coffin."

"You must not do this!"

Dohosan's knife plunged into Adoeette's side. "Find the others. Bring them or kill them." He jerked Ann toward the tunnel out.

"You will bring no more troubles to our village." Adoeette drew the knife from his side and lunged. The two men and Ann fell into the colored beads littering the ground. The other warriors stopped to see if their chief would be overthrown.

Stephanie sunk her teeth deep into the arm that held her. Ehawee kicked her heel into her captor's groin. The man doubled. "RUN!" Ann came up and plowed over the warrior, who grabbed Ehawee by the ankle. Ehawee crashed to the hard earth. Another warrior recaptured Ann.

Adoeette straddled Dohosan. "You have seen your last day." He attempted to push the knife into his chief's heart.

Dohosan pushed back against Adoeette's wrists, twisted violently, knocked Adoeette over, and rolled out. The knife slid away. The men scrambled for it. Adoeette came up with the blade. The men circled each other. "Yield, and I will let you live," Adoeette snarled.

"You are a puny nothing. I will never yield."

The dagger soared from Adoeette's hand, without a doubt to sink deep into Dohosan's heart.

BLAM!

The knife flew sideways. All eyes turned. A man with three red dots across his forehead and two red lines from his nose to each ear strode down the tunnel. He wore a breechcloth, moccasins with ermine tails at the rear, bones and eagle feathers tied in his hair, and a mink cape over his shoulders. He held a Lefaucheux revolver in each hand. In Kiowa, he boomed out the words Tapco had taught him on their way from Horse Canyon. "YOU CANNOT HAVE MY PEOPLE!"

Also wearing war paint, Tapco, Adahy, and Eli swarmed in to forcibly remove their loved ones from the clutches of the warriors who still stared at Tahatankohana. Nikki and Oscar, with their faces painted for war, peered out from behind Tahatankohana's legs.

The men immediately let go of Stephanie and Ann. Clutching her belly, Ehawee laid in the pool of her water. Dohosan looked away from the Mystery Man toward the white woman, wearing a smile and soft eyes as she looked at her powerful husband, who she had summoned. *Very strong medicine.* He looked at Adoeette. "You defeated me. You chief now." He turned to Tahatankohana. "You give me my life. I your servant."

Forty Two

Adahy scooped up Ehawee. "Save them!"

The fearsome Mystery Man got right into Dohosan's face. "You still may lose your life." With the boys hot on his heels, Tahatankohana pulled Ann and Stephanie with him to the other side of the tipi curtain. "Bring her," he told Adahy. "And somebody, tie him up." He pointed at Dohosan.

"Tie him too." Ehawee pointed at the man who had accosted her and grabbed her ankle.

Adoeette defended the man, "He did what chief told him. Dohosan only guilty one."

Tahatankohana instructed Tapco and Eli, "Keep a close eye on all of them." He sent the boys to get their friends. "Nikki und Oscar, hol unsere Freunde."

Ann asked, "How did they get with you?"

"I'll tell you later. Boys, don't bring them back until I tell you." He took off his cape, the bones, and his feathers, then held Ehawee's hand. "I need to feel inside you."

"Go ahead."

Still wearing his war paint, Noah felt Ehawee's abdomen then her cervix. "You're body isn't ready to deliver. The baby can't stay in there with the water gone. I have to cut the baby out. We'll give you the sedative, but if we wait twenty minutes for you to go to sleep, the baby won't be alive."

"I had a couple more weeks before he was due. Are you sure?"

"Yes."

"Husband, get me something to bite, then hold my hand. Brother, do what you have to. Save my baby!"

Adahy's face burned red. "Bring that man in here!" He ordered Tapco. "For every cut on my wife, you cut that man."

Tapco and Noah turned to Adoeette. Adoeette nodded. "Do it." Adoeette and Tapco carried in Dohosan and laid him on a bed beside Ehawee's bed.

Ehawee signed, "May you hurt much more than I do."

Adoeette turned to take his men outside. Noah stopped him. "All of you stay. You see what we do to Dohosan, and let me see your injuries." Noah examined Adoeette's side and the bitten flesh on the arm of the man who had tried to restrain Stephanie. He signed, "Bind each other up. I fix you better later."

Noah and Tapco prepared. Ann brought two cups of painkiller, which she gave to Adoeette and the man her sister had bitten. She passed Ehawee and Dohosan cups of the sedative they had previously made for the injured wagon train people. Ehawee stared into the eyes of Dohosan. She refused to let him see her pain. As Noah's scalpel sliced her skin, she clamped her teeth on the doeskin in her mouth. Her eyes narrowed ever so slightly. Tapco's blade cut into Dohosan. He equally hid his pain.

Adahy turned Ehawee's face toward his. "Don't worry about him. I'm here for you."

It was the fourth time Noah had cut into a human. He thought about the thickness of the skin of Kangee, Warren, and Henrietta. "Cut him shallow. I want him to get just as many cuts." At the uterus, Noah told Tapco, "This is what the baby is inside." Noah hated inflicting pain on his sister, but he wanted to make sure that he did not cut the baby. He carefully cut shallow slices. Ehawee's uterus opened. Everybody watched Noah lift out her baby. He examined the child. It wasn't breathing, so he smacked the baby's bottom. It drew in a breath and then screamed of its displeasure. Noah pushed all the blood in the umbilical cord into the baby before he tied it close to the baby's body and then cut the baby free. Noah laid the child on Ehawee's chest. "Meet your son."

Noah pulled out the placenta and clamped every bleeding vessel he could find. He did not sew Ehawee back together. He wanted to allow her to fall asleep without inflicting more pain.

He joined Tapco beside Dohosan. "Make sure fix large blood vessels." They found only small ones. "We burn these." He got one of the clean cooking spits he had placed in the fire before they started. A vessel sizzled as he touched it with the red-hot metal.

"Let me." Tapco cauterized the others, then

sewed closed the four-inch-long incision and dressed the wound, all before Dohosan became unconscious from the sedative. As Tapco practiced on Dohosan, Noah stitched the stab wound and then the bite.

Finally, Ehawee slept. Adahy breathed a sigh of relief that she was no longer suffering. Noah told him, "Take your son before the sedative gets into your wife's milk." Noah turned to Stephanie. "When he's hungry, would you feed him?"

Stephanie knew drinking milk from an animal that had been sedated would sedate the milk consumer. It had happened to her, their friend Lola, and the man who had kidnapped Lola. She also knew that Ann was already feeding three babies. "I surely will."

Adahy took his healthy baby from Ehawee's breast. "You are Etu." He wrapped, then rocked his son in his arms while Noah carefully demonstrated to Tapco how to stitch blood vessels together and close up a uterus and abdomen. Both patients lay covered in their beds. Noah called out, "Bring everybody back."

Forty Three

All the patients returned to their beds or activities in the same pit house with Ehawee and Dohosan. Adoeette and his men went with Ann, Stephanie, Akea, Tapco, Noah, Eli, Nikki, and Oscar to look at the horses. Adahy stayed with his wife and child. They went into all the pits that contained wild horses, each time entering and exiting from the outside. Adoeette said to the Mystery Man, "I want make the trade. One tame for two wild horses. Fifteen for thirty. I and my warriors smoke with you."

Tahatankohana replied, "I did not catch them. You must trade with horse owners."

Adoeette wasn't sure which of the two he was more in awe of: the Mystery Man who had taken a baby out of a woman or the woman who had conjured the Mystery Man, opened his eyes, and given him the strength to fight with a knife wound and win. "You, or her," he pointed at Ann, "might kill us. I want all smoke for trade and peace."

Ann had seen that the clay bowl had broken

when dashed from her hand. "I have no Calumet. Dohosan broke it."

Noah looked into Ann's eyes. He spoke in English, "There was only one here."

"I used it. I'm sorry, my husband. I was trying to save our lives."

"I'm not upset that you used it. I'm sad that it's broken. It meant so much," he paused, "to all of us."

Adoeette signaled to his village Mystery Man. "Get Calumet." He looked at Noah. "May my people come?"

"Your people offended them. Ask them." He pointed at Ann and Stephanie.

Ann looked at her sister. No words were spoken. "We agree, all your village and all here smoke. Bring plenty kinnikinnick."

One man rode away. Noah walked between Stephanie and Ann back to the living quarters. He whispered to Stephanie, "I hope you never have to, but if you do, bite just as hard." He spoke more loudly to his wife. "You will still have seven horses after the trade."

"Only half are ours. Half belong to Jedidiah's people. There are more in the meeting room that neither you nor the Kiowa have seen, and Nikki and I have two in the tunnel. The colt was breech. We helped it give birth. How did Nikki and Oscar get with you?"

"You know how big that herd was. It blocked us. When I saw a golden eagle flying this way, I knew I needed to get here. We lay on our horses and Ace.

We worked our way across the herd. We were almost to the river crossing when we saw people on the prairie. I thought they were very far because they appeared small. We got closer. I recognized Nikki's voice, 'Noah, hol mich.'

"I called out, 'Nikki.' We hurried over. Nikki and Oscar let out a flood of German and English all scrambled together. I told them, 'Nikki, halt. Oscar, tell me what's happening.' Oscar told us about the men arriving. When Ehawee told them to hide, they knew there was trouble. They were trying to get us. It's a miracle that we came across them. Anyway, we hurriedly painted our faces, and I changed my clothes, then we mounted up and came as fast as we could. We got here not one second too soon. Adoeette had time to win."

Stephanie said, "If you had gotten here one second later, you would have been too late to save a life."

"The boys are heroes," Noah patted the top of their heads. "They were very brave."

Inside their quarters, Noah went with Nikki to see the horse with its colt. Nikki and Ann had taken it more water and oats before the last warriors had arrived. "I do this. They like me." Nikki showed Noah how he slowly moved closer then performed the breathing procedure. "They like me." Nikki's smiling face looked up at Noah.

Noah realized the two horses had to go with them. "Let's introduce them to our animals." He tied the other end of the net to the door, going to their animals. He picked up the bucket of water and pointed to the lighter grain. "Bring that." They placed the two buckets just inside the door of the far tunnel. The mare watched its food leave. Noah and Nikki went all the way into the animal pit and greeted their animals. Safely separated on their side of the net, the dam and foal went to the food. Nikki and Noah pulled the buckets to the inner door, then went outside and reentered their quarters. Nikki walked past everybody. "Howdy. We move Mama and baby."

Ann smiled, "Much obliged."

Noah and Nikki returned to the door from the meeting room into the tunnel to their animals. They closed the door and walked toward the animals in the corridor. As they came up from behind, the mother and baby moved into the pit. Noah and Nikki watched for a long time. None of the other animals paid any attention, not even when the mare drank from the water trough. "They'll be fine." He closed the inner door. They went back to their family.

The warrior with the bite wound returned with the rest of the village and more horses before sundown. The Indian women set up their tipis. Dohosan's family already knew that he had chosen poorly and was no longer chief. They didn't believe the story that a white woman had conjured a powerful Mystery Man to her side from across the prairie.

Dohosan's family wanted to see him. Tahatankohana and Adoeette took them to the sleeping man. His wife wiped his brow with a wet cloth as the newly arrived Mystery Man prepared for the ceremony. Oscar, Cleo, and Nikki had watched Ruben smoke with the men. When told they were to be included in the upcoming ceremony, they were thrilled. The ceremony wasn't exciting like Ann's had been. However, neither Nikki, Cleo, nor Oscar had seen that. For the boys and all of Jedidiah's people except Ruben, it would be the first time they smoked a peace pipe. Everybody smoked in agreement to peace and fair trading, at least of the horses and maybe other things as well.

After securing the peace, Ann, Akea, Stephanie, and Abigail served roasted cow leg and vegetables to everybody. After eating, Dohosan's family took him to their tipi. Noah explained to his wife, "When awake, give one drink." He held up a wooden cup. "Short time, he sleep again. Not feel pain."

Dohosan's wife asked, "Why you help him after you torture him?"

"We cut him because–"

The woman stopped him. "He make you cut sister. He deserve cutting. Why you not give him pain now?"

"My sister sleeps. His pain equals her pain. That is the punishment."

Dohosan's wife nodded once. "It is fair." She left with a jar of sleeping magic.

Neither Ann, Stephanie, nor Ehawee felt inclined to trade anything other than the horses. However, Ann did speak with her family and Jedidiah's people about two specific individuals. "Adoeette risked his life. Akea guarded you. First, I want every one of us who wants one of the wild horses to take one. We'll put them with our animals until we leave. Nikki and I want the one we helped, along with the colt. Then, as a wedding present and a thank you for their help, I want to give Adoeette and Akea the rest of the wild horses we still own after the trade."

Ruben, Abigail, and Cleo had been instrumental in catching the horses, although not as much as Ann had been. Ruben had previously decided that he, Abigail, and Cleo each owned ten of the tame horses he had gotten. Without asking, Ruben replied, "Untamed horses would be a nuisance. We don't want any."

Cleo spoke up, "Nikki gets to have two. Me and Oscar want a mother and a baby."

Noah helped the boys pick horses with a foal able to run and then moved them in with the goats, sheep, and injured animals.

Both groups posted guards and retired for the night.

Forty Four

The sun was at its zenith when the people who had been trapped at Horse Canyon arrived at the pit houses with two wagons. Before the wagons continuing to the west had been taken to the south side of the river, they had been restocked. All the food that remained from the deceased's wagons was loaded into the wagons returning to Horse Canyon. Adoeette determined that it would be best to rope their sixty new horses to the wagons and go to Horse Canyon with Guipago when he left with the food. Noah, therefore, decided to stay in the pit house for a few more days. They all wanted Ehawee and the others to have extra time to heal more comfortably. Noah also thought it would be beneficial for Tapco to receive more training caring for the injured.

Tahatankohana helped Adoeette rope the last horse. "You and Akea come talk after tie this horse."

"About what?"

"Give you and Akea gift."

"We come."

Adoeette and Akea joined the white folks. Ann spoke words and signed, "We heard you will marry. All want give wedding gift."

Akea hugged Ann then started over to Stephanie. Ann held Akea's hand. "And you both risked lives for us. We give you second gift."

Nobody had yet given them even the first gift. Akea asked, "What gifts?"

"More horses we caught. Seven for wedding. Seven for thank you."

Neither Akea nor Adoeette knew what to say. With the four horses Adoeette had from the original trade, they would have eighteen horses. They would be very rich. Tahatankohana put his hand on Adoeette's shoulder. "We will help you get them."

"Where more horses?"

"Follow." It was hard to toss a lasso inside, but it was much easier where the horses had nowhere to run.

Jedidiah helped. "Doc, would you ask Tapco if his family will care for my injured horse and the second one until I come back? It would be a struggle to take them. If they will, I'll let them keep the other one. Maybe they would let me spend the winter with them."

"I'll ask." Noah led a horse into a tunnel.

Even though they jostled and tugged, all the wild horses finally stood on the other side of the river attached to the wagons. Even with thirty-seven of them secured to each wagon, the wild horses couldn't take control away from the fewer horses that had already worked together and pulled a wagon to Horse Canyon and then back to the pit houses.

Everybody knew they were in for a long, slow journey traveling at the speed of a horse walking with a metal cage around a broken leg. They weren't going to get to Horse Canyon before dark, but the Kiowa separated from the white folks anyway.

Dohosan woke. "Are we moving?"

"We're going to Horse Canyon to get far away from those pale-faces. We're with our people."

"Do you have any food ready?" Dohosan asked.

"I do."

"It doesn't matter how far we go. Tahatankohana can send himself where he wants."

Dohosan's wife handed him a jug to relieve himself. "Nobody can do that."

He returned the jug to her full. "I saw it. He was in Horse Canyon. That woman called him, and then he was here. He made a flying knife take a new path. They called Jehovah to help. What spirit is Jehovah? I will learn of this Jehovah."

The woman held out a cup. "Even if he can, he doesn't want to hurt you more. He gave me plenty magic."

Dohosan gratefully drank the liquid. "Tahatankohana training Tapco. Tapco be Mystery Man in Haungooah's village. We go live with them. Learn of Jehovah."

Dohosan's wife passed her husband a bowl of pemmican stew. *It would be good to have a powerful Mystery Man. More important that Dohosan have good reason to say why we move and not be reminded of his defeat.*

When he started to feel drowsy, Dohosan drank the large jug of water his wife had ready for him. "You are a good wife. Are you going to stay with me?"

"Yes. Now lie down and go back to sleep."

"You're a goo…." Dohosan slept.

His wife kissed his lips. "You are a good husband. I hope you learned to do the right thing."

Forty Five

Every day, they hitched up the new horses and took short training trips, the injured people and animals healed, and Ann sifted the dirt floor to recover her beads. It had been a week since the storm. Noah and Tapco looked at the stub of Ruben's arm. "Ruben, have you been using the wash twice a day?" Noah asked.

"It hurts."

"It's going to hurt much more, and you might even die if you don't get rid of this infection."

I don't need to be invisible to Ruben, and he is in the pit house my family is using. Sally stated her opinion, "He probably should have stayed outside when we were shoveling all that manure."

Roscoe also looked at Ruben's arm. "We need raw meat."

"For heaven's sake, why do you need that?" Ruben's wife asked.

"Maggots," Sally informed them from across the room.

"Maggots!" Ruben and his wife both exclaimed.

Sally gleefully sang, "Maggots. Maggots.

Everybody loves them. Maggots. Maggots. They eat an infection, but they don't eat you."

Noah laughed. "That's the answer."

"All right, Doc. You know what's best." Ruben drank a cup of the willow tea painkiller, then slid the arm he still had into the shirt sleeve his wife held out for him.

"I'll scrub him real good."

"I'll do it myself, Hortense. You'll scrub my shoulder clean off." The two of them left.

Sally stood up. "I know where there's a covey of prairie chickens. Don't tell anybody else I'm going out."

"You shouldn't go alone. I'll go with you. Let's try to shoot some with our bows." Eli reached for his.

Jedidiah walked in. "What's the chance of another dust storm?"

Tapco answered, "Had rain. No dust storm few months."

"Do you think everybody is well enough for us to move on?" Jedidiah inquired.

Noah answered the second question, "I'd like to make sure Ruben's infection clears up."

Tom didn't want the groups to split. *I'm just an old man to her, but maybe if we're all together, Emily and Oscar will have more time to like me.* "You could go with us," Tom offered.

Sally stopped in her tracks. *That will be a disaster. How am I going to prevent that?*

"These people paid me to take them west. I'm going to be the one to do it. Don't get me wrong. I'm not saying that I don't appreciate everything you folks have done for us."

Noah breathed out a sigh of relief. *I'm so glad we won't have to hide our identities for months.*

Tom sighed too, but for the opposite reason. "Emily, you and Oscar can go with them if you want. I won't try to stop you."

Jedidiah looked at Emily.

Tom wants to get rid of us. It's too bad he finds me so distasteful. She said, "Maybe." *I hope I can get Tom to see something he likes before they're ready to go.*

Heath saw Sally with a quiver on her back, carrying a bow into the prairie. With his rifle, he ran after her. "I'd love to join you. My brothers and I want some fresh meat."

I can't breathe. Sally put her hand to her throat. *This is as scary as caves.* Sally replied, "My brother will be glad to take you with him." She turned on her heels and fled.

Eli knew Sally feared another lost love and was blocking any chance she might have with Heath. "I don't know where the prairie chickens are."

"You're a smart man. You can find some." She practically ran away.

Heath looked at Eli. "I don't know what I'm doing wrong."

"It's not you. She's left behind too many men she cared for because they couldn't come with us."

"But I can."

"Her heart isn't healed enough to allow anybody in."

More days later, the maggots had done their work on Ruben's shoulder. Jedidiah looked at the river, then Ken. "There's not enough current to push a dead grasshopper. Should be easy to drive the wagons across."

"I'm gonna tell Emily and Oscar that they're welcome to join me and Cleo."

Tom made himself scarce. He wanted Emily to have unpressured freedom to decide what she wanted to do. Emily looked for Tom. She couldn't find him, so she separated the clothes given to her and Oscar. "Roscoe, is there any way I could have one of those packs for our clothes?"

"I'm glad to give you one or two, but why don't you stay with us?"

"It doesn't seem like that's the right thing to do." Emily put her two packs in Ken's wagon beside Abigail's bundle.

Everybody went back and forth, transporting the wagons and horses in Jedidiah's wagon train to the river's north side. Emily saw to it that Oscar and Cleo played in the back of Ken's wagon while Jedidiah organized his people.

Heath walked over to hear Jedidiah's instructions. *It's too bad she's so closed off. She's the most beautiful woman I've ever seen. She never even told me her name. Come to think about it; I don't know any of their names.*

Across the river, Sally and her nameless family rode into the dry expanse between the river bend.

Several minutes later, the wagon in which Oscar

played moved. "I have to go. I'm sorry you have to be alone. I'm going to miss you." Oscar jumped out of the wagon and looked across the river. He saw the wagons across the river far ahead. "Ma!" he screamed, "We have to run! They've already left."

Emily knelt beside Oscar. *He's going to be devastated.* "We aren't going with them."

"Yes, we are."

"They don't want us."

"I don't believe you. They love us."

"I can't be with them. Tom doesn't love us."

"He does too." He pulled out of his mother's hands and ran to the edge of the river. "I'm here!" He jumped up and down, waved his arms, and shouted. "Come back." Tears streamed down his face, and Emily's too. "I want to be with them."

"I do too. Tom told me to go."

"He didn't. You're lying."

"Oscar, I wouldn't lie about this. I want Tom to want us just as much as you do."

"But I have his spyglass."

"It's a gift. Get on the wagon."

Oscar sat in the driver's box and stared across the river through the looking tube.

Forty Six

Eli tried to convince his father. "You're making a mistake, Pop. She must not realize how you feel. I think she loves you. I'm sure Oscar does."

"If she wanted to stay, she would have."

They traveled across the dry land for two hours, moving farther and farther from the river that looped to the north. Every one of them attempted to persuade Tom to go back and tell Emily how he felt. Helen finally put her foot down. "Thomas Yates, what were the exact words you told her?"

"You can go with those people. I won't stop you."

"Son, I'm telling you. You practically told her to go. If you don't go tell her you love her, you'll regret it for the rest of your life."

"I don't want her to think she has to be with me just because I helped her."

"You are not a stupid man. You can figure out what to say. Now, go tell her before I beat you with this whip."

"Will you wait here until I come back?"

"We surely will," Noah assured Tom.

Tom wheeled Spirit around and rode diagonally toward the river.

Ehawee prayed, "God, thank you that we stopped moving. I can't take any more bouncing."

Forty Seven

It had been hours, but Oscar hadn't given up. He felt sure that it was all a mistake. *As soon as Tom realizes that me and Ma aren't with them, he'll come for us.* He continued to scan the other side of the river. A tiny blur appeared. Oscar focused intently. It grew larger. "Ma, he's coming!"

"Oscar, he is not coming. Give me that spyglass. I'm putting it away."

"Look, Ma. It's him."

"It is NOT him," Emily grabbed the thing, "but I'll look, so you'll stop this." She peered where Oscar pointed. "Something is there!" Her heart leaped into her throat.

Oscar held out his hand. "Let me look again." After several minutes, Oscar waved at the approaching rider. The rider waved back. "I told you!"

Emily jumped into the back, grabbed their packs, stood on the seat, and held them high.

Oscar told her, "He's saying, 'Yes.'"

Emily ran to the men farther ahead. "Ken, thank you for your offer. We're getting off here."

"In the middle of nowhere?"

"Our ride is coming."

"It's the older one who fixed the wagons, isn't it?"

"Yes."

"I had the feeling that's where your heart was. Do you want me to wait to be sure he gets you?"

"No. I'm sure." When the wagon caught up with her, Oscar handed his mother their packs and jumped down beside her. They stood at the edge of the river.

"Jedidiah, may I borrow your spyglass for a few minutes?" Ken watched Tom hold Spirit's tail as the horse swam the river.

Tom came out of the stream, slowly meandering across the prairie. He stood before Emily and Oscar. "I want to tell you something."

Emily looked into Tom's eyes and hoped.

"Emily, I want to be sure you understand exactly what I feel. I absolutely want you and Oscar. I love you both, but I do NOT want you to feel forced to be with me because you think you owe me something for helping you. From the bottom of my heart, I hope you both want to be my family. If it's not what you want, I understand. I want you to do what makes you happy. However, if you'd marry me, you'd make me a very happy man."

"Oscar, what do you say?" Emily asked.

"Let's marry him, Ma!"

"I agree. Let's marry him." Emily stepped over, put her arms around Tom's neck, and accepted the kiss she had wanted ever since she had opened her sunburned eyes and seen his face.

Tom eventually let Emily out of his arms. "We can get Jedidiah to marry us, but I can't use my real name. I don't want Judge Hall to have any way to find us."

"Noah can marry us. Let's go."

Tom put one of the packs on his back and tied the other on Spirit. He picked up Oscar and sat him on top. "Hold tight to Spirit's mane. Emily, hold tight to his tail." Tom led his horse into the Cimarron. When the water became too deep to walk, he and Emily took ahold of his horse's tail. "Spirit, forward swim."

Spirit took the three of them back to the correct side of the river. Tom picked up Emily and put her behind Oscar. He swung up, sat on the pack, put his arms around both the people he loved and hugged them tightly. "We'll follow my tracks back. They're waiting for us."

Ken handed Jedidiah the spyglass. "They're safe. He has them."

Forty Eight

Spirit carried his riders into camp. Oscar waved. "I'm glad we're home."

"I am too." Emily turned her head to kiss Tom's lips.

Everybody in camp smiled. Confident that Emily and Oscar would be returning with Tom, they had already planned their group response. "Welcome! We love you!"

Emily slid off the horse. "I hope we can prepare for a marriage."

"Today?" Helen asked.

Tom's grin spoke the answer.

Helen looked at Roscoe. "We decided it wouldn't be safe for Jedidiah to marry us because he'll turn in the record in St. Louis after he goes back."

Roscoe spoke up, "Let's prepare for two weddings. I'll bake a cake in the new stove. Since we're going to fire it up, I'll put together a nice meal and bake bread too."

Noah had been sure there would be some

marriages before they arrived at the western sea and that the women involved would want a ceremony of their own culture. Therefore, he had bought marriage certificates from Jedidiah and had copied the words of Jedidiah's ceremonies.

Ann pulled out the dress she had worn when she had married Noah.

Stephanie exclaimed, "I didn't know you had that! Does Noah know?"

"He does not. I asked Sally to buy it from Minnie when she got you from Harmony. It's still configured to fit me." Ann slid the dress on, then carefully fitted on the green hat that she had worn in the wagon when Nikki had found it.

Sally put on her red evening gown and the ruby necklace, which she been given legal possession of back at Fort Gibson. She also put on a wide-brimmed red hat with maroon-colored satin ribbons that had previously belonged to one of the Pennyworth women.

Each of the other women put on evening dresses and high-society hats and as much of the Hank Butterfield booty and Dr. Pennyworth jewelry as they had a place to wear it.

The men and the boys put on white linen shirts, black linen breeches with matching black vests, colored sashes, and black top hats, along with all the gold necklaces they had acquired from the same places as the other jewelry. They gathered for the ceremony as if attending a grand ball.

Noah stood in front of the two couples. "This

truly is a glorious day that the Lord hath made. Today you are blessed with one of God's greatest gifts; the gift of love and devotion between a man and a woman. Mankind did not create love. God created love as a representation of the union of Christ and the Church. God's unconditional and free love shows us that true love is freely given and freely accepted. May these marriages be adorned with true and abiding love.

"Marriage is not living merely for each other. It is uniting and joining hands to serve God. Seek His kingdom first and His righteousness, and He will add all other things to you. Do not expect perfection from each other--that belongs solely to God— You need not minimize each other's weaknesses, but always be swift to praise and magnify each other's points of strength, and see each other through kind and patient eyes.

"God will lead you into such situations that will bless you and also difficult times that will develop your characters as you walk together. As you look to Him, He will give you enough tears to keep you tender, enough hurts to keep you compassionate, enough of failure to keep your hands clenched tightly in His, and enough of success to make you certain that you do walk with Him so that He remains the central figure in your relationship together.

"God, we gather in Your sight to unite Roscoe Bacon and Helen Yates; and Tom Yates and Emily Stringer in holy matrimony. We ask that You be glorified by what takes place. Might this ceremony honor You. Might it reflect the seriousness of the vows to be spoken, be a reminder to us who have spoken similar vows to our spouses in the past, and be instructive to those considering such a commitment in their future. We ask it in Jesus' name, Amen.

"Family, are you willing, now and always, to support and strengthen these marriages by upholding Roscoe and Helen; and Tom, Emily, and Oscar with your love, your concern, your counsel, and your prayers?"

"We will," the group answered.

"Is it your purpose to establish a home where the Word of God is read and obeyed; a home that is welded together by prayer, in which the Holy Spirit is your constant Guide?"

Roscoe, Helen, Tom, and Emily all replied, "It is."

"Please join your hands. Roscoe and Tom, God has ordained the man as the spiritual head, the responsible provider, and the initiator of love in a human relationship. The woman whom you hold by the hand is to be your wife. She has given you one of the most sacred things under heaven: a woman's life and a woman's love. It is not what you bring in a material way that will make true happiness--riches without love are nothing. What you show her as her lover will keep her heart won. By His enablement, your strength must be your wife's protection, your character her boast and pride, and you must so live that she will find in you the haven for which the heart of a woman truly longs. Do you vow that you will be true and loyal, patient in sickness, comforting in sorrow, and forsaking all others, keep yourself only unto her, so long as you both shall live?

Roscoe and Tom said, "I do."

"What token do you give as a pledge of the sincerity of your vows?"

Roscoe had the emerald ring of his mother that he'd had since he was a boy. Tom had given Eli the wedding band of Eli's deceased mother in exchange for one that Eli had taken from the Butterfield Gang's stolen loot. "A ring," the men replied.

"Helen and Emily, it is God's purpose that you be a loving wife, that you respond to your husband's love with tenderness and a deep sense of understanding through a great faith in Christ who brought you together. It is His desire that you have that inner beauty of soul that never fades; that eternal youth that is found in holding fast these things that never age. This man whom you hold by the hand is to be your husband. Upon your life, your love, and your devotion, he will lean for strength and inspiration. He is going to look to you for encouragement, for cheerfulness, and for confidence. No matter what the world may say or think, people may forget him, lose confidence in him, or turn their backs upon him, but you must not. May your life and love be the inspiration that will constantly lead him to greater dependence upon our Lord. Do you vow here that you will be loyal in adversity, ministering to him in affliction, comforting him in sorrow, and forsaking all others, keeping yourself only unto him so long as you both shall live?"

Helen and Emily replied, "I do."

"What token do you give as a pledge of the sincerity of your vows?"

Helen and Emily had both exchanged the rings of their previous marriages for Butterfield loot. The women stated, "A ring."

"A ring is a fitting symbol. Not only are these made out of the finest of metals to remind you of the purity of your relationships, but they are also a circle, a line unending, to remind you that your love, devotion, and commitment to one another are to be unending."

Noah read the words and paused each time for the men to speak their vows one after the other. "Men, repeat after me: I, state your name, take you, say the name of your betrothed, to be my wife, before God who brought us together." The men spoke as instructed. "To love and to cherish you, even as Christ loved the Church, and gave Himself for it." Noah waited for Roscoe and Tom. "To lead you, and share all of life's experiences with you, by following God through them." Again, Noah paused. "That through His grace, we might grow together into the likeness of Jesus, our Savior and Lord." The men completed their vows.

"Women, repeat after me: I, state your name, take you, say the name of your betrothed, to be my wedded husband, before God who brought us together." As he did for the men, Noah waited while Helen spoke then Emily. "To love you and to cherish you, to submit myself to you in all things." The women repeated the words. "To follow you through all of life's experiences as you follow God." Noah waited. "That through His grace we might grow together into the likeness of Jesus, our Savior and Lord." The women completed their vows.

"May you never take each other's love for granted, but always experience that wonder that exclaims, 'Out of all in this world, you have chosen me!' When life is done, may you be found, then as now, hand in hand, still thanking God for each other."

Noah led Tom and Emily to a table taken from Dr. Pennyworth's wagon and assembled. "Oscar, please join us." Noah had been planning for this since he had made a copy of the ceremony. He had searched everywhere for pure sands of different colors. After Tom had asked Noah to include Oscar in the ceremony, Noah had found a third color of sand. On the table stood four jars. One with pink sand, one with black, one with yellow, and one was empty. Noah continued once Oscar stood beside Emily and Tom. "To bring the happiness God designed for your home, there must be the merging of these lives into one life. From now on, your thoughts shall be for each other rather than for your individual selves. Your plans, your joys, and your sorrows shall be shared. As you each take a jar of sand and pour them together, your jars will empty and mix into one container, thereby symbolizing your lives and hearts entwined. Once combined, just as the three of you are joined together, the sands cannot be separated. Neither shall your lives be divided, but be a united testimony in a Christian home."

Tom, Emily, and Oscar each took turns pouring thin layers of their sand into the empty jar until it was full and theirs were empty. Noah concluded, "May this be a testimony of your unity in the Lord Jesus Christ. I pronounce you husband, wife, and son." Oscar carried the new jar away from the table.

"Helen and Roscoe, please come to the table." Noah put the empty jars into the wagon and brought out a clear glass vase, a bottle of red, and a bottle of white wine from Dr. Pennyworth's wagon. "Within the Bible, nothing is of more importance than love. We are told 'God is Love.' We are assured that 'Love conquers all.' It is love that brings you together today. As you travel through life, remember that the true avenue to joy and peace is to be found within your love for each other, so hold the key to your hearts very tightly. This is what the Lord meant when He said, 'On this account, a man shall leave his father and mother, and be joined to his wife, and the two shall be one flesh.'

"Roscoe and Helen, merge the rich and flavorful wines that represent your individual and separate lives into something new and delicious; a new creation better together and unable to be put back into separate containers."

The wine from the two bottles flowed into the

vase. The red and the white swirled in beautiful patterns as they mixed. "As your lives continue to interweave as one, remember that it was love that brought you here today, it is love that will make this joining glorious, and it is love which will cause this union to endure. Roscoe and Helen, I pronounce you husband and wife." *

"Everybody present here today wishes each of you all the joy, happiness, and success that the world has to offer. Let us now celebrate one of life's greatest moments." Helen poured the mingled wine into everybody's tin cup, including Oscar and Nikki, who were each given one swallow.

After they had eaten the delicious meal that Roscoe had prepared, Ehawee asked, "Stephanie, if brother will give me the sleeping potion, will you feed Etu tonight and tomorrow morning?"

"Of course." Stephanie held her arms out to receive the child. Ehawee slept as the others played the piano and the fiddle and danced under the light of the full moon.

Tom helped his bride into the wagon. Emily's shirt slid away as Tom's hand glided across the skin softer and more tantalizing than the billows of silk hanging above them or the silk sheets that covered the soft feather mattress upon which they lay. It had been fifteen years. He desperately wanted to bury himself in her softness.

Tom's touch and muscular body set Emily's desire ablaze. She felt his hardness against her and opened to him. The rest of the world disappeared.

In the other bridal wagon, the heart of the

fifteen-year-old boy, devastated by the rejection of the woman he had loved, healed at the age of sixty-one as he gave his heart to and shared his body with the women he desired more than he had any other.

Forty Nine

Before the sun rose, Noah whistled in their trained animals. The new horses, along with the goats and sheep that always ignored his summons, as well as their five cows, grazed in the large netted space.

Tapco sipped coffee at the morning fire. "Travel time wrong. Four miles in but not water full. Must take long ride to river. Water animals. Fill containers. Then, start across. Hope will work."

After only a few hours, every possible vessel contained all the water it could hold. As the group waded into the expanse between the river loop, the dry, rustling grass cut tiny slices on their arms.

"Ground not dusty. Follow right behind." To prevent their animals from getting lost in the tall grass, Tapco tied them to the wagons.

Tom rode beside Roscoe. "I hope we get far enough. If I hadn't been so hard-headed, we wouldn't be out of kilter."

"Some things in life aren't simple. Don't fret. We'll make it."

"But Tapco says we have to travel twenty miles each day. Even if that lame cow didn't slow us, I don't think we could do it. We should have decided either to not come this way or to not bring that cow. We didn't even pray about it."

"True, but yesterday we did vow to trust God. That's what I'm going to do. Even if we don't get that far, somehow He'll make it work out."

Mid-day came. The animals attempted to stop as had been the usual procedure. However, since they had to cover many miles and only have water once per day, they didn't pause. The donkeys brayed their irritation, joined by the mules' hee-hawing and the rest of the animals' general discontent. The wagons pulled the resistive animals along.

Noah shared water from his canteen with the cow struggling to walk with a heavy metal cage around its leg. Noah carried Adele because she weighed the most. Beside him, Ann had Joy. On this day, on his other side, Sally carried her nephew, Chris. Sally asked, "Will she be able to make it if I give her some of mine too?"

"I'd rather you drink your water," Ann told her sister.

Noah contemplated aloud, "I don't think she'll have the strength to go as far as we need to go. Maybe I can rig up one of the spare harnesses to help pull her. I'll need somebody else to carry Adele, and we'll need to stop for a short time while I set it up."

Ann hurried ahead. "Noah's going to rig a harness to help the cow. We need to stop."

Roscoe pulled on King's reins. He remembered his previous trip across the plains. "Don't let the animals eat any grass. It'll drain their water digesting it." Since Noah was behind him, conserving energy, he strolled back. "What if we let the other oxen pull her? They'll walk as slow as she does, and we have that harness you got from Jedidiah."

"Good plan. Help me rig it up."

Unknown to any of them, their horse, June, managed to reach and nibble sprigs of grass for the thirty minutes it took to get the cow ready to be pulled and for everybody to put on long-sleeved shirts for protection from further grass cuts.

The women directed the animals harnessed to the wagons. The men surrounded the cow to help it learn the new method of travel. Noah and Eli pulled the cow's halter as the oxen drew it forward. Each time the injured cow needed to move a leg, one of the men tapped the back of that leg's knee. The going was even slower as the cow struggled to coordinate its movements while being pulled.

When the sun went down, they were only thirteen miles from their starting point. Noah looked at Tapco. "This is a far as she can go today. How much of a problem is this?"

"Can't change it. We drink milk. Use no water for cook or clean. Save water for animals."

The following day, they traveled through the heat partially shaded by the tall grass. Sally asked, "How is Gimpy doing?"

"It's not so hard for her, and she is going faster, but we haven't made up much time."

"What's going to happen?" Sally asked Noah.

"One day without water shouldn't be a major disaster."

"I hope not. Tapco said we should kill her, but I don't want to. You know how I feel about defenseless animals."

"I don't think it will come to that."

Sixteen miles farther across, the day ended. Tapco told them, "Short water again. Won't get to water tomorrow."

On the third day, they made seventeen miles but were still fourteen miles from the watering hole and had only fifty gallons of water. Noah stood beside the water barrel with two buckets. "We need to give the milk cows their full dose of water. I don't want them to dry up, and we need to water the chickens too. Whiskers can drink milk with us."

"That's going to be all the water." Roscoe set a number ten tub beside Noah. "But I think the others will be all right with one dry night."

The women arrived with milk cans, stools, and milking buckets. "I'll milk Gimpy." Ann sat beside the lame cow.

"I'll milk Courageous," said Stephanie.

They had plenty of milk for dinner and breakfast and still had a fair amount for the covered bucket they attached to the bouncing wagon to make butter.

The thirsty animals walked slower. Still, they arrived at the water hole before the sun went down. Tapco discovered a problem. "But, it's always got water."

"Obviously not!" Roscoe stared at the emptiness.

Tapco felt horrible. He had gotten them into a deadly situation. Most of the animals had already gone two days without water. If they traveled at the same speed, they had four more days to get back to the river. "We won't make it."

Roscoe remembered what they had done decades earlier. "We still can't let the animals eat. Load the slow animals into the wagons, including Gimpy. We have to walk straight through, day and night, as fast as we can without sweating."

"We can go much faster if the slow animals aren't walking, and most will ride all right, but the cows never have." Ann asked, "Do we have enough sedative to put them to sleep?"

Everybody looked at Ehawee. "Probably. I haven't had any since the weddings."

Two hours later, one wagon carried all the sheep and goats. A second contained the five sleeping cows. The third had the two miniature donkeys, the chickens, and the cat, along with all of Dr. Pennyworth's previously owned items crammed into the front end. The other two wagons were stuffed to almost overflowing with the remainder of their goods. "At least the moon is bright." Roscoe cracked his whip in the air. "Forward, ho!" The alternate set of teams pulled the wagons away from the dry waterhole into the night.

They traveled at a fast walk. Roscoe peered ahead through the spyglass. "I see a dry wash. It'll be easier to travel in that than this tough grass."

"Do it," Tom told him. The others followed the lead wagon. When the sun came up, they had traveled twenty miles without a drop of water lost to sweat. However, they still had forty miles to go.

Roscoe unharnessed the team that had pulled all night. "Don't waste a second changing the teams."

Sally hurried to the cows with Noah and the last of the sedative. "I hope this is enough to put them to sleep one more time." She attempted to harvest the milk. She got only three-quarters of the normal amount. In record time, they set off across the water-starved land.

The sun rose. "It's getting hot," Ann commented.

Noah walked beside her. "I know, but we need to walk. We need to make it as easy as we can for the animals."

The heat of high noon arrived. Sweat rolled down their backs. Noah pinched the skin on the back of Ann's hand. The peak of flesh remained. "You'll never be able to walk thirty more miles. Making milk for the babies and all this sweating is dehydrating you. You need to stay out of the sun. I'll check the others." The three nursing mothers and all the children got into the wagon with the sleeping cows.

"Is there a way we can catch our sweat?" Emily asked as they trudged along.

"No, but don't talk and breathe through your nose," Noah instructed.

A few hours later, Roscoe called out, "Halt!"

"Why?" Tom asked.

"These animals can't pull any more. We need to swap them."

Those not riding walked to the front. "Why we stopping?" Tapco asked.

"Swap animals."

"We're not going to make it, are we?" Helen asked.

Roscoe checked her skin. "Get in the wagon." He checked the others. "We all need to ride."

Twenty-seven miles from water, they swapped the animals and started out again. When the day ended, none of the animals had the strength to pull a wagon. The horrible problem was that they had twenty miles to go. Tapco thought about what to do. "Cows have water inside. Cows pull one wagon. Little animals and people inside. Other animals walk. Leave other wagons. Go river. Drink plenty. Rest plenty. Fill up water. Come back for wagons."

Ann knew they all needed something to drink, and the babies were all asleep in the wagon. "Let's get the milk from the cows before we start." Once the cows stood on the ground, Stephanie and Ann milked them. Stephanie held out her pail. "It's not even full."

Sally looked in Ann's bucket, "You, Stephanie, Ehawee, Nikki, and Oscar share it."

Oscar held out a cup of milk to his mother. "Mama needs it. I already had some."

"Thank you so much, Oscar, but you must drink it," Emily told him.

"I won't."

The bucket of milk slipped from Ann's hand. Sally caught it as Ann crumpled. Noah caught his wife. "She's nursing three babies." He carried her to the wagon.

Oscar looked at his mother. "Maybe we should give my milk to Ann."

"Mine too."

The four healthy cows slowly plodded through the night, pulling the one wagon. Being careful not to waste any, Ann was carefully given milk until she revived. The moon sat on the horizon when the horses with foals appeared to be at their end. They stopped, got all the sheep, goats, and the two little donkeys out of the wagon, then led the weakest of the animals that had been walking into the wagon. The exhausted animals willingly lay close together.

Ten miles from water, Spirit gave out. Tom got him into the wagon. "That's it. There's no more space."

Four miles from salvation, Eyanosa and Zi could walk no further. Noah climbed off the wagon. "I'll stay with them. Come back with water as quickly as you can."

Sally pulled on his hand. "Get back in this wagon. We are not leaving you."

Ann joined her, "What about your promise to me?"

Noah remembered how Ann had felt when he had saved Rose from drowning. "This is different, Ann, but I'll stake them. We can follow our tracks back and bring water."

Eli spoke up, "A large group is safer. We should leave all the animals we think won't make the last few miles."

The donkeys and Indian horses looked like they could keep going. Most of the horses they had brought from the east did not. Noah rode away from the group of water-starved, exhausted animals. "I hope they'll be alive when we get back."

The shallow river was silent, and the tall plants prevented all but anybody standing on the driver's seat from seeing beyond the grass being plowed over. Everybody was too dehydrated to bother climbing up to look.

The sun rose. A mule fell over. "Oh no! We've lost Hector!" Roscoe exclaimed.

Tapco ordered, "Keep going. Be there soon." As the words left his mouth, the grass around them changed.

Several steps later, Noah noticed. "The river has to be just ahead. I'm sure the grass is greener." He climbed onto the seat. "I see it."

Eli's mule stumbled and went to his knees. "Ace is down." He jumped out as the oxen plodded on. A minute later, they broke through to the river. Animals and people sucked down water.

Nikki and Oscar took water to Whiskers and the chickens while Noah filled two canteens and grabbed a bucket. With all the water he could carry, Noah hurried back to Eli and Ace. He handed Eli a canteen and set down the bucket. As Ace gulped, Roscoe and Adahy went past with water for Hector. Several minutes later, Hector and Ace stood in the river. Tapco and Tom took the animals from the wagon into the river. Tom asked, "How long before we can go back with water for those we left behind?"

Noah dipped two buckets into the river. "Let's start filling the water barrels and mattresses. I don't know how I'll stand it if I lose Eyanosa or Zi, especially after losing Arabella. I'm afraid the cows will be too slow going back. I'm sure none of the others can pull the wagon full of water."

Stephanie asked, "What would be faster: letting the cows start pulling now or letting the Indian horses drink and rest and then using them? Should I go ahead and milk the cows, so you can take them?"

To Roscoe, that sounded like a good plan. "That's it. After they've had plenty of water, we start with the oxen pulling the wagon full of water. We let the horses drink and rest. After two hours, don't run them, but come quickly with the Indian ponies. When you catch up, the water will already be a few hours into the ride and probably more than halfway to our horses. We switch to the horses and quickly travel the last few miles while one of us brings the oxen at their pace. I think we can get back to our other animals in four hours."

Tom replied, "It's already been eight hours. I'm afraid some if not all of them have already died."

"We have to try." Noah poured two more buckets of water into the wooden barrel on the side of the wagon.

Ann weakly called from inside the wagon.

"Noah." Noah stuck his head under the edge of the cover. Ann touched his face. "Save the horses and come back. Don't go to the wagons. We can get them later. Did Stephanie get any milk?"

Noah helped Ann out of the wagon. "The cows have dried up. I promise that we'll only go to the horses. We should be back before morning."

Fifty

Noah cracked the whip. "God, I beg You. Let us get there before it's too late." He and Tapco reentered the dry expanse, carrying water.

For three hours, Noah dreaded what he would find. "They were so weak. I don't see how they can still be alive." He tried to think about something else. His mind repeatedly returned to his fear.

The Indian horses finally caught up. Roscoe dismounted. "We thought it would be best if we start the cows back. The wagon won't have much water coming home. These horses should be able to pull it." He unhitched the oxen from the wagon's falling tongue. The three men attached the six-horse harness and got the horses into the traces. "I can go on if one of you wants to take the oxen back to the river," offered Roscoe.

Noah tightened the harness strap. "I have to know."

"It's my fault. I do everything to help," Tapco explained.

"Very well, we'll see you at the river. Fire your revolver if you need us to come to you." Roscoe led the oxen, still joined in the harness.

Noah told the horses, "Forward, ho."

Forty-five minutes later, they saw the horses, all flat on their sides on the ground. Noah cried out in anguish, "All of them are gone!" *I'm strangling Tapco.* Noah knelt beside Eyanosa and stroked his neck. The horse whimpered a neigh, barely vibrating his lips. "He's alive! Check the others." Noah ran to the wagon and got his canteen. He poured water from the canteen into Eyanosa's mouth then hurried to Zi. "Zi's not dead either. We may be able to save her too." Noah gave his mare water then checked all seven horses. "June is gone. She's one we bought in Ann's hometown."

They made round after round giving the horses water from canteens. The water level of the first barrel dropped below half. Tapco tried to dip his canteen in again. "Can't reach. I open another."

The second barrel dropped to half. Promise, one of the horses Noah had bought at Fort Smith, sat up. Noah grabbed a bucket, filled it, and put it in front of the horse. It slurped the water. The men didn't hurry or push them but let them take their time regaining their strength. One by one, they revived. Hours later, the animals were ready to walk. By the light of the waning moon, they slowly led the horses along the path of flattened grass. Every half hour, they and the horses rested and drank water.

Before the sun rose, they returned to the camp, with all but the one horse they had lost. They released the animals to eat the lush grass and drink all the water they wanted. Noah carefully stepped over the people surrounding the babies. "It's me. I'm coming in."

"I'm glad you're back." Ann drowsily moved over to allow Noah to lie beside her.

"How are you, my lovely wife?"

"I'm fine now that I've had plenty of water. I didn't dry up like the cows. Neither did Stephanie nor Ehawee."

"That's an answer to my prayers."

"How were the horses?"

"We only lost June."

"I'm sorry about her, but I'm glad we didn't lose more. Go to sleep, my love. I'm sure you're tired."

Ehawee heard the morning discussion. She felt thankful. While the wagons were recovered, she would have days to heal without bouncing. Adahy told the others, "Less people drinking water; more water for the animals. I'll stay here and protect women."

"Who says I'll be staying here?" Sally asked. "As you said, we need men here, so half the men go and half stay."

Emily put breakfast on Tom's plate. "Oscar and I want to be wherever you are."

Tapco held out his plate. "P'ahy and I help get wagons."

Tom gobbled eggs lain by their chickens. "Emily, Oscar, Sally, Tapco, P'ahy, and I should be enough to get the wagons. The animals need more time to recover. We shouldn't go until tomorrow."

Noah suggested, "Or maybe you can leave

tonight. Even without much moonlight, you shouldn't have a problem going back. You have an easy path of flattened grass to follow."

Tom motioned for Oscar to sit beside him. "We'll do that. We'll take the Indian ponies and donkeys. They'll do the best. We should be back by tomorrow evening."

At sundown, they left. Not long after, Ann and Noah lay on the ground with Nikki, Chris, Joy, and Adele between them. Whiskers purred as Nikki rubbed her head, Eli and Stephanie protected Hattie between them, and Adahy and Ehawee did the same with Etu. Soon, everybody slept.

Lisa Gay

Fifty One

Nikki's screaming woke everybody in camp. "Sie ist gegangen! Whiskers ist weg! Sie ist gegangen! Sie ist gegangen! Whiskers ist weg! Sie ist gegangen!"

Noah tried to determine what had upset Nikki. He noticed that the cat wasn't there. "Nikki, sie ist eine Katze. Katzen hunt at nachts. Whiskers will come back."

"You sure?"

"Yes. Go back to sleep."

Nikki lay awake, wondering if the cat would find its way back. He finally fell asleep sure that he had lost something else he loved.

Something touched Nikki's hand, so he opened his eyes. Orbs glowed only inches from his face. *Whiskers ist zurück.* Sharp teeth drew closer. "Too big!"

A ball of orange, black, and white pounced. Long claws punctured skin. Sharp teeth sunk into the exposed neck of the creature that hadn't been aware it wasn't the only one stalking.

HISS, RRRAWOW, SPITTTT.

Tan fur and blood flew into the air. Everybody in camp bolted to his or her feet. Whiskers flew backward through the air, landed on her feet, and darted back. Nikki's assailant turned from him. It focused on the cat barreling down at full speed. With claws fully extended, the bobcat swiped Whiskers' face. Blood spattered Nikki and the babies before Ann could react. She scooped up the three babies, clutched them to her chest, and ran. Noah aimed his revolver. The two ferocious cats tangled into one ball of vicious claws and teeth.

"Rette sie! Save her!" Nikki screamed.

"I can't get a shot." Fur flew in every direction. It was impossible to tell if the flying blood belonged to Whiskers or the bobcat. Both grew redder by the second. "She can't win against a bobcat."

Every person encircled the two combatants. Nikki cried as the battle raged, and Ann cried for both Nikki and Whiskers. Before anybody knew what she was doing, Stephanie kicked the bobcat. The claws of one of the felines ripped into her ankle.

Eli jerked her back. "What are you doing?"

A streak of tan shot away. Whiskers hissed threateningly, arched her back, and puffed her fur. She appeared twice as big as she actually was. Nikki started toward the cat. Noah grabbed his arm. "Hold on, Nikki. Let her calm down. Are you hurt?"

"No, but I almost food for mean cat!"

Noah hurriedly got out the medical supplies. "I know Stephanie is hurt. Is anybody else?"

Nobody was. Noah looked at Stephanie's ankle.

"Let me quickly look at Whiskers." He slowly walked toward the cat, collapsed in a heap. Whiskers let him approach. "Stephanie, do you mind if Roscoe stitches your ankle? Whiskers needs a lot of help immediately."

"I don't mind. Please take care of Whiskers. She's a hero."

Nikki asked, "Is bad cat coming back?"

Ann still clutched all three babies. "If that bobcat is as injured as Whiskers, it's probably dying."

"I'll make sure." Adahy followed the trail of blood.

Nikki knelt beside Whiskers, "You saved me. Me and Noah save you."

Noah got the canteen with the sedative they had in case Ehawee needed it. *How am I going to get it to drink the sedative? That won't work anyway. I can't wait twenty minutes for Whiskers to fall asleep. Maybe the sedative will absorb through the cuts.* He handed Stephanie a cup of the liquid, then gently poured the sedative onto the torn-up cat. Noah didn't want to inflict more pain on the poor creature, but he needed to stop the bleeding. He wrapped her tightly in bandages soaked with the knockout medicine.

A few minutes later, Adahy came back with the mangled remains. "Bobcat did not get far before died."

Nikki held out his hand. "Give to me. I make rug. Walk very hard on bad cat." He stomped his foot and ground his heel. "Eli, you help me?"

"The salt is in the wagons."

"$@%t!"

Ann turned her head. "Nikki, where did you hear that?" She swung her arms as if sweeping the world then pointed to Nikki's ears. "Where word come from?"

"Cleo."

"Naughty word. Don't say it again. Do you understand?"

"I understand. Don't say $@%t."

"Nikki!"

"Sorry."

The cat slept. By the light of lanterns, Noah carefully shaved Whiskers and saw how badly Whiskers had been injured. He knew what he needed to do. Noah and Nikki washed their hands and then the cat. "Nikki, hold together." Noah demonstrated how to squeeze together the two pieces of deeply cut shoulder muscles. Nikki kept the parts together as Noah stitched the worst injury. After closing the skin over her shoulder, they moved on to the next slice. When the sun came up, with Nikki's help, Noah had worked for hours sewing up the many lacerations from Whiskers' ears to her tail.

Nikki picked up the cat and carefully placed his hero in the crate he had lined with his buffalo hide and a clean shirt to make it soft. He sat on the completely horse-hair encased bundle of his parent's bones and watched over Whiskers.

It wasn't long before the wagons rolled into camp. Nikki ran to Oscar. A scramble of words spilled out, "Oscar, bad cat hat versucht mich zu essen, but Whiskers hat fight und sie bobcat died, but Whiskers ist verletzt very bad."

"What?" Oscar looked at Noah.

Noah started the story, but everybody who had been in camp added details. Oscar looked at the shaved, mangled, sleeping cat in the crate and the equally torn-up carcass of the loser. "That's a big bobcat. How did Whiskers win?"

Emily put her hand on Oscar's shoulder. "Whiskers fought for somebody she loves. Just like your Pa did. He didn't stop trying either, not even when he knew they were killing him."

"Noah, Pa was all cut up just like Whiskers. Could you have saved my Pa?"

"Maybe, but I'm not even sure if I saved Whiskers."

Fifty Two

Roscoe changed the subject, "Was everything still in the wagon?"

Tom answered, "As far as I could tell, no person or anything else went near them. I asked Tapco to examine the area carefully. He didn't see anything either."

Ann watched Roscoe's face. *I wonder if he's told Helen about all the money he has in that satchel.* Roscoe's face remained expressionless. *He'd make a good poker player.*

Ann found Roscoe alone by the river. "You shouldn't keep big secrets from your wife."

"What are you talking about? I'm not keeping any secrets."

"I happen to know that you are." Ann walked away.

Which one of my secrets could she know about? Roscoe followed her. "I'm not saying that I've ever done anything wrong, but nobody tells everything about themselves."

"I'm talking about your very heavy satchel. I

269

opened it at the Butterfield House and saw what you had in there."

"I earned that money running Bacon's Trading Post. I didn't do anything wrong."

"I'm not saying you got it inappropriately. I'm saying you should tell Helen that you own thousands of dollars."

"She already knows I'm well off."

"Not that well off."

"If somebody tries to rob us, it's safer for everybody and the money if nobody else knows about it. Please don't tell anybody about the money. That includes Helen."

"All right, Roscoe. If we're ever robbed, I hope I'll have as good of a poker face as you do, and I hope keeping that secret doesn't go bad on you."

They left the next morning without June, and also minus the milk that the cows were no longer producing, but they had gotten everything else one hundred and twenty miles in six days. Tapco walked beside Noah and Gimpy. "Sorry about June. How Gimpy?"

"Slow, but knows how walk in harness now. Not your fault waterhole dry."

"Save ten days not travel river loop."

"That very good."

"How Whiskers?"

"Wasn't sure yesterday. Nikki and Oscar give good care. I think she live."

"Almost at end Kiowa land," Tapco held up two hands of fingers, "Days to end."

270

"Something you need learn yourself. I promised you be Mystery Man at end of Kiowa land, so you must figure out soon."

"You said so before. I don't know what."

Fifty Three

Nikki walked beside Noah, "Why you and Ann not marry me?"

The question took Noah by surprise. "Marrying is for big people."

"You marry Oscar to Tom."

He wants assurance of his place in our family. "I know of something better. I can't do my own. Tapco must do this for us."

"When?"

"At the end of Kiowa land."

When they were alone, Noah told Ann about the request. They decided they should include Joy. Noah privately asked each adult to pray and ask God if they should be the one to give Nikki, Adele, and Joy their adoption names.

Tom had included Oscar in his wedding. Still, he didn't want the boy to feel slighted. "Noah, how many people may be adopted in the same ceremony?"

"I don't think there's any limit. Why?"

"First, I want to ask Emily if she would mind if I more officially adopt Oscar. If it's all right with her, and it wouldn't be a problem to add him, I'm going to ask Oscar."

"It wouldn't be a problem at all, and it's a wonderful idea."

Tom knew where he would find Oscar. He went to the wagon that carried Whiskers. "Oscar, may I speak with you out here?"

"I'm coming." Oscar jumped into Tom's arms.

Tom carried Oscar as he walked behind the wagon. "This is the perfect place for you to be, here with my fatherly love around you. I know you mixed your life and sand with mine, but Oscar, I want to adopt you, make you my son, and let the whole world know how much I love you. Noah and Ann are going to adopt Nikki, Adele, and Joy. I want to adopt you at the same time, but I want to be sure you understand that I don't want you to stop loving Warren. I just want you to add me. What do you say? Will you become my official son?"

Oscar hugged Tom's neck. "I told Ma you love us."

"I surely do."

"I love you back, and I want to be your son, but right now, I need to make sure Whiskers is all right."

"I understand." Tom put Oscar back into the wagon.

Nikki moved over so Oscar could get back in his spot watching the cat. "What happen? You say $@%@? Ann no like $@%@. Maybe Tom don't like it."

"I didn't say that word. You should stop saying

273

it. Tom asked if I would be his son like Noah and Ann want you."

"You say Ja?"

"Yes. Ich sagte ja."

Roscoe had been adopted by Ann, Stephanie, Sally, Eli, and Noah in Noah's village. At that time, Nikiata had given him his secret name. Only the people at the ceremony had the privilege of knowing Roscoe's adoption name. Roscoe felt highly honored to have a Quapaw name. Not even Ann, Stephanie, Sally, or Eli had a Quapaw name. He felt he didn't need to ask God if it should be him, but since he had been consulting God about everything for months, he did so about this matter as well. He did, however, immediately start planning the celebration feast.

Ann wanted to make something for the children that could continue to be used as they grew. She thought about it for days before she had formulated a plan. "…I won't be able to get three done before the ceremony, but I can get them far enough to use and keep working on them afterward. What do you think?"

Stephanie spoke up, "That's an excellent idea. I'd love to make one for Oscar if it would be all right."

"I want to work on each of them like we did for Roscoe." Sally went to the wagon for her sewing kit. *This is as close as I'll ever get.*

"I can help too," Ehawee told her sisters.

Sally sewed. *The only way I'll ever have a child is adoption, so I don't have a chance. God is giving them all to Ann.* She jabbed the needle through the material. "Yow!" And also into her finger.

Nikki ran over. "You all right!" Sally put her arms around him and let out a flood of tears. "It hurt very bad?" Nikki asked.

"Yes," *but it's not my finger.*

"I get bandage." Nikki scurried into the wagon. He rubbed an uninjured part of Whiskers in her cage, mostly to keep her still while recovering. "How you, Whiskers?"

Whiskers rubbed the inside of the cage closest to Nikki. "Meow."

"I come back. First, fix Sally." He jumped out of the wagon with a roll of gauze. Nikki carefully wrapped Sally's finger, which hurt much less than her heart. He cut the end a few inches the long way down the middle and tied the strips to keep on the bandage. "All better!"

Sally stroked Nikki's check. "Much obliged, Nikki. I love you very much."

Roscoe still felt that he should find the adoption names of the children. He told Noah and Ann first.

Noah accepted, "Roscoe, I'm delighted that you are the one God has chosen."

Tom also accepted Roscoe's offer.

Noah spoke with Tapco. "Have very important ceremony. Ann, Tom, and I need you. Nikki, Joy, Adele, and Oscar need you. Have you seen adoption?"

"No."

"You taught how?"

"No."

This will be his final test. "All through life, many

275

things needed that Mystery Man not know. What you do?

"Tahatankohana, you told me to make person feel what I want. This ceremony need to make people feel loved and part of family. I think about how? I tell you first."

The Mystery Man, Tahatankohana, signed back. "You may." *He still doesn't understand, but I'll see what he comes up with.*

Every night, Stephanie signed what Eli read from the Bible. Tapco sat thinking about the words of the Bible. He had an idea. *I ask Great Spirit's son again. He not give me viper. He gave me something better. Great Spirit and son, Jesus, I ask you to show me how to make this family know they are one in love even though they are not of one blood.*

Emily and Helen joined the creation of the adoption badges. The family was happy. At least, everybody appeared content.

Sally looked at the happy couples with smiles and kisses for each other. At night, she sometimes heard one couple or another making love. She had no one. It wasn't that she didn't want them to be happy or that she didn't want them to enjoy their mates; somehow, their contentment felt like salt in a festering sore. Every one of them had something she had come to believe she would never have. *I miss you Chaska. Justin and Gad, and Edwin, too, but Melvin, I miss you the most. I wonder if you've already found somebody. I wonder if you're kissing her the way you kissed me in Little Rock. Have you made love? I haven't. I wish it could have been you.* She sewed cloth beside the other women. With smiles and jokes, Sally hid her pain and loneliness. Inside, ice continued to grow around her heart.

The days and the wagons rolled. Tapco hadn't come up with a plan. Roscoe didn't know that every Indian on the planet didn't already know how an adoption ceremony was conducted. He sat beside Tapco. "I gave Nikiata a gift for my name. Children not have gifts for names. I not want gift. What we do?"

The answer smacked Tapco inside his head. *That is the answer. I need to make a ceremony and Noah says there is something important I have not learned. It is so simple. Here is somebody who knows. I help him, and I get the information I need. If I do it right, he will not know I am getting information.* "Roscoe, does it matter if everything same as before?"

"I guess not."

"What you feel when you get name?"

"I became part of family and part of tribe."

"What make you feel that?"

"Nikiata put much thought and much work to find my name. Not easy for him. He did anyway."

"Other things make you feel part family?"

"Stephanie made and wore medicine bag. That very hard for her back then. Girls made beautiful white buckskin clothes and moccasins with beads. Eli made ceremonial knife. Noah climbed into eagle nest. Gave me eagle feather on red ribbon. The words they said—"

"He went in eagle nest!? He truly brave!"

"Eagle spirit sent eagles away. They warn us must leave home. Eagles not there, but he not know when they come back."

"All this help you give names make children feel part of family?"

"It does. Much obliged."

Tapco spoke with Noah, "What you feel when you adopted Roscoe?"

Noah explained, "I felt very humbled that the man, who helped me during a very difficult time, wanted to be part of my family. I felt fiercely devoted to Roscoe when we joined our lives, and I still feel that way."

Tapco spoke with Tom, Ehawee, and Helen, who had been observers. He extracted information from Eli, Ann, Sally, and Stephanie, who had also adopted Roscoe. Next, he asked P'ahy if she had been to an adoption ceremony. It had been when she was a small girl, but she told him what she remembered. Tapco put it all together and then revealed his plan to Noah. Noah approved. They explained what Tapco suggested to the other adults. The plan was set, and everybody was ready enough.

Noah walked away from the cooking fire with Tapco. "What you learn?"

"I not need know everything. Ask, so people think I help them with THEIR questions. Ceremony of any kind cannot always be same. Find what works this time with these people."

"Perfect! You become Mystery Man tomorrow night. Next night, you do adoption."

Fifty Four

They set up the tipi. Noah laid the hide of the bear he had killed at Fletcher Creek on the floor, put on his breechcloth, painted his face white, and tied on one of the tanned coyote faces he had made at Fletcher Creek. He attached his Mystery Man bones in his hair, along with the two eagle feathers plucked out by the eagles he had saved at Pine Bluff. Around his shoulders, Noah hung the mink cape given to him in his home village when Wakanda had named him Mystery Man to the world. In front of him, covered with the hide of the elk that he and Ann killed at Pine Bluff, Noah had the items he wanted to give Tapco.

When Tapco saw the door flap open, he went in. He sat on the bear fur, facing the Mystery Man, and waited for Tahatankohana to speak.

Tahatankohana spread the tanned hide of one of the antelopes they had killed over Tapco's shoulders. He tied the straps that held the antelope's fur-covered skull so that its long horns pointed up from Tapco's head. "Be Mystery Man to your people. You know ways of people, know how to heal, help, and learn. The antelope is symbol of wisdom." Tahatankohana pointed to the round scar on Tapco's arm. "He marked you. He is still your totem."

Tapco did not inherit the grandmother medicine bag of the village in which he had grown up. That bag had gone to Gomda. Tahatankohana had made a new one out of the antelope hides they had killed. He handed the empty bag to Tapco. "You start with nothing." One at a time, he handed Tapco a small pouch of plants. "Tell me about this?"

If Tapco knew what the plant was, how to use the plant, and what kind of place to get more, Tahatankohana declared, "You earned," and then gave it to Tapco to add to his grandmother bag. After the many plants, he took two Canada goose wing fans from under the elk hide. "Tell me about these?"

"Goose: sacred circles of year and of life, selfless dedication, the coming of winter, communication, time to lead, and time to follow."

"You earned." He brought out some bear teeth.

"Bear: strength, power, leadership, courage in hard times, solitude, time for healing, respect of boundaries."

Tahatankohana pressed them into Tapco's palm. He opened his other hand and revealed alligator teeth. "These?"

"Alligator: keeper of secrets hidden in water and the ancestor and universe secrets, patience, and ancient power."

"You are worthy." Tahatankohana dropped them into a pouch of alligator skin and placed them in front of Tapco before revealing coyote paws.

"Coyote: trickster, bringer of life, deceit, playfulness, beware of darkness of soul, selfishness, greed, cowardice." *Fits Gomda well*.

Tahatankohana pulled out a second coyote mask, tied it over Tapco's face, and handed him the two paws. "Like coyote, sometimes we must trick people into learning. Beware others do not catch you with their lies." He felt under the hide and drew out elk molars.

"Elk: strength, stamina, patience, dignity, survival, hunting skill."

Tahatankohana drew out a two-foot-long, cherry rocking chair spindle that he had split the long way and then had gouged a trough in each half to make a hollow tube once he had secured it back together. A clump of horsetail hair hung from it, as well as kestrel wing feathers strung to drop open like a fan. "The pipe stem?"

Tapco answered, "This symbolizes the male principle, all plants, and straightforwardness of mind, body, and speech. This horsehair represents all four-legged creatures. Also, this is from horse that Warren worked to death. To me, this also means respect for animals that help us. Also, that Great Spirit makes good things out of bad. Warren killed that horse. Great Spirit used that to bring you and your family. These kestrel feathers stand for all the winged ones."

Tahatankohana removed a piece of the red catlinite that he had gotten during the wagon train disaster trading. He had carved it into a spiral with a

281

fat bowl that rose an inch at the center. "And the bowl?"

"The bowl is the earth, the people, and the female principle. They bring life. The bowl holds the eternal fire of the sun. When they are joined, the Calumet represents creation. The smoke connects everything and carries our prayers. The pipe is the bridge between man and the Great Spirit, who created the four directions, Mother Earth, and Father Sky.

"From the Calumet, our prayers, our agreements, our peace, and our war plans travel on the kinnikinnick smoke through Father Sky to the Great Spirit. The Great Spirit is the one called Jehovah. I must store the stem and the bowl in their separate compartments of the bag you laid there and only connect them to perform a ceremony."

"Tahatankohana say all this medicine yours." He pushed the pipe bag across the bear fur. "Tapco, that is not all. Great Spirit, Jehovah, and son, Jesus, call you to be their Mystery Man. They put in your heart desire to help all people. They give you wisdom. You say make Gomda Mystery Man at home. You want learn more. You help Tahatankohana. Tahatankohana help you. You want be Mystery Man P'ahy village. You find way make her your wife. When you pay bride price, you help your people, and you help white people. Jehovah say, 'Give this.'"

Noah drew from under the elk hide a Bible that he had gotten at Polk Preaching Station on the road to his home village. "Like Noah, you servant of

Jehovah, Jesus, and Holy Spirit. You share them to all Spirit shows you. Great Spirit put in my heart to tell you about Jesus. Jesus, say He want you learn more about Him. You must learn white man language. When Jedidiah get horse, you ask him stay and teach you. You tell Jedidiah teach you with this. You will have power of Great Spirit, Jehovah, **IF** you learn what is in this Bible and follow His commands. Then, He will go through every joy and every trial of your life with you." Noah placed the Bible in Tapco's hand.

"Reveal yourself." Tahatankohana stepped out of the tipi, "Mystery Man, Tapco," he declared.

Wearing the antelope hide over his head, shoulders, and back and the coyote mask over his face, Tapco carried his grandmother bag and the Bible. He dangled the bag from one hand and raised the Bible in the other. "Great Spirit, guide me," he requested.

Fifty Five

Nikki and Oscar shined their shoes as best as they could and then donned them, as well as their best breeches and shirts. Emily tied a bowtie from Dr. Pennyworth's wagon on Oscar. After Ann had dressed Joy and Adele in the adoption dresses that Helen and Sally had made for the occasion, she tied Nikki's bowtie.

Nikki and Oscar carried Joy and Adele into the tipi. Tapco smudged them as they entered and sat inside the inner ceremonial circle of tobacco on the ground. Both rings had an opening to allow the people to enter.

Tapco beat the furless hyena hide he had stretched over a small wooden crate he had found in the wagon he had earned. The rest of the family entered into the sweetgrass-smoke-filled tipi. They sat in the outer circle. Once the last person was seated, Tapco ceased drumming. "All mischief-makers of the spirits have been driven from this circle." He closed the outer tobacco ring with everybody inside.

Tapco brought the stem and bowl of his new

pipe from their pouch. In his right hand, he pointed the pipe stem to the east. He held the bowl in his left hand. Tapco joined the two and then raised the Calumet toward the sky. He lowered it to the ground. "Earth and Sky, four-legged, winged, and swimming things, I bind you all to witness this ceremony." He added kinnikinnick to the bowl each time he raised it in one of the four directions. "Four winds, the sons of the Great Spirit, I call on you to seal what we join together today."

With a tong, Tapco drew an ember from the coals beside his position inside the tipi. He lit the pipe and drew smoke into his mouth, which he exhaled onto Nikki. "Smoke, purify Nikki for this joining." He did the same to Adele and Joy. "Who will be purified to join with Nikki, Adele, and Joy?"

Noah and Ann stepped forward, both saying, "I will."

"Come into the circle of joining." When Noah, with Christopher in the cradleboard on his back, and Ann stood beside the children, Tapco blew the pipe smoke over them. "Smoke, purify Noah, Ann, and Christopher for this joining." He told Noah and Ann, "So Nikki can stand, each of you, hold one of the babies." They did so.

Tapco blew the smoke on Oscar and repeated the command to purify Oscar for joining. He asked, "Who will be purified to join with Oscar?"

Tom and Eli replied, "I will."

"Come into the circle of joining." He purified them with smoke. "Kinnikinnick, purify Tom and

Eli." He placed the Calumet on the stand beside the pit of hot coals and then enclosed Tom, Eli, and Oscar in their circle of tobacco.

Tapco asked, "Noah Swift Hawk, what do you offer for this joining?"

"As Nikki, Adele, and Joy's father, I offer these medicine bags that I made, and I promise to care for, and teach, and love these children as if they were my own blood." Noah hung around the necks of Nikki, Adele, and Joy the pouches he had made from the tanned skin of one of the antelope they had killed during the stampede.

Tapco turned. "Thomas Yates, what do you offer for this joining?"

"As Oscar's father, I offer this medicine bag and promise to love, teach, and care for him as if he were my own blood." He put the pouch on Oscar.

"Ann Williams, what do you offer for this joining?"

"As Nikki, Adele, and Joy's mother, I offer these badges of joining and promise to care for and love them as my own blood." Just above their hearts, Ann pinned an embroidered and beaded circle of antelope skin onto Nikki's, Adele's, and Joy's clothes.

"Eli Yates, what do you offer for this joining?"

As Oscar's brother, "I offer this badge of joining and promise to care for and love him as if he were my own blood." He pinned the badge on Oscar.

Next, Tapco picked up a bowl filled with a slurry of red clay. He dipped his hand into the clay, "Oscar, I put this on your face," and then smeared

red over Oscar's whole face. "You are joined." He took another handful of red and covered the faces of Nikki, Adele, and Joy. "You are joined."

Tapco set down the red clay and retrieved the blue clay paint. This time he went to Tom and placed a blue thumbprint in the middle of Tom's forehead. "Think equally about all those in this group." Tapco pushed a large dot of blue into Tom's chin. "Speak out of love to all those in this circle." He drew two blue lines across each of Tom's cheeks. "See each of the people in this joining as equal but with his own personality and characteristics and accept them as they are."

Tapco put the same blue marks on Eli's face and issued the same commands as he had to Tom.

He walked to Oscar and circled the edge of his face with the blue paint. "You are new person. Now, you get secret joining name. Only people in this ceremony know it. Do not speak name often, and use only during special ceremonies. Who has Oscar's name?"

"I, Apenimon, have the name," said Roscoe, using his own secret adoption name. "Oscar, in your first family, you were the only child. You have joined your second family and are now one of two sons. Your name is Nuka, which means younger brother."

"Thank you for my name, Apenimon. I like it very much."

Tapco brushed an opening in the tobacco ring around Oscar. "Nuka, you are joined with Tom and Eli. Go into the world united as one family."

"Come along, Father and Brother." Nuka exited, followed by Tom and then Eli.

Tapco turned his attention to Nikki's new family. He put the blue marks on Noah and Ann and spoke the same words as he had to Tom. Tapco stood before Nikki and circled the edge of his face with the blue paint. "You are a new person," and repeated the same words as he had said to Oscar. He did the same for Adele and Joy before he asked, "Who has Nikki's, Adele's, and Joy's new names?"

"I, Apenimon, have the names," said Roscoe. He went first to Adele. "Adele, you are Winona, the oldest daughter." He slid two steps over. "Joy, your secret name is Meli, which means daughter." Roscoe turned to Nikki. "Nikki, you are now family with Noah, Ann, Adele, Joy, and Christopher. Your name, Sidanelv, means family."

Nikki hugged Roscoe around his legs. He wasn't completely sure what Roscoe had said, but he heard the names of everybody inside the tobacco with him. "Vielen Dank, Roscoe."

"Sidanelv, Meli, and Winona, you are joined with Noah, Ann, and Christopher. Go into the world united as one family." Tapco brushed an opening in their tobacco ring.

Sidanelv exited with Noah right behind him, carrying Christopher and Winona, and then Ann carrying Meli.

While Tapco again drummed, Stephanie, Sally, and Helen hurried off and then returned with the food that had been prepared. Once the feast had been laid out, Tapco stopped drumming. "The four-legged, flying, swimming, and two-legged have consented with the four winds and the Great Spirit that you are all one family! Celebrate!"

They did, all feeling loved, loving, wanted, and a true and equal member of the family.

Fifty Six

Tapco prepared to separate from Tahatankohana and his family. He knew the bond he felt would not lessen with the distance they would soon have between them. "Five sleeps to cross this part Comanche territory. Not likely you see any. If do, say you help Haungooah catch many ponies." Knowing the cutoff's water hole was dry, Tapco and P'ahy crossed to the northern side of the Cimarron and then turned toward Horse Canyon to join their people breaking wild ponies.

Just as they had left behind people they loved in Harmony, Fletcher Creek, Maumelle, Little Rock, Fort Gibson, and Noah's village, they left in the Kiowa prairie people they loved but would never see again. Ahead the river ran through the lands of the Comanche, a people closely aligned with the Kiowa.

Roscoe spoke up, "It's too hot during the day. We need to change the way we travel. Now that we corral the animals that don't come when called, we'll call in the others and leave as soon as the sun comes up. We can eat leftovers while we walk. We'd sweat out all our water if we kept going, so we'll stop at ten-thirty and get out of the sun. After the animals have grazed for five hours, we'll walk until eight. In the afternoon, the sun will be right in our eyes, so be sure to wear goggles.

"To have clean air for all, we'll travel side-by-side with a rope strung from one wagon to the next and the animals tied along the rope as usual."

The sun rose behind them while they traveled. They stopped beside a knoll two fingers before the sun was directly overhead. Roscoe and Sally cooked a meal.

Noah surveilled the surrounding land from the top of the rise. He noticed something strange. *Is that a bear way out here?* He peered through his spyglass. *I can't tell.* He closed the telescope. To not alert the bear, he slithered through the grass with an ammo belt across his chest and two Lefaucheux revolvers in his gun belt. He approached so slowly that he believed he had caused no grass movement and had not aroused attention.

A sudden rapid parting of the grass drew Noah's attention. He sprung to his feet. His revolvers flew out of their holsters. Also now aware of danger, the gray grizzly rose to its full ten feet and let out an ear-splitting roar.

In camp, those dozing woke.

The unhappy bear charged. However, Noah focused his attention on the giant mass of silent, tan-colored death making its final bound to sink its fangs into his neck. "God, help me!" Noah squeezed the trigger with his left hand.

Guns were grabbed. People jumped from the wagons.

"It's a grizzly!" Tom screamed. *I've never seen a bear so tall.* He sprinted with his guns blazing.

"Help!" Noah screamed.

Ann leaped from the wagon. "Watch the babies!"

People streamed from camp. Not knowing what was happening, Ehawee hollered, "Adahy, don't leave us!"

I need to protect the women. Adahy stopped at the top of the knoll, where he could see both groups.

Something's to my right. Noah's attention swiveled. *The grizzly's almost on me!* His right index finger drew in again and again, but the bear didn't slow. "Help!!"

Attempting to take down the monstrosity he could see, Eli ran at Tom's right, firing rapidly. Roscoe fanned out to the left. Unable to shoot for fear of hitting the men ahead, Ann charged with drawn Lefaucheux revolvers in both hands. "God, save him!"

The giant cat soared through the air, slammed Noah to the ground, and knocked his breath from his lungs. Ten claws pierced Noah's chest as revolvers rose to the sides of the feral head only inches above him. Bullets crisscrossed through feline brains. The puma's claws withdrew from Noah's flesh as it dropped. Blood flowed from both of them.

Bullets and arrows continued to riddle the grizzly's body. It bellowed its pain and anger, dropped to all fours, and fled.

Hot on its trail, three men followed. Eli, however, stopped beside his brother-in-law. The giant cat still lay on Noah, but Noah's eyes were open. "Are you all right?!" Eli asked. Noah didn't speak. Eli shoved the animal off. Blood saturated Noah's shirt.

Ann arrived and saw the blood. Her eyes wild with fear, she dropped to her knees beside her husband. "How bad is it?!" Noah raised his hand to her face. Barely with a whisper, he said, "Can't breathe."

Ann pulled up Noah's shirt. "Two sets of claw punctures — thank You, God — deep but not gashes."

Finally recovering the ability to take air into his lungs, Noah replied, "They still hurt."

With Tom and Roscoe, a Comanche raced behind the bear he had been stalking. He shot arrow after arrow into the retreating rump ahead. The other men fed more rounds into their revolvers.

The shredded muscles of the bear's rear ceased to function. The grizzly pulled itself with its front legs. Soon upon it, Tom put the creature out of its misery. He signed, "Friend, this bear for you."

The Comanche replied in sign, "I not see puma. Very brave man, save my life. Bear for him."

"We share," Roscoe replied.

"I have travois. Take to your camp."

"Tom, stay here. We'll be right back." Roscoe walked away with the Comanche. He pointed to himself, "Roscoe."

The man pointed at his chest. "Pecos."

Roscoe and Pecos took the travois to the bear.

With his arm over Ann's shoulders, Noah made his way back to the wagons. Eli carried the dead puma over his.

Adahy hurried into camp. "Set up the smoke racks."

After Noah showed his injuries to the people in camp, he helped Eli skin the hide off the animal that had put holes in his chest. Ann made willow tea to kill the pain, and Sally cooked cedar for the poultice to keep the wounds free of infection.

Roscoe, Tom, and Pecos arrived with the bear. Roscoe introduced the unknown person. "This is Pecos. He says his name means pecans." He then named each of the many people of his family. "Many names. Many times, you can ask names."

Due to the short, summer fur of the grizzly and the many holes through its hide, Tom took little care when removing the skin. He looked at the mangled bear meat. To include Pecos in all their conversations, Tom signed, "I guess we'll have to clean intestines and make this mess into sausage."

Sally had sworn she would never again clean intestines but had already done so twice since. She signed, "Not again!"

Roscoe jammed a spit through an intact front bear shoulder. "If we clean the intestines in the river, it won't be too awful."

"I don't want to. I'll watch the babies," signed Sally.

Ann sat on the seat of the wagon where all their babies played in the rear. "That's all right with me."

As they did with the elk at Pine Bluff and the bears Noah had killed at Fletcher Creek and in his village, they cut intestines into six-foot sections.

Nikki took a piece. "Smells very bad." Nikki followed Noah into the slow-moving Cimarron River behind the other people carrying a portion into the water.

They spread across the shallow water and squeezed out the contents of the intestines. The droppings sunk slowly and barely moved away. Noah told Nikki, "Back away as you push it out."

Even mostly empty of contents, the slow water did not flow through the empty tube. "Spring River did this much better. Maybe we need to pour water through. Hold this." Ann handed her piece to Nikki. Soon she returned with the coffee pot. "Noah, hold one end open." Ann dipped the pot into the river and then tried to pour the water into the open end. It barely entered.

"I've got an idea." Noah handed his piece to Nikki. He came back on Eyanosa. He pulled Nikki up, facing toward him. "I'll hold. You pour." The water still did not go in. He drew his knife from the alligator-covered sheath. He cut the intestine in half, lay one piece over his shoulder, and then held the other open again. The tube of intestine hung straight down and ended above the river. Ann refilled the coffee pot and gave it back to Nikki. The water went through. Noah spoke up loudly and signed too, "Cut your part in half and bring it over. Ann, get another pot."

Ann and Stephanie filled the pots repeatedly. Noah and Nikki sat on Eyanosa and poured water. Pecos signed, "Water in my village no longer comes."

"What do you mean?" Tom asked.

"Hills come apart. Now, stream goes other place."

Sally asked, "Why don't you move?"

"Every year, we wait for the buffalo in this place. We must not miss them."

Roscoe thought about the talc rubble that had circled the canyon of Pine Bluff. "Maybe it was a mountain slide. We could go see. We do have all that dynamite."

Pecos asked, "What is dynamite?"

Noah replied, "Something with much power. We move mountains and return water. You take us across your land."

"I take you to chief after get meat ready. We ask him."

Once reasonably clean, they pulled the outer flesh off the thin inner membrane of the short pieces of bear guts. In the river, they thoroughly cleaned the delicate tissue they needed. Afterward, they flushed all the intestinal membranes with the cleaner rainwater from one of their water barrels.

While Ann, Stephanie, and Ehawee fed their babies, Sally ground puma and bear meat together with spices and lard. Emily and Helen stuffed the mixture into the intestine tubing and knotted it into strings of sausages. The men cut other pieces of the bear meat into strips. Then, during the early evening, they kept the coals red-hot and the racks in the white smoke of the hardwood boards of the wagons ruined in the dust storm. By morning, the sausages and bear jerky on the racks had been smoked. As the meat cooled, they filled every water container they had to the brim. They planned to bring all they could to the water-starved people.

Fifty Seven

Pecos tried a sausage. Sally had never eaten puma and bear meat mixed. "Is it good?" she asked.

"Good!" He sampled a few more, then led them beyond the trail of bear blood.

Before the sun reached its zenith, they arrived at the rock slide. The hill wasn't high. However, the boulders that blocked the ravine through which the stream had previously flowed were much too large to be moved by people. Roscoe stood on the tall mound of stones. "Years ago, I spoke quite a bit with a demolitions man, who came to my trading post. I think I can clear this."

Sally stood beside Roscoe. "It's going to take time to climb down, and you also have to get out of the blast zone. I don't want you to get hurt. Are you sure you can get away fast enough?"

"Yep. It's just a matter of cutting the fuse the right length. Guaranteed; exactly one foot in thirty seconds, every time. A man named Bickford just invented it."

"If it was just invented, how do you know it always works right? Maybe we shouldn't do this."

"It's not exactly JUST invented. It was nine years ago. It's saved a lot of lives because it always burns at the same rate. Get a pocket watch. We'll time how long it takes for me to get far enough away." While Sally fetched a watch, Roscoe surveyed the rock slide and contemplated where to plant the charges.

At the end of their five-hour rest, Roscoe had a plan. They set off toward Pecos's village.

Pecos stopped just before the village sentry's vision. "I tell people I bring you. You wait here."

Noah didn't believe that Pecos had any ulterior motive, but he thought it best not to assume. "I'll go with you." He looked at Roscoe.

He'll signal if they try to attack us. Roscoe nodded his head ever so slightly.

Noah took off the cradleboard holding Chris. "I'll see you again soon, my white eagle boy." He propped the carrier up beside Ann and whispered. "As soon as we're out of sight, take everybody and hide. Shots just like the knocks."

Ann wrapped her arms around Noah. "I love you too." Under her breath, she added, "I understand."

After Noah and Pecos were out of hearing, Ann asked, "Eli, how do the knock signals work?"

Eli explained. "Three knocks with a long pause between each knock means it's us, and it's safe to open the door. Ten fast ones mean we're in trouble, so open the door cautiously. Two knocks with no pauses between means it's us, but don't open the door. Anything else will not be us."

Lisa Gay

Fifty Eight

Pecos secretly took Noah to his chief's tipi. He spoke in Comanche and signed. "Nacoma, this half pale-face brings water in wagons."

"Why?" Chief Nacoma asked.

"Tahatankohana wants me to take him and his family safely across our land. His family will also move the rocks blocking the stream."

"Nobody can do that!"

"He has a thing he calls, 'dynamite.'"

"Will you take him if he brings back our water?" asked the chief.

"I will."

Nacoma looked into Noah's blue eyes. He signed, "Can you move the boulders and return our water?"

"Have you asked the Great Spirit to bring back the water?" Noah replied, with a plan in mind.

"We have spoken many prayers for this."

"If we move the mountain, would you believe the Great Spirit sent us to answer your prayers?"

"That is what I would believe."

"Then you would believe who we say is the Great Spirit?"

"I would. The Great Spirit sent you. You must know who He is."

"We remove the boulders. Water will again flow in the stream by this place where you wait for the buffalo. After we leave your land, I will send Pecos to Tapco of the Kiowa. Tapco will teach him about the Great Spirit. Pecos will come home and teach the Comanche.

Nacoma spoke. "We will smoke to this agreement. Then, bring your water and family. Tonight, Pecos will tell of his vision quest and how he found you. Tomorrow, restore our stream."

"Agreed. How many people, families, and animals here?"

"Fifty-one people, eleven families, and thirteen ponies."

"Tell all to gather in meeting lodge. Bring one cup each person and one water-container this high," Noah tapped the side of his knee, "for each family. Don't come out of lodge once inside."

"I will pass the message."

After the three men confirmed the arrangement, Noah followed Pecos out of the tipi. Together, they sneaked away from the village. At the wagons, Pecos saw no people or animals. "I didn't know anybody would take them! Don't kill me!"

"It's all right. I told my family to hide." Noah fired a shot, paused, fired another, paused, and then fired the last shot. "Now we wait."

Thirty minutes later, Noah's family returned. He informed them, "All is well. Let's water all our animals now and set aside the water we need for tonight and tomorrow. Then, we'll go to Pecos's village and give them the rest of our water. He's going to tell the story of his vision quest tonight."

When they had arrived at Noah's home about this same time the previous summer, Roscoe, Ann, and Sally had served bear meat sausages as he had told his quest story. They explained to the rest of the family as they rode to help Pecos relate his tale.

The people gathered in the meeting lodge for a reason unknown to them. Before long, they heard the jiggling of harnesses and the plodding of many animals. "What is that?" asked the chief's wife. She rose.

"Woman, sit!" commanded Nacoma.

The door flap opened. Pecos returned home after a three months manhood vision quest. "I will tell you of my journey. First, I bring friends to serve you sausages and a drink of water."

As planned, with their babies in cradleboards, the eighteen people of Noah's family entered with pitchers, coffee pots, and pails of water. The boys had a pouch of sausages at each hip. After they had filled every cup and given every person a sausage, they sat in the space that had been reserved for them. Pecos took a bite of the sausage in his hand. "Eat and drink." He gulped the water in his cup, then related his story as his people ate tasty sausages of unknown meat. Pecos finally arrived at the part of the story where he had stalked the bear. "My new friends, refill the water cups and give another sausage." Quanah, the chief's daughter, batted her lashes and smiled at the storyteller. Without mentioning that he had not seen the puma, Pecos told how they had killed the bear and puma. "Puma-killer is that man." Pecos pointed at Noah. "He wears the proof of his bravery on his chest. Show them, giant cat-killer."

Noah rose and removed his shirt. Five red wounds arched just below each shoulder.

Pecos looked into the eyes of Quanah. "You are eating that bear and that puma." He turned back to Nacoma. "The Great Spirit led me to these people to give us back our water. Tonight, we filled your cups twice. Now, we will fill your water jugs. Tomorrow, we will bring back the whole stream!" Pecos triumphantly led his people out of the lodge, where water was portioned into the large water jugs and ten-gallon tubs for the village ponies. Everybody slept saturated.

Fifty Nine

In the morning light, every man, woman, child, animal, and wagon started toward the rock slide. At high noon, the group set up out of blast range. With eighteen sticks of dynamite, blasting caps, and a roll of Bickford Fuse, Roscoe rode King to the obstruction. *One giant explosion would be more impressive, but the rock pile is full of space, and I'm not sure if I can get these deep enough.* For hours, while the mid-day sun beat down, he shifted moveable stones.

Inside the wagon previously owned by Dr. Pennyworth, Nikki poured some of their remaining water into Whisker's bowl. "It's too hot."

With him, Oscar watered their chickens. "We could lie in the wagon, but I don't want to miss the explosion."

"Me neither."

Roscoe lowered six sticks with their blasting caps attached in different places of the rockslide close to the stream's new turn. Each hung on four-feet of fuse, then all tied together at the end. *That's two minutes.*

Roscoe tied the new end of the roll of fuse to the

knot. Making sure he placed the fuse where the preceding explosions would not snuff it out, he moved toward the downstream side of the stone blockage — *two more minutes.*

Meanwhile, Nikki stood beside Ann. Waves of hot air rose from the expanse of flat land around them. "Too hot, may I go in water over there?"

"There isn't any water. We've trying to bring it back."

Nikki pointed. "I see it."

Ann stooped and looked where Nikki was looking. She saw what he did. "It's not really there."

"You wrong. I see it."

"It's called a mirage. It's not real."

"I see it."

"Let me get Chris into a cradleboard. Then we'll walk over. Go tell Noah where we're going."

Nikki told Noah his plan then asked Oscar, "Want to come with me and my Ann to the water?"

"No, I want to see the mountain blow up."

Nikki hugged Ann. They walked away. Several minutes later, he asked, "Why we not getting there?"

"In Roscoe's journal, he wrote that some people thought they saw water. They tried to go to it. It kept moving ahead of them. It wasn't really there."

"We go back. It really not real." In German, he thought, *My Ann knew it wasn't real. She still walked with me, so I would know. She like my Mama.* Nikki hugged Ann again. "Thank you for bringing me."

As they walked back to the wagons, Roscoe planted six more charges just as he had the first set.

That'll add four minutes. He continued the fuse to the last group and positioned them close to the downstream edge. *This is where it matters. I need three minutes to get away once I light the fuse. This set will only give me two.* He tied the fuse to the last group, then unrolled it as he climbed down the boulders he hoped to blow to smithereens. *That's four more minutes. Better to be safe.* He cut the fuse, mounted King, lit a match, and held it to the end. The black powder ignited. Roscoe dropped the line. "Forward run!" King flew toward the large group of people, far away.

The black powder in the shellac-coated twine sparkled as it burned. Through her spyglass, Sally intently watched. "Here he comes! I've never seen dynamite explode. I'm so nervous!"

Ann observed through her own telescope. "I am too, but it's also exciting."

Roscoe blew past the camp then wheeled back. He jumped off King. Sally hugged his neck. "I'm glad you're safe."

"I promised you I wouldn't kill myself."

Helen hugged him. "I'm also glad you're safe." She held his hand as the final segments of fuse leading to the closest set of dynamite ignited. Two of them burned around the twist of the knots. Four immediately started down the lines. One fuse sparkled its way toward the next set of charges.

Nacoma stood up. "YOU FAILED!"

KABOOM!! Tons of rock flew sky-high. Nacoma threw his body to the ground and his hands over his head.

All eyes riveted on the portion of the earth in the sky. It started back toward the place it had just left.

"It's going to resettle and resume blocking the water," Roscoe huffed.

The other two sticks ignited.

Kaboom!

The enormous boulders behind the explosion directed the blast forward, forcing the descending pieces away from the newly created void.

The lines down to the next sticks of dynamite ignited. With a larger knot and less of a run to the last group of explosives, the wicks to the final set ignited before the designed two minutes. As a novice demolitions man, Roscoe had also not gotten the final bundle of dynamite sunken as deeply as he had assumed. After four tense minutes of waiting, all twelve of the final runs grew short.

Nacoma again felt tempted to declare failure. This time, he held his tongue.

KABOOM!! The closest six sticks blew together.

Two seconds later, **KABOOM!!** Four more exploded followed by, **Kaboom!**

"The water isn't coming!" Nacoma started toward the site of the mountain removal attempt.

Roscoe held out his hand. "Better wait to be sure they've all exploded," he signed.

Kaboom! The last boulder split. Water splashed between the halves, over the remaining stones, and then covered the bits and chunks of rock blasted into the dry stream bed.

Rubble covered a wide swath of land around the water, now flowing in two shallow streams. "That real?" Nikki asked.

Ann assured him, "That's real."

"May I lie in it?"

"Yes."

Noah called to Ann, "I'm taking our animals over for a drink."

"I'll stay here and keep an eye on Nikki."

Ann dipped only her bare feet into the stream. Nikki, however, remained true to his words and lay flat in the cool water.

When the water flowed clear, animals and people sucked it down. Once sated, the village Mystery Man handed a pouch to Pecos. "Take these people across the land. If any of our people are against you, smoke this pipe with them. Bring it back to me before you go to learn new things about the Great Mystery. I will go with you and also learn these things."

"I do as you have asked." Pecos received the carrying bag containing three pouches holding the two halves of the Calumet and a measure of tobacco.

Nacoma led his daughter to Pecos. He put her hand in his. "The water again flows beside our village. You have done this great thing for your people. I give Quanah to you as wife. Take these people to dividing of river, then return and make her yours."

Pecos drew the girl to him, briefly kissed her lips, then pressed his cheek to hers, and whispered, "Now we can be together."

The hottest part of the day had passed. The sun, however, was still scorching. With all their water containers filled, Pecos left with the Great Spirit's servants, who had moved a mountain.

Sixty

That night, Pecos watched Ehawee sign the words Stephanie read from the Bible. Ehawee stopped, "Wait, I don't know how to tell this. How do I explain this image of the anti-Christ?"

Stephanie thought. Everybody else thought, but Sally spoke up. "I've never thought about what it is. The only thing I can think of that is an image of you, but not you, is a picture. Like what we have of Papa and Mama, but how would it come to life? If I could do that, I'd bring our parents back. I don't think that's what it means." She went into the wagon and got out the tintype of her parents. She handed it to Pecos and then drew her hand across her body. "Real." She pointed to the picture. "Image."

"Like what I see in water?"

Stephanie signed. "Yes, that is image, but I not think that is what this is. Still, we know it looks like the real anti-Christ but is not him." They spent the rest of the evening thinking and offering what they thought the likeness would be. Just before they lay down to sleep, Pecos signed, "Whatever it is. I not want real anti-Great Spirit or image to come. Will Tapco tell me about that book like you do?"

Noah replied, "Tapco will have his way of telling. Maybe sixteen moons," Noah displayed the corresponding number of fingers, "Jedidiah go to Tapco village and teach all who want to read these words." Noah held up the Bible. "And to speak this language. All will have many questions. If you try to know this book, over many seasons, Great Spirit will open many answers. Nobody finds every answer."

Pecos signed, "I will be one to learn." He closed his eyes. *I want to learn everything I can from these people the Great Spirit brought to move the mountain but not from a white man. It will only be a few days before these people are across. How do I make that longer?*

That night Pecos dreamed – Up on their hind legs, bears and wolves danced in a circle under the moon. The bears and wolves looked like their own type, but each was unique. Pecos ran into the middle of the animal ring. He shouted, "You are not the same things. You hate each other. You will destroy each other." One of the bears circled past. It turned its head toward him, and then with its giant paw, it drew off its face. A beautiful face of light shone out. Its glory overtook and then converted the entire bear into a shining being of light. Pecos clenched his fists. "What are you?!"

The tallest wolf danced into view then removed its face. From within, the same light overtook the animal before it peered intently into Pecos's eyes. "I Am who I Am."

One by one, each of the dancers touched his shoulder. He spun toward each tap. The face of indescribable beauty converted each of them. No longer able to tell which was a bear or which was a wolf, Pecos sweated. "Who are you?" He fell to his knees. "Tell me who you are!"

"What is your concern with the outside when I Am is inside?"

"I need to know if you are a bear or a wolf."

"I am neither. You must see Me."

The dancers returned their original faces. "I can again see what you are. Thank you." Pecos saw the face of light still within each of them. "But it doesn't matter. You all have the light." Pecos woke, understanding that the person's skin didn't matter. He had to look for the beautiful being within. He related his dream while they ate eggs scrambled together with the sausage they had made.

"That was a beautiful vision, Pecos!" Sally took his empty plate. "Did the light really say it was I AM?"

"Yes, those were the words."

Stephanie picked up Eli's Bible. "Let me read something from the Bible. Thousands of years ago, a man named Moses wrote about what happened to him." She flipped open the Bible. "Exodus 3:1-14 – Now Moses kept the flock of Jethro his father in law, the priest of Midian: and he led the flock to the backside of the desert, and came to the mountain of God, even to Horeb.

"And the angel of the LORD appeared to him in a flame of fire in a bush: and he looked, and the bush burned with fire but was not burned up.

"And Moses said, I will go over there and see this great sight, why is that bush not burning away?

"And when the LORD saw that Moses went over to look, God called to him from out of the bush, and said, 'Moses, Moses.' And Moses said, 'Here am I.'

"And He said, 'Don't come close: take your shoes off your feet, for the place where you stand is holy ground.'

"He also said, 'I am the God of your father, the God of Abraham, the God of Isaac, and the God of Jacob.' And Moses hid his face; for he was afraid to look upon God.

"And the LORD said, 'I have seen the affliction of my people which are in Egypt, and have heard their cry by reason of their taskmasters; for I know their sorrows;

"And I have come down to deliver them out of the hand of the Egyptians, and to bring them out of that land to a good land flowing with milk and honey; to the place of the Canaanites, and the Hittites, and the Amorites, and the Perizzites, and the Hivites, and the Jebusites.

"Now, therefore, behold, the cry of the children of Israel has come to me: and I have also seen how the Egyptians oppress them.

"Come now, therefore, and I will send you to Pharaoh that you may bring my people the children of Israel out of Egypt.'

"And Moses said to God, 'Who am I, that I should go to Pharaoh, and that I should bring the children of Israel out of Egypt?'

"And He said, 'Certainly I will be with thee: and this will be a sign to you that I have sent you: When you have brought my people out of Egypt, you will serve God upon this mountain.'

"And Moses said to God, 'Behold, when I come to the children of Israel, and say to them, The God of your fathers has sent me to you: and they say to me, What is his name? What shall I say unto them?'

"And God said to Moses, 'I AM THAT I AM,' and He said, 'This is what you should say to the children of Israel, I AM has sent me to you.'"

Sally explained, "So you see, God must have spoken to you in your dream. You would not have known that He calls himself I AM."

Four days later, when Pecos bid the group goodbye, he believed he had recognized I AM within those he had escorted to the fork of the Cimarron River by the gracious and generous way they had behaved ever since he had met them.

The servants of I AM crossed the river and then continued west into the land of the Arapaho. With Joy in the cradleboard on her back, Sally walked beside Ann. "I wonder what else will happen along our way. Do you think God will take us to other people He wants us to meet?"

Ann answered, "I'm sure He will."

"I wonder who He wants us to meet next."

Acknowledgments

I acknowledge God the Father, Jesus the only begotten Son, and the Holy Spirit as my savior and inspiration.

* wedding ceremony sample 17, modified, accessed 4 April 2021, https://www.Bible.org

* traditional Christian wedding ceremony, modified, accessed 5 April 2021, https://www.weddingsbyphyllis.net

Chapter Headings and Dream Dance
W.R. Michael Mattingly

Follow Me Online
https://www.ChanceandChoicesAdventures.com

Did you like this story? Please write a review!
https://www.amazon.com/Along-Way-Lisa-Gay/dp/1945858192/

Chance and Choices Adventures
by Lisa Gay
Pray for Justice
Choose Your Consequences
No Remorse
Means of Escape
Torn Hearts
Xida People
Stone Cold
Goodbye Hideout
Along the Way
The Western Sea
Sally's Sketchbook

Books by The Traveler

Provence: a land of lavender and olives